MY ALIEN PROTECTOR

ROTHA MATES OF XAVIA | BOOK TWO

REVERIE HARWOOD

MY ALIEN PROTECTOR

ROTHA MATES OF XAVIA | BOOK TWO

REVERIE HARWOOD

Cover design by Mayhem Cover Creations
Editing by Headlight Fluid Press

ISBN-13: 978-1-950439-80-5

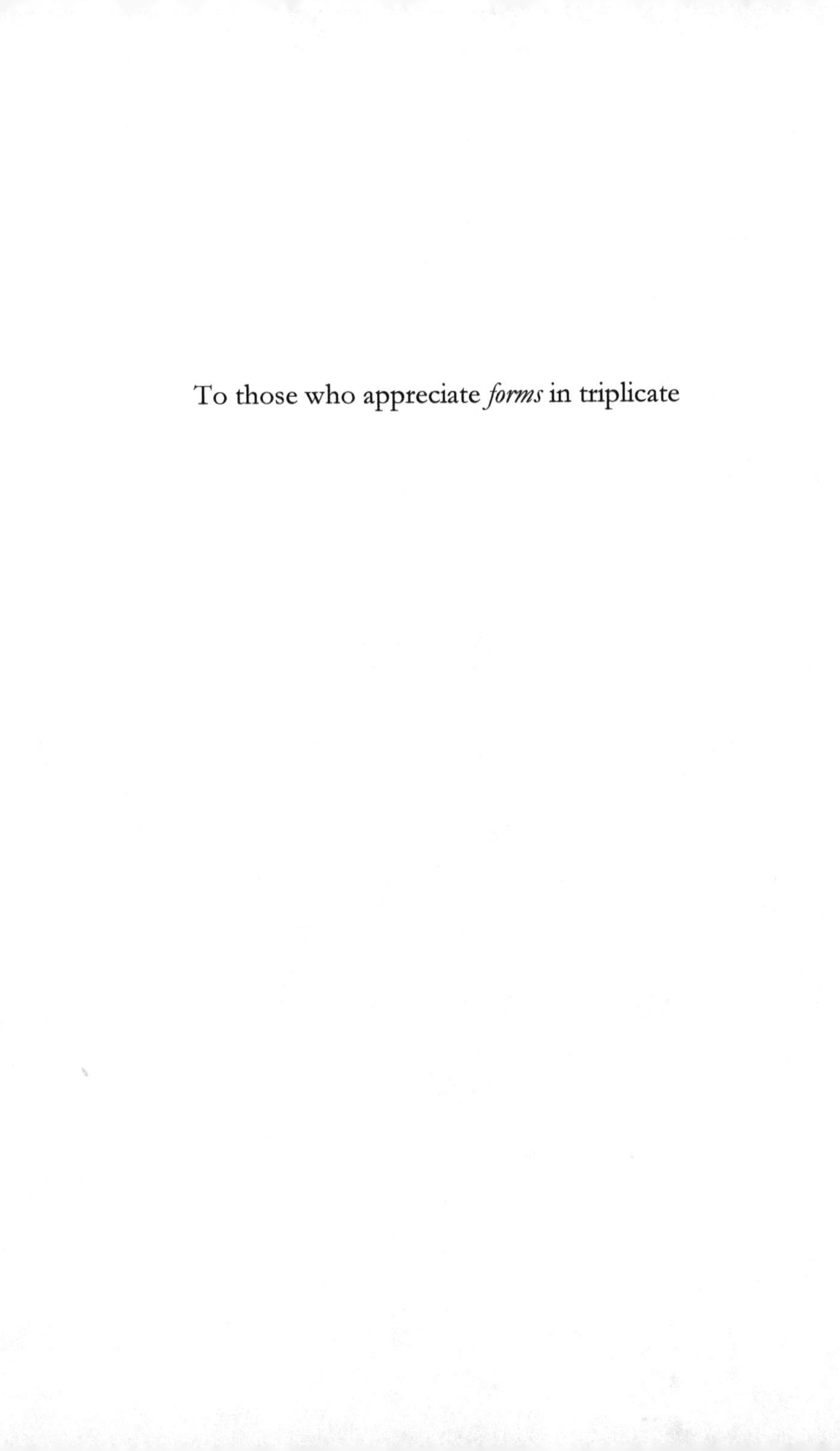

To those who appreciate *forms* in triplicate

Chapter One
#XaviaBound

Sara

Doom-scrolling through my social media wasn't my first choice on a Saturday night. The second glass of cheap red wine helped though. What people don't tell you about the insatiable need to travel is that leading up to those unforgettable weekends, there's like a year's worth of really boring weekends in which you have to stay home and save money.

This was one of those weekends.

I had a keratin treatment warm in my brown hair. Only my lips and brown eyes could be seen, for all else was resting underneath a collagen cream face mask. I took another sip of wine to fend off questioning whether I had made all the right decisions in my life. I'd been through those. There were regrets, but I had done the best I could. Couldn't ask for more than that.

Chad could have happened to anyone.

I'm sure he was happening to someone else right now.

Good riddance.

He was wickedly handsome, though.

I decided against looking up his profile (again). See, progress?

I had met Chad when he walked into my fast-fashion clothing store…not a store I owned. This wasn't a Hallmark movie. And he wasn't a Hallmark guy. Working retail wasn't glamorous, but it paid the bills, and it allowed me as much time as I wanted off to travel. It was a pretty transferable skill too. I had traveled across the United States, into Mexico and Canada. If I needed to make more money, I'd hop into a store and get a job for a while. The jobs were easy to get and easy to leave. I got my fulfillment from adventures, not traveling up some corporate ladder in the same dry place for years.

I lived in a studio apartment on the west side with lofted ceilings, decorated cowboy bohemian. My roommate's cat, Leslie, hopped onto the fabric couch arm next to where I sat. Leslie was a small, old gray cat that only liked three people. Fortunately, I was one of those blessed few. Before I could stop her, she stuck a paw into my face cream. She pulled it back immediately, glaring at me as if I'd betrayed her.

"What did you expect? It's cold cream. It's cold. And creamy." I laughed as she licked the minute amount off her claw indignantly.

Perhaps she had been expecting cream.

I adjusted on the couch in case she hadn't learned her lesson and wanted to wipe more of the valuable stuff off my face. As I did so, my thumb caught on the screen of my phone and accidentally 'liked' a post. I scrolled back to 'unlike' it, and that's when the post actually caught my eye. It was a travel influencer I had been ignoring. She had stopped being an inspiration for me, and instead was starting to make me feel anxious about not making my travel goal next year. I wanted to hike the Inca trail and visit Machu Picchu. It would be my first time outside of North America, and I was really excited about it.

Gabriella Travella was a solo female traveler who really seemed to have her life together. She was everything I wanted to be…glamorous and adventurous. I tried to remind myself that Gabriella Travella probably had other funds and wasn't supporting her lifestyle with a retail job. At least, I didn't think she was. Screw me if she was pulling that off. Maybe I was jealous because I hadn't thought of that handle and brand…Sara Travella would have worked just as well. OK, maybe not.

The post I accidentally 'liked' was some sort of contest entry hash-tagged #XaviaBound. Where the hell was Xavia? I clicked the hashtag and was relieved to know that I wasn't failing basic geography. I was failing galactic…-ography. Xavia was one of the many planets we'd explored since meeting our very first aliens who happened to be used ship salesmen. No, really. Shortly after their arrival, the Arqal sold the U.S. and Chinese governments faster-than-light spaceships.

As if I didn't feel traveled enough concerning my own planet. I now had other planets to worry about. But I didn't think that even the super successful Gabriella Travella would be able to afford a trip into freaking outer space. Who'd ever heard of space tourism? That was for billionaires and their washtub creations.

Then I read up on the contest for which Gabriella had created the video. Xavia was an out-of-this-world getaway—an entirely tropical planet. The U.S.

government was sponsoring trips to promote tourism there. An entirely free trip?

This was better than Machu Picchu. Instead of visiting the remains of an ancient civilization…I could meet another civilization. Apparently, there were Xavians on Xavia. And they'd agreed to a cultural exchange—hosting winners of the contest. I couldn't think of a better travel experience. I would meet new people living on a completely different planet.

I saw myself sunning in the tropical paradise which looked a lot like South America or Hawaii. I'd be there for six months—nowhere else I'd be able to sustain a trip that long. I wouldn't be a retail worker who had managed a vacation. I'd be a galactic traveler. I'd be able to get to know the local people and learn a new culture and language. This wouldn't be a vacation. This would be a life-changing experience.

I continued scrolling and watching the entry videos, while I walked to my bathroom and turned on the shower. My wine was left forgotten on the coffee table. The television screen waited for a program to be chosen on Netflix, also forgotten. I had the whole apartment to myself, my roommates out enjoying themselves. I now had a plan for tonight…and for the next year. I was going to make a killer video.

Screw Machu Picchu. I was #XaviaBound.

Chapter Two
Negotiations

Vance

I relaxed into one of the many chairs around the spaceship's conference table. My green-blue skin, a shade paler than was usual for Xavian males, clashed with their upholstery, which was green too but more yellow, like the sea on a sunny day. At first, convening in the spaceship had felt uncomfortable and alien, even if it was grounded. However, I soon realized the humans didn't feel much more at-home than I did. They hadn't developed the technology, built the spaceship, or chosen its color scheme—which served to wash out their complexions as well.

I shared this opinion and many other perceptions with our prince, Drex. Despite my constant reminders, he remained staunchly upright, as if he was on trial. I didn't know why he was so nervous. He could take any or all of these men on his own. Drex and I were government, but we were in warrior-shape. Unlike the humans, we actually fit into the chairs which were clearly built for a taller and broader species. We were probably twenty percent taller than the humans. Drex was taller than me—although I often claimed his horns only make him *look* taller by boosting the height of the hair along his temples. No matter how you measured it, my shoulders were broader. They were my best feature.

"Second to your humility, Vance," Drex would joke.

We grew up together, and then had grown up much faster together when our planet came under attack by an alien species, the Orkain. As such, we'd been thrust into government: the prince forced to lead after the passing of the king and queen. Me, his best friend and resident goofball, suddenly adviser and government leader. I wasn't sure if I was their best choice, but I was always by Drex's side. And I could at least help him here. This was just a negotiation.

I mimicked the faux-casualness of the human leaders, of which the table was full. Some of whom had yet to speak, despite days of negotiations. I had no idea why they were there, except to maybe fill the table and outnumber us. For the Xavians, it was Drex, myself, Davian—our communications officer, Lowree and Elza—our eldest Xavian women. They were stand-ins for the government positions we had lost and the women that held those positions. Our government had been reduced to a Prince and a handful of appointees.

Our women were generally smaller than men of our species, and they were still larger than the humans. As opposed to Drex and my green skin, their skin was delicate and yellow. They had nubs along their hairline but no horns. The humans had no horns of either species, I was told, but for not having any population issues of their own, there were not any women at the table for the humans. They were all men, as we understood it. Men in desperate need of holmium, the metal that our mines were full of. As much as I struggled with the idea, we had reached a crisis point. We needed a population injection to ensure the continuation of our species. The Orkain had taken up residence and hunted us to near extinction.

These were the final negotiations. The deal was basically sealed. The humans were trying to walk away with as much good-faith glor, or, as they called it, holmium, as they could manage before they left to bring back the women.

"You have only given us enough for the travel back with the women. That is effectively net-zero for us," said Captain Smith. He was a thin-boned man with a hefty beard. They had explained to us the three-month stasis that caused their hair to grow long. Indeed, their badges showed them with short-cropped hair and no facial hair.

"We can give you more when you return," I said.

"Then how do we know that your production levels are up to snuff?"

"Snuff?"

"Figure of speech," he said without any further explanation.

I assumed he meant within acceptable production levels. I noted to check for 'snuff' rate in the final contracts.

Anyway, I didn't trust them. I knew it was a tactic. It didn't mean that it wouldn't work though.

#

Several hours later, Drex and I walked from the spaceship with the deal complete. It was midday, and the jungle was hot and bright. The path from the spaceship had been worn from our constant negotiations. Tomorrow, the ship would be gone.

"Are you relieved the negotiations are done?" he asked.

"I am. You were right. We have nothing to lose at this point."

In the end, they'd taken almost our entire stockpile of glor. It didn't matter. Our reduced population would never use that much, and we had the ability to mine more. However, it was one thing to give the humans all of our glor. It was another to spend the next hundred sols preparing for the humans' return. We would be spending the next of Earth-time's six months, the time in which the ship would go to Earth and return with the volunteers, to adapt our mines to accommodate for the increased production for our (hopefully) ongoing deal with Earth.

If we redirected our efforts with the mine into building a tunnel system for us to use, to be able to walk to neighbors and create a community underground, where the winged Orkain wouldn't be able to swoop down on us, we would create a safe place for our people.

But Drex firmly believed the most critical problem was our population. He believed there was no point in building a tunnel system if no one would be here to use it in two or three generations. He had a point. Still, it was putting a lot of trust into the humans. We could be accelerating our extinction by wasting our time and resources on a mine that we wouldn't need immediately. Or ever. I didn't trust the humans to return with the women.

On top of that, we had to prepare for the women's arrival. We had an entire language to learn. And I would have to listen to Drex's complaints the entire time.

"As Prince, I really shouldn't have to *do* anything." Drex whined.

"If you'd *do anyone,* you wouldn't have to be a part of this," I chided.

Drex and I were both single, eligible men, and as such, the deal with the humans and the program to meet single, eligible human women was, well…for us.

I would be hosting one of the potential-mates if they did arrive. It was pretty much a necessity of participating in the programs we were designing; I needed to do it for some of the same reasons that Drex had to do it. But I was also excited for it. It wasn't really a hard thing to volunteer for. Host a guest who might become your mate. Yeah, I could get behind that. I thought about how brave she would be. I'm not positive I would travel across the skies to find a partner. I'm not sure if I was that adventurous. I was, however, close enough to be impressed by anyone that actually did so.

For the most part, I was ready to fulfill my obligations. You know—anything for my people. Drex was a lot more nervous about it. But I told him that he couldn't expect his people to trust in the humans and the program if he didn't *personally* invest in it.

We would both host a guest when they arrived. He could complain all he wanted, but our prince had to take a mate if the ship did return. He couldn't ask more of his people than he'd ask of himself.

Plus, he'd have to do it anyway, eventually, as royalty or whatever. I mean, if they even kept it a monarchy for that position. I had a feeling that Drex didn't want the tradition to continue, given that our population had reached such small numbers that Prince/King/Queen weren't really necessary positions…but they could be again. I understood where he was coming from. There was so much done as a group or board now that his position wasn't much different from any appointed one. Why should his bloodline be given a spot? But there wasn't anyone currently vying for his position. We had higher priorities.

"Vjann wants to organize another scouting trip," said Drex.

"Of course he does. It's what he does."

"Will you go with him? I think his reports are…" He hesitated.

"Overly optimistic," I offered.

Vjann was against the tunnels. He had also been against evacuating the towns. He held tight to the old image of Xavia. And in this old image, we send a scouting party to find the Orkain, gain information about them to create a successful plan of attack, defeat our enemies, and return to the old ways of life. There was no need to move underground or build enemy-free tunnels. Unfortunately, this would likely be the hundredth unsuccessful scouting trip.

I respected Vjann because my father respected Vjann. He was one who I knew my father's opinion of—one of the few left. However, his old ways hadn't been helpful with the Orkain. That's why I was adviser to the prince of Xavia, and there was no king or queen. Maybe Drex figured, between the two of us, he would get a realistic report.

"Should I bring Lian?"

"No, I think he still needs to cool down from not getting selected for the program. Take Chelk."

Lian was a junior officer we had been considering promoting, or at least providing him more experience. It was a lack of experience that had him cut from the list of hosts. He was too young, too immature. His reaction confirmed our decision.

However, another boring scouting mission with a stubborn old Xavian and a dumb mid-ranking soldier wasn't going to damper my spirits. Tonight, I was going to dig into all the English-language programs we'd been given.

I wondered how you said, "May I eat you out?" in English.

Chapter Three
Space Center

Sara

I snapped a selfie in front of the new U.S. Space Center building. The sunshine reflected off of all its sleek windows and made my brown hair extra shiny. The government had spared no expense in recreating the program, including erecting this fancy new pro-space tourism annex.

I posted the photo to social media, but it was hardly newsworthy. I had walked into this building several times now for the selection process. I had gotten this far in the contest as a "plain regular" person promoting space tourism on socials. I guessed they figured the best way to do this was to pay people to vacation to beautiful, tropical planets.

I was on board.

Well, not yet.

After signing in, I was sent into a familiar side examination room. A petite olive-skinned lady measured my weight, height—as if that changed— blood pressure, and body temperature.

"What's on for today?" I asked as I pulled down my sleeve but pulled it back up when she gestured at the blood collection equipment.

"Just the usual." She wiped the crook of my arm with a cold alcohol swab.

That was definitely the usual. It seemed they could never have me come in and *not* take some of my blood.

"No treadmills, right?" I joked nervously. I always did when needles were involved.

"You've already passed our physical. If selected, we do recommend that you continue your typical physical activities in preparation for the flight. There will be some minor atrophy of muscles, but nothing like in the past. The stasis pods are great."

So, continue doing two push-ups to earn a third glass of merlot…when I remembered. Got it. I could handle that for sure. After pulling several vials of blood from me, she directed me to hold a cotton ball to the trusty vein while she scanned the barcode on the vials and the one on my wristband. She put an adhesive bandage on my arm, freeing my hand.

"Please wait in the lobby with the others while we run the numbers on your blood work. That will determine what you do next today."

I jumped down from the examination table and exited into the bright, all-glass lobby. I hoped my bloodwork told them that I was perfect for lounging in Xavia. How do you study for a blood test? I'm sure my sister would try.

I sat near a woman with blond hair and blue eyes…very Hollywood to the brunette mid-western look my mom had given me and my sister. I didn't recognize her from my other lobby-time. She gave me a big, bright-white smile.

"Hi, I'm Anna James."

"Sara Shylock. Do you know why we're here today?" The process had really started to get drawn out. I guessed that was the government for you.

Anna lowered her head, and with a conspiratorial whisper, she said, "I think they're measuring us for our stasis uniforms today."

"Oh yeah?" I brightened. I had been trying not to get my hopes up. While this would be a great (free) adventure, it wasn't a guarantee.

She nodded. "That would mean that we're basically in."

I didn't know where she got her information, but I liked the sound of it. If I didn't get picked, I wasn't sure what I'd do. Everything else really seemed to pale in comparison. At this point, I was just waiting for a 'yes' or 'no.' I wasn't going to plan for two vastly different futures. I'd wait for the answer and then figure everything else out after.

"Why are they still taking our blood?"

"I don't know. They're always taking our blood. Monitoring something, I'd assume."

I shrugged. It *had* become pretty routine. There were two other women on the other side of the lobby. I only recognized one of them. It didn't make too much sense to make friends yet. We were all being pulled this way and that every few minutes, and possibly some of us weren't going to be accepted into the program. I tried not to view them as competition, but I also really wanted one of the spots.

A vacation like this was astronomically out of my price range.

Anna got called into another room, different from the examination room I had been in. I sent my sister some silly video of a cat in a makeshift space helmet, telling her that would be me soon enough. I didn't get a response before Anna returned and I was called in. She gave me two covert thumbs up by her sides as we walked past each other.

I was getting measured for my space suit!

Or measured for something. A lady who appeared more comfortable working with a computer than wielding a tape measure clumsily measured my body. She tucked the measuring tape underneath my arms and measured my chest above my nipples. She measured my waist and hips, then my arm diameter much to my chagrin. At least the space suit would hopefully fit. I hated sleeves that were too tight.

My sister messaged me as the lady was recording the numbers onto her electronic tablet. She raised the tablet to show me a full body image of me they had taken previously. She dressed it like an electronic paper-doll and showed me inside a silver-clad jumper that I hoped was at least flexible. Maybe I shouldn't have sucked in my stomach when she measured, I thought. I gave her a happy little nod. "Does that mean?"

She shook her head. "We're measuring everyone at this stage, but we're getting close to making our final decision. You've got a good chance if you've made it this far. Most people still here will be going. Some of them might be going on a later trip."

"I'm still trying to convince my sister to come," I said as the woman picked up my chart and jotted down some notes.

"Katherine Shylock," the woman recalled, not even looking up from her work.

"Yes, Katy." She was my older sister.

"You should really have her talk to your recruiter. She can be fast-tracked because of your shared genetics. And it'll help your application too."

"How so?" Was I in danger of not making through on my own?

"Even though most space travel occurs in stasis, being so far from home can sometimes be distressing. Sisters provide a built-in support network."

That made sense. I definitely wanted my sister to come with me. Although they'd spouted the jargon at me several times, I still had no idea where Xavia actually was, but it was three-months travel in stasis. More than wanting the company for me, I wanted it for *her*. Katy needed a change in her life.

And there were worse things she could pick than vacation on a tropical planet. The brochures showed gorgeous flowering tropics. And the men...wow. Alien, but exquisite. Screw little green men. Maybe they were green, but they were freaking bodybuilders. Broad shoulders, expansive chests. They had devilish horns framing their angular faces and thick hair. I had also been assured that they were proportionally equipped below...and compatible.

If my sister didn't come, she was the one missing out, that was for sure. I wouldn't be. This opportunity had come just in time for me. I had been starting to panic. I had a birthday coming up, and I was starting to feel...I don't know...old? It seemed it was becoming more and more difficult to travel with each passing year. I still hadn't been to Europe, like all my other friends. Nor had I settled down like many of my other friends. As an adventurer, I felt like I was falling behind on my bucket list. Visiting another planet would really put that into perspective though. It's like a dozen birds with a space-traveling stone or two.

"Thanks," I whispered. It all seemed conspiratorial here. I still wanted to improve my chances. I glanced at my phone to see my sister's message. She wanted to know if we were still on for movie-and-popcorn night. That would be perfect. I could bring it up again then. I knew she didn't want me to go alone, and I hoped that getting this far into the program would light a fire under *her* butt to join the program.

I was going into space, and I needed my sister to come with me.

Chapter Four
Saf

Vance

As I expected, Vjann and I found nothing on our scouting trip. For whatever reason, Orkain were active at night, so we suspected caves were their first choice for shelter upon arrival. Caves provided instant shelter and a good hiding spot from creatures who were active during the day like us. Unfortunately, there were a lot of caves in the area, whole systems of them, and many scouting missions were unsuccessful.

On the evening's return home, I walked the path alone but remained careful to listen for any sounds above. I would not get lazy and let the thing I couldn't find track *me*. The ground was close to its warmest, I'd likely be safe returning to my home. The Orkain hunted with their temperature-based vision. Even for my size, I still blended in a bit with my surroundings.

As soon as I opened the door to my humble underground abode, the saf bounded from wherever she hides while I am away. Her shiny cream coat looked almost smoky near her eyes, which were a pale-blue. She came at a hurried pace, as if she'd been doing something naughty. Either that, or she wanted me to refresh her food. As much as it pained me, I pretended to ignore her.

My home was very much the opposite of the human's spaceship, small, underground, and cozy. In the living room, the urish was oversized so it could be lodged upon at different angles by even a large being such as myself. I had stuffed the communication device, settit, in the corner for my official remote work. Otherwise, the place was full of things that brought me comfort. Natural fiber, woven textures and potted plants covered every surface.

I walked into the kitchen and prepared a cup of fah, turning on the oven and stove, and filling the kettle. The kitchen was just as bright and green as the living room. I pulled out the tin of fah before I got a gentle swat on my ankle. That was the signal. I looked down and widened my eyes in surprise, as if I've just noticed her there.

"Oh! Hello, Moyuki."

Moyuki purred and rubbed against my leg. I pretend she is appreciating my return and not celebrating incoming dinner treats. I never expected to care for a saf, but so many pets had been orphaned. This one belonged to my neighbor when I lived in the city. I knew the saf's name was Moyuki but not much more than that. It had taken a while for Moyuki to learn to trust me and for me to trust her, but we had figured it out. I learned she didn't like me looming over her, which was difficult…because I was massively larger and taller than her. She only came up to my knees. We had this one ritual—me ignoring her until she demanded my attention. Any other approaches had her scampering away in shyness. I didn't know if she had always been this way—she had been alone for some time before I heard her in the neighboring apartment. No matter. We had each other now.

I pulled out a snack for both of us, some cured meat, leftover fish from last night, and some fyg. I made two plates, and put hers down on the floor. She rubbed appreciatively on the previously swatted ankle. Then she slinked to the edge of the plate and stalked the food which sat upon it.

I did much the same after sitting down at my table for one. I laughed at the impulse to bring her food onto the table with mine. Still, I felt particularly lonely in the moment. Something about seeking out people and not finding them had me feeling like I was missing out.

I imagined the humans had communicated with Earth and were calling for volunteers and preparing them even as I munched on my early dinner and watched the fah dissolve in my mug. Who was she? What would she be like? Would she like me? And would she like Moyuki?

It was too late today, but tomorrow, heshiev. I needed to pick fyg and harvest the nele near my house. Also, the plants inside needed to be rotated with the plants outside so they could get some real sunshine, fresh air, and stimulation. Thoughts of preparing the place for my potential mate distracted me.

After Moyuki's hunter prayer, she attacked the food on her plate. I gave up appreciating my own dinner and pulled out the language pamphlets again. I still didn't understand subject-verb agreement. I'd work on my English, then maybe redecorate the guest room. I stayed up late readying myself and the place every night. I wanted her to see I could provide a suitable home environment. I was being given this opportunity, and I wasn't going to take it for granted. I would be a good provider and a good partner. She would want for nothing.

Moyuki had no complaints, at least. She had torn at her food and left the remnants surrounding the turned-over plate. She growled as she exited the room, which, if anything, was a compliment, not a complaint. Yep. Who wouldn't like Moyuki? I picked up her scattered food and poured a glass of fage for myself. It went well with subject-verb agreement.

Chapter Five
Trip of a Lifetime

Sara

Popcorn-and-movie night went way better than I thought it would. After some prodding, I found out my sister had already been speaking with the recruiter. I spent the next week pushing her, and she finally went in for the tests. Just in time too, I was told.

Next month, we were settling into another popcorn-and-movie night at my place. Katy had brought the white wine this time, which was good, because I was out. Katy wasn't on Leslie the cat's incredibly short list of tolerable people, and thus Leslie was nowhere to be seen. I kept out an ear for butter-flavored popcorn popping in the microwave while I flipped through the movies.

"What are you in the mood for?" I asked, speeding through the list faster than either of us could interpret.

"I dunno. I feel like I've seen everything. I guess that's what happens when you sit at home all day," Katy replied, equally unmotivated.

I made a noise of acknowledgment but didn't want to beat a dead horse, even if she did open the door for it. My sister's lack of work had been going on for nearly a year now, and that's why I was glad she had applied for the Xavia trip. She needed something…different. Anything.

I wasn't used to feeling like I knew better than my sister or that she needed help. She was not only older than me, she had always been decidedly the more serious and responsible of the two of us. For example, I took photos and posted them to social media. I chronicled my travels, and that helped sponsor a trip or two. Meanwhile, my sister had built a real business as a freelance wedding photographer. However, when her jerk of a fiancée left her at the altar—good riddance, the ass—weddings obviously left a really bad taste in her mouth. It had been a year though, and she still hadn't been able to get back to work. I couldn't blame her, but I also hoped it was because she had wanted to do something different…and not because she still hadn't gotten over Mike.

"OK. Well, I need a rom-com to distract me from all this nervousness," I said, moving to that genre on the screen. Happy Caucasian couples smiled from the preview images surrounded by baked goods and fall festivals.

We were supposed to hear from the trip program director any day now, though I felt like we probably should have heard from him already. It made me anxious. I really wanted this, and I hated getting my hopes up for nothing. There was no way I was going to pay my way to another freaking planet. I couldn't even afford to get to Europe for a backpacking trip. I'd be back to saving up for Machu Picchu.

My mom had always talked about traveling, but never did. Perhaps she thought she would have had time after her kids had grown. Perhaps if dad had stuck around, we all could have traveled together. Whatever the reason, she couldn't and didn't travel. I wasn't going to make the same mistakes. For her, she had the entire world. I had more than one. I needed to get going.

Our mom had been stuck raising my sister and me after our dad left. Even though we were different personalities, we looked like hers and looked like sisters. We had our mom's hazel brown eyes. Katy's hair was a lighter brown than mine but with the same slick texture. We were all around 5'7". Katy would be quick to point out that she was half an inch taller than me. Whatever.

My phone buzzed on the counter.

"No phones during movie night!" shouted my sister from her designated spot on the couch, but she made no movement to actually stop me.

"Heck no! Movie hasn't started yet, and…shit! It's a government number. This is it!" I accepted the call with a shaky hand. "Hello, this is Sara Shylock," I said in my most professional phone-voice.

"Hello, Sara. This is Captain Smith. I'd like to cordially invite you to join my flight to Xavia."

"Oh my gosh! Yes, yes!" I shouted, pulling the phone away from my face, but I'm sure it was still plenty loud for him. He probably did the same on his side.

Another beat later, I was asking about my sister. "She's right here. I can save you a call…" I said ending it with a question's inflection.

"She is my next call. Would you like to hand the phone to her?"

I trotted over to the couch and presented my phone eagerly to my sister.

After a moment, she smiled and nodded her head at me. "Yes, sir. Thank you, sir," she said.

She managed to keep a professional volume until the phone call's end. I grabbed both her hands and pulled her off the couch, my phone falling between the cushions. We jumped up and down and screamed… Okay, I jumped up and down and screamed, and my sister just gave a big smile. But it was a happy smile.

This was going to be great. This was going to be awesome. I just knew it.

Chapter Six
Heshiev

Vance

I checked the time again, but it only made Lian later. I had taken a special interest in the young Xavian when he had barely missed the cutoff for the prospective mate selection process. Lian had lost his family. He had a lot of potential, and that's what drew me to him— he'd be an easy project. It felt good to teach someone…made me feel like I had expertise to share. Really, there weren't many qualified Xavians around. Unfortunately, his attitude had quickly come to a head when he realized he wouldn't be selected for his age.

He would have some excuse when he arrived, but I wasn't going to wait any longer for him. He could find me at whichever heshiev plot. In fact, it would benefit him to locate them on his own. We had scattered our plots so that they'd be less likely to be noticed by the Orkain. We all planted and tended areas near our homes. There were some community plots as well. I hoped Lian was taking care of the ones near his home, but I suspected that his respect for our future had been spread thin since receiving news that it wouldn't include a potential-mate.

I gathered the small hand tools I would need. We were harvesting the last of our crops before the rainy season. Crop yield wasn't critical this year. We had plenty of food stores from supporting a much larger population, but it was important to perfect our systems before we were completely dependent on them to sustain—and eventually, hopefully grow—our population.

I purposefully chose the farthest lot from the house, so Lian would have to work extra hard to find me. I dug up the mature nele root, shaking dirt back into the holes. I was mostly done when Lian arrived.

He was tall, lanky, and carried himself like he was self-conscious about it. He would probably have another growth spurt that would fill him out. His horns would thicken and darken as well. He had deep blue-green skin, many shades darker than mine.

"Haellea," Lian greeted me. "I was working out and didn't realize how late it had gotten."

I noticed that was not an apology. "If you spent as much time tending the food your mate would eat as you do yourself—"

"I am what she's going to eat, right?" He smirked and flexed his arms for me.

Even if he had been punctual, I was unimpressed. He had been spending too much time with his young, underdeveloped peers. He was standing next to an elite specimen. "You'd be better tending the nele."

I tossed him a hand shovel, and he got down on his knees without complaint or further excuses. I let the rest of lecture die. His age group was more disenfranchised than mine. They had been through trauma at a much younger age. How should I tell him how to cope? His generation had to find its own way. He dug around the roots of the nele plant to find the tubers for our tables. I took the opportunity to sit back against the bank and supervise. Perhaps Lian knew what he was doing when he didn't care about tending *my* vegetables.

I basked in the sun, the smell of freshly turned dirt filling my nose. I combed the soft green grass with my fingers. The rainy season would be upon us shortly. Then, after crops were back in the ground, it would be time for the human women to arrive. That is, if the Earthlings hadn't just flown off with our glor to never come back. I thought over the negotiations. There were other ways to pull off what they did with less trouble. They seemed intent to return for more glor, at least.

Something large swooped down toward Lian. Launching from the bank, I smashed into it before I could even process what was happening. The Orkain were large beasts. I knocked this one off balance, sending it tumbling. It hadn't been able to grab Lian, only knock him over. He was flat on the ground, unable to help. I scrambled to my feet, reaching for my dagger and for the Orkain. The Orkain was faster to its feet, or else didn't need them, as its wings helped orient itself. It had a Xavian torso and arms, but its hands formed talons. Massive wings sprouted from its back. Horns grew from its head and reached down to mirror its long fangs.

I attacked but was no longer in range anymore. It kicked me with its hocked beast foot. The flesh on my arm ripped open from its sharp nails, its powerful wings beating around me. There was a flurry of swings as I found my dagger and swung with my injured arm. I missed when it retreated. Lian recovered, standing up. The Orkain's advantage of surprise was now gone, and it took off as quickly as it had arrived, leaving them in a swirl of confusion and blood.

Lian cursed loudly and took stock of his body. He wasn't bleeding. I was. I staunched it as best I could with my hand. I still clung to my dagger, which hadn't even touched my enemy. Lian and I crept deep into the jungle, making our exit too. We would return later for the tools and the harvest, but we wouldn't use this plot next season. It had been spotted, and it would no longer be safe to go there.

"Thank you for saving me back there," said Lian. His head drooped in shame that he needed to thank me. I was glad he was alive. It wasn't his fault. I hadn't seen the Orkain either, and I should have been looking out while he worked. It wasn't either of our skills that had saved us. We didn't have a chance against it. We were only alive because it stopped attacking. Life with the Orkain was hard. Even when there weren't losses, there was never any clear victory. I felt shame too. And pain.

My arm was cut open. It would need stitches. I took off my shirt and wrapped it around my limb, tying it tight. Lian averted his eyes from my wrapped arm as he turned a shade closer to my complexion.

"Let's get you to the medic," he said.

I considered the cut's prominent location. "No, I'm going to someone good. An old friend."

#

I knocked on Bolin's door with Lian hovering around me like a lost, slightly pale pet. One of Bolin's housemates, Kalen, took one look at my wrapped bleeding arm and called over Bolin. "It's either about the blouse or the arm," he reported as he let me and Lian inside.

"An Orkain attack," said Lian, panic still simmering at the edge of his voice despite us not having seen sign of the Orkain since it took off at the heshiev plot.

Kalen directed Lian to the settit where they could alert the others. Vjann might go looking for it. He had hopes of following one back to its cave and then killing a whole nest of them. We didn't have methods for killing one, much less a group of them, but Vjann had yet to find them anyway.

Bolin appeared at the door. He was an old friend in that we'd known each other for a long time. And that he was old. It seemed he had thinned again since I had seen him last. He gave me a warm smile framed by leathery, faded green lips.

"I don't think that shirt is salvageable," he said.

He supported my arm as if it was a delicate garment he was taking to his machines. I felt silly, but maybe it was just the blood loss. He escorted me to the kitchen. The shirt was discarded.

We cleaned the wound together, huddled over the laceration on my forearm.

"This is deep. Perhaps you should see about this muscle. It's injured too." He looked at it underneath a magnifying light, brought to him by Kalen.

"Just sew up the skin. Make it pretty. That's why I came to you." I dismissed him. I didn't want to see the medic.

Bolin was a seamster. The greatest in town when we lived in towns. He was also one of my apartment neighbors. That's how I'd gotten to know him.

Bolin took stock of me, then acquiesced. "How much of a scar do you want?" he teased as he began his patchwork.

"Just enough to start a conversation," I joked in return.

"Lian's unhurt." He said it slowly and appreciatively, not taking his eyes off my wound.

I didn't feel like accepting the comment at the moment, even if it was the truth. We had been lucky the Orkain had changed its mind for whatever reason. What was that reason? Was it just reminding us we could be killed whenever it pleased?

I squeezed my fist and felt more pain than I expected. Bolin paused his work to give me another chance to renege. There was possibly some tissue or muscle damage. I did not. He continued his work.

Internally, I cursed. Now the rainy season would be spent healing and recuperating my arm. What about preparing for my mate? I had so many plans, and what were they for?

I heard Lian in the next room, reciting the story with some exaggeration for his role. I squeezed my knee with my free hand. Lian was unhurt this time. But I should have done more…what more could I do? I felt powerless against this enemy. The Orkain were looming larger and larger over our shrinking community. We'd lost the apartment and town where Bolin and I had lived. Now, he was patching me, hidden underground.

Where would we be next?

"How is Moyuki?" he asked, pulling me from my reverie.

"I think she eats half my protein portion," I joked.

"Thank stars, you are not suffering." He raised his shaggy gray eyebrows as he looked pointedly at my shirtless torso.

I smirked at the praise. "Woman's gotta be able to bounce a berry off these." I wiggled my pecs.

"That's really stupid," said Bolin.

It was.

There was little point if I wasn't going to be able to protect said woman.

Bolin gave me a pat on the shoulder after he finished with the bandage. He didn't ask me to recount the proper tale as he cleaned the table. It didn't matter. We were both a bit jaded. We saved the optimism and righteous anger for later in the day with Xavians who required such emotional responses.

"Thank you, Zroso." I used the term for respect.

I was not given a shirt to straighten, so I settled on clearing my throat before heading into the other room with Lian, Kalen, and whichever government official they had on the settit.

Chapter Seven
Take-Off

Sara

On the morning of the launch, I was a bundle of happy nerves. I thought there'd be a meet-and-greet with the staff and the other selected guests for Xavia, but unfortunately it was for more serious safety checks and technicalities. There'd be plenty of time to meet and hang out with everyone when we reached our destination. Six months of vacation!

I had already been familiarized with my stasis pod and had tried on my suit, which fit perfectly. I'd enjoyed taking pictures of myself in it and posting them to my social media. *#Xaviabound, finally!*

It seemed strange to be posting to social media for the beginning of my trip when I wouldn't be able to post anything during the trip. Some of our photos might be transmitted and posted to the government's official channels, but my ever-present personal channels would be quiet for a year. That was insane to me. I was sure I would get right back to it when I returned though. I would have six months of vacation photos to upload. That was freaking awesome. I would have content for like a year.

I was really excited for my adventure. My room had a sturdy cot and a television. They had several care-kits for when we woke up. Along with the usual water and rations, just in case. There would be plenty to enjoy in Xavia. Tropical paradises always meant tasty fruit. I was promised there was an alcohol substitute there too, but without the hangover! I was looking forward to that. I was also able to bring several bags of personal belongings. I really struggled with what to bring. How do you know what to take with you on such a long adventure where you really know so little of their culture and what they have available. Fortunately, I was able to bring a wide collection of movies on a data pad, which took up little room. For clothing, I focused on tops so that I could look like I was wearing lots of different things in my photos.

With our suits on, I was able to say goodbye to my sister once more. She would be just down the hall from me, as if it really mattered. We would be put into stasis prior to ship launch—that way they could make sure everyone was handling everything well prior to being launched into space away from extra medical personnel.

"Finally, you've got some taste in clothes," I said of her identical form-fitting suit.

"It feels like I'm wrapped in a reflective space quilt," Katy complained. She was joking, but I could see the wrinkles on her forehead. She was worried.

Worry was good. We were doing something unique and awesome. I wrapped her in a big hug and our suits made some synthetic rubbing noise together, which made me laugh.

"Don't worry. I'll be right over there." It would be the longest we would have gone without seeing each other, although we'd still be physically close and we wouldn't remember any of it.

Katy and I had always gotten along despite our different personalities. My sister was older and wiser and oh-so-patient. I kept her fun. When our mom died a few years ago, we had only gotten closer. We were all we really had in the world, family-wise, and so it became important to me to keep my sister close, even if it meant dragging her to the other end of the known galaxy.

"I love you. Be careful," she said, as if either of us had any choices to make for the next three months.

"Oh, about that," I said.

"You didn't!" she squealed and smacked my silver-clad arm. Her brown eyes were wide. She knew exactly what I was I talking about.

"They took it out." My vibrator was removed from my personal belongings. Katy said I should ask or not bring it. It could mess up the rocket science or something. I told her if it was really life or death, they'd search my belongings and remove it.

Apparently, it was life or death.

I had thought so too, that's why I thought it was important to try to bring it on board. It really felt like I needed it some days.

"Serves you right."

"I told them it was yours," I laughed.

"That's…even…weirder… Gross—"

"I love you too." I had told them no such thing. It was just gone when I opened my bag to immediately check for all my contraband.

I gave her one last hug and rushed off before she could decide if I was telling the truth.

In my room, there was a staff member waiting for me. I didn't recognize her. Maybe she would accuse me of trying to sabotage the whole flight with my vibrating toy, like a space pirate—it was at least sword-like...

No. Surprise. She took my blood before helping me settle into the semi-upright stasis pod. The top leaned back a bit. She told me some things about fluid equilibrium and gravity changes, but I wasn't really paying much attention, honestly. I'm sure my sister had taken notes.

The next parts were uncomfortable. She hooked me up to the stasis pod with an IV. I knew I would wake up with even more tubes inside of me, but they would wait until I was asleep to put those in, thankfully. I would have to deal with them when I woke up though, possibly. The assistants weren't coming. Only so much room on the ship, I guessed.

Anyway, off to sleep, or quiet nothing, I escaped.

#

Before I knew it, I was waking up alone. The assistant hooking me up to the machine was gone. I felt uncomfortable. My body felt heavy, empty, and sluggish—sluggish because it was tied to this coffin-size pod in many ways I cared not to talk about.

After I unplugged myself, I stumbled out of the pod. When I first stepped in, I didn't feel particularly uncomfortable with it, but now it felt large, ominous, and I didn't want to be in it for any longer. Next to the pod were grooming supplies. Immediately, I clipped my nails. They had begun to curl! Gross, gross, gross. Lots of things felt gross. How long had I been asleep?

With my nails a safe length, I splashed water onto my face and looked in the mirror. Maybe it was the suit or the small room, but none of it or me felt extremely familiar. Were those crow's feet so pronounced? I shook my head of the cobwebs and left to find my sister and whoever might know what was going on.

Several women crowded the hallway, all wearing the same silvery suits and confused looks. One looked familiar.

"Katy!" I shouted and ran to her.

"Do you know where any of the crew is?" she asked me, already worried about the next step in the process. At what point would 'vacation' actually begin for her? I didn't know. For me, it would begin once I showered. Yuck.

I had just finished re-dressing from my shower when all the televisions turned on with an announcement. I quickly joined my sister in her room with a few others.

I had the feeling it had been pre-recorded. Captain Smith didn't look a day older than I'd last seen him.

"Welcome to Xavia, ladies. Thank you for participating in our cultural exchange mission. We have been very clear on the importance of this program, but not exactly clear on how it is important. You see, you have been chosen to save this planet in a genetic exchange. This planet has two important resources. One is holmium, known to us as a rare Earth metal. It's critical in all of our industries, space-travel, surface-travel, medical, communication, computers, defense. The second resource is the natives that maintain the mines. You are here for the second.

Their species is on the edge of collapse. They are lacking females, and your wombs are the only things that can save this species."

"We will be back in one year, Earth-time, to see how you are all faring. We hope you can build connections with the natives and create some biological ties that will reinforce our relationship with them and, of course, access to the holmium we desperately need. You women have been chosen for a special mission. We depend on you."

Then, the television screen went blank, and the ship rocked, landing roughly on what I assumed to be Xavia.

The supposed vacation of my dreams.

"We were abducted and trafficked," said a woman.

Incubators. Our government sent us here to be wombs for aliens. And what for? For some rare Earth metal I'd never seen. Fucking bastards.

Chapter Eight
Arrival

Vance

We watched the skies for their arrival, and also for our enemy. In late morning, the ship appeared, orbiting above. It did not land as it had before. Instead, part of the ship separated and fell to Xavia. Even for the fire and smoke, it seemed to occur as-designed. It was just one section, and the rest of the ship—intact—left orbit without any sort of signal or sign. With permission from Drex, I led our people into the jungle to find the pod and greet the women of Earth.

During the rainy season, I had almost convinced myself Earth's ship wouldn't return at all. They would take off with our glor and be done with it, forgetting all about their promises of women. However, that was not the case. The Earthlings had surveyed our mines. If they could find the women who would be willing to travel for a metal of which they wouldn't directly benefit, we'd be their solution.

I wasn't sure who would volunteer for such an adventure. And even as we approached the silvery nugget of a ship, I wasn't sure who to anticipate. A ramp had already been lowered for entrance, and Drex sent in our elder women—who were not necessarily old—to check on our arrivals. We waited in the clearing. I hoped it would not take long, but had no idea how long such a process would take.

Lowree reappeared, unaccompanied, and drew close to Drex and me.

"What is delaying this process?" asked Drex. He was concerned we were all gathered here. The longer we stayed together, the greater the risk.

"The women are on board. There's a problem, though." Lowree hesitated. "They were told this was a cultural exchange program. They were only informed of our population crisis in a video after they arrived here."

"I don't understand," said Drex.

"They knew nothing of our need—" Lowree began to explain, but her voice cut out as a shadow flew over us.

"Orkain!" someone shouted as Xavians began running for cover, back to the jungle's edge.

Had it followed the pod's landing? We had no idea how intelligent they were. Intelligent enough to be a bane to our population when they arrived on this planet.

The men chosen as part of the program were all warriors of some degree. We had to be. We pulled out weapons and assisted Lowree up the ramp. "Bring them out. We will escort them to the host homes," directed Drex.

After what felt like an infinite amount of time, Lowree and Elza had gathered the women and escorted them outside.

"They're on their way out," said Lowree.

"Good. You all go home. We will take care of it from here," I said.

"Are you sure? We can help." Lowree said.

Drex agreed with me. It was important all the women get home. At least two of them were pregnant too. It didn't take much convincing. Lowree led her women away.

"We will help," said one of the human women. She had long brown hair and small brown eyes. I hadn't known who would volunteer for such a program…I still didn't. All of my insides twisted within me. She was volunteering now. I had never been one to lose sight of what was going on, but I couldn't see anything past her pale coloring and subtle features. She had a small nose, and dark eyes with an even darker center. Her lips were delicate, and crinkled as they moved, and I realized she was still trying to communicate with me.

"Let me help," she said.

She and I directed women to Xavian men to escort them off the ramp and underneath the jungle canopy. The skies seemed to darken, and a buzzing sound echoed through the trees as if many Orkain surrounded us. Knowing it could be trickery of a single Orkain does very little if one cannot locate it. And more could be coming. We had to go.

"More?" I asked.

The woman stuck her head inside, and after apparently not seeing anyone else, started down the ramp. She stumbled as she turned, and I instinctively grabbed her by the elbow to stop her momentum.

Her head rose high to see who had touched her. She said something that wasn't quite a thank you and wasn't quite rude and pulled her elbow away. I hadn't even realized I was still touching it. I held my hand dumbly in front of me. It tingled where it had met her soft skin.

"Where can we go?" she asked me.

I reached for her elbow again and did my best to encourage her to follow me. I wasn't sure what sort of body language would be understood between the two of us. I wanted to take her through the depths of the jungle. She would be safest there, underneath the canopy of trees.

She seemed to understand, and she let me escort her willingly. She looked back once at another woman with brown hair who was being pulled by Drex toward the jungle's edge. He would be taking her to his home. I was taking this one to mine. Seeing the last woman being escorted, she seemed content. She grabbed my arm and tucked her body close to mine.

Her short legs moved quickly in silvery fabric to keep up with me. The Orkain rushed the pod as soon as we stepped off the ramp. It ducked inside, much larger with wings high on its back. It swept through the interior and dragged out a woman who had been hiding. She grabbed the sleek edges of the ship to prevent her egress. Her screams were strange but undeniably terrified.

I almost didn't turn back to help. Not because I was scared of fighting the Orkain, but because it meant deserting the woman beside me. I wanted *her* to be safe. And I didn't care what happened to anyone else. It was an intrusive thought I had to fight.

I took a deep, creaking breath in my chest, filling it with all the courage I could muster, and pulled my arm from the grip of the woman I escorted. I was torn.

"No, please stay. I'm scared." Her eyes were wide. Her words pierced me, but I was resolved.

"I'll be back. I promise." I didn't even know why I had said that to her. She was a stranger. I didn't even know her name, and yet I knew it to be true. I would do everything I could to keep her safe. Something about her connected with me. I couldn't abandon her any more than I could abandon my own heart.

I directed her into a thick flowering bush, trying to get her to hide. I didn't want anything to happen to her. It took everything that was in me to turn my back to her.

The Orkain showcased its find. Its claws ripped at her soft skin, and I could see that humans bled red. She trembled. Its hocked feet, mottled gray and white, were spread wide like an open coffin around her. I knew the pattern. It was the same Orkain that attacked Lian and me. I felt a surge of anger—I charged it. I wasn't the only one. Drex was at my side. Together we were fierce fighters, but we had been in this showdown before. We'd never get close.

The Orkain waited until the last minute and spread its wings and scattered us. There was no way to get close. Our blades were not long enough to find their way into anything weak behind its talons, feathers, and wings. It was a whirlwind of sharpness, and then it took off into the air, giving it the height advantage as well.

We had not brought any projectile weapons, but we hadn't been able to get them to hit either. The Orkain were a formidable enemy. Our people were strong, and were becoming stronger, but we hadn't figured out how to defeat this bane.

Warm blood sprayed on my face and chest as it took off with the woman. And just like that, she was gone. The Orkain capable of flight and capable of emasculating me in one visit. I felt my heart wrench as I stared up at the Orkain who was now half the size due to its distance. My face burned hot, and I wasn't sure I even wanted to turn to face the woman that could have easily been taken by the Orkain instead. I was unable to save her travel companion, and she would now know that I had no capability to keep her safe either.

No matter what they had or hadn't told her, I was sure she hadn't fully understood the danger the Orkain imposed. It didn't matter if she'd been warned, she was in desperate danger here. I ripped my eyes away from the departing Orkain and searched behind me for the woman. For a moment, I wasn't sure if I would recognize her, but that was insane. Everyone was a blur in the excitement except for her. Her eyes locked onto mine. She knew who I was too. We were paired, somehow, in some way.

I wiped my face with the back of my arm, refusing to see how much blood had transferred from the woman to my body. I hoped it wasn't much. I didn't know how much they could bleed. And I didn't know what the Orkain was going to do with her now that they had taken off with another. Would it realize that it was a different species? Would it hunt more fervently knowing that others had arrived here?

The woman still at the jungle's edge approached. She wasn't as warm as the females of my species. A coolness swept over me as my heat drew toward her. I yearned to close the distance. She was a complete stranger—an alien—but my body and my zarata were already connecting with hers. I couldn't imagine rotha hitting so soon. Who knew if it could even exist between our species? But if it wasn't rotha, it was sure as heck something like it. I hadn't felt this way next to any of the other human women. Just this one.

"Are you OK?" she asked. She reached with the smallest hand. I felt her smooth skin catch on the rough skin on my face. It felt like jolts of electricity. I had forgotten why I might not be OK.

I didn't dare return her touch. I stood staunchly, but my countenance melted. "Are you OK?" I asked her dumbly.

"I'm fine. Let's get you out of here. Come on," she said as she grabbed my arm again and hers melted seamlessly with mine. It was something I should have been saying to her. She blindly led me in the direction that she had come from, where I had led her.

She was beautiful. I had never seen anyone like her. And while I was supposed to be taking her to safety, I was amazed that she was touching me and that I was touching her. She seemed like an ephemeral being, her legs spinning to keep up with me, her soft core seemingly attached to my arm.

She didn't ask about the Orkain, or about the fate of her companion. She might have been in shock, but for the moment, I was thankful to not have to answer those questions. They were questions I didn't have good answers for. I was thankful for the distraction. My new goal was to get this woman to the safety of my place. The place I had built with my own hands, which was strong, hidden, and safe. That was all that mattered in that moment.

"My name is Sara," she said.

Okay, *that* was all that mattered in the moment.

She was Sara.

Sara.

And she was undeniably my mate.

Chapter Nine
Introductions

Sara

My rescuer didn't say anything when I told him my name was Sara. I didn't know if he hadn't heard me or understood me. Maybe he had said something—I could totally be in shock.

That *flying thing* was a thing of nightmares and definitely not in the brochures. A giant beast with the wings and horns of a devil, the fangs and legs of a werewolf, and the torso and arms of a human. It took off with one of my shipmates. She must have thought hiding in the ship would be safer than running off with one of these green men. With all the blood spilled, I wasn't sure that she was correct. If she'd had any idea that *that* was what was after her, I think she would have risked a Xavian. I hoped that she would be okay.

My alien protector led me into the depths of the jungle where there was no clear sight of the skies. He seemed to think that would keep us hidden and safe enough, although we didn't stop moving. His large eyes were bright and alert, with a sliver of greenish silver around the irises. They were gorgeous, like the rest of him. His face was cut and angular, and his horns shaped his face nicely, framing it. The long hair caught in the horns gave him a wild look.

"My name is Sara," I said again. I didn't know why I thought it was important for him to know. I…needed someone to know.

He abruptly stopped walking. Did he understand me? The woman alien had understood us, but perhaps she was a translator.

I pointed to myself. "Sara," I repeated.

He pointed to himself. "Vance."

Vance. That wasn't too hard. I pointed to him. "Vance," I said. And I pointed to myself. "Sara."

"I am very glad to have met you, Sara," he said.

My mouth dropped open. He did know English. He must have thought my interaction idiotic. I blushed.

If he did think me stupid, he didn't say anything. He gently touched my elbow again as we continued our trek.

"Where are we going?" I asked, now full of questions.

"To my place will be the safest. Is that OK?"

Perhaps it shouldn't have been okay, but I really wasn't getting any bad vibes off of him. I didn't have any better ideas. I would go with him, and we would get all of this straightened out.

"You know we aren't here because *MARS NEEDS MOMS*, right?"

"Pardon me. I don't understand."

Right. Making stupid jokes when nervous was not a transferable skill for another planet. "We told that lady. We were tricked into coming here. We didn't know you needed females. We thought this was like…a tour," I finished lamely, leaving out the joke that had popped into my head.

"Yes, she told us. I understand. I am not here to…claim you…or anything like that."

"OK, good," I said. "And your friend?"

"The prince? He knows too. No one will be harmed further here."

The prince? Well, that was fine. I should have been worried for my sister, but I wasn't. I imagined the prince was even more proper than Vance. And, given his physical build, she was probably far safer with him than with me.

I couldn't quite place it, but I felt bizarrely comfortable by Vance's side. I couldn't imagine anything harming me when I had such a rock of a person beside me. Our eyes met several times, and it sent warmth into my chest. This man wasn't just fine as hell. There was something special about him.

I could really get used to this alien thing.

And it seemed like something I was going to have to get used to. I couldn't believe that video from the government. I had so many emotions running through me, most of them worthless and not useful to the situation at all. First off, I felt embarrassed that I had been tricked, and ashamed that I had convinced my sister to come. It was one thing for me to get myself in this situation. I had wanted to take the risk to come. My sister, was just tolerating the risk to be with me. I deserved whatever was coming to me, but she didn't.

My government had put me in a ridiculous situation. Surprisingly, at the moment—still, could be the shock thing—I didn't feel scared. I guess the Xavians had made a good impression. Besides, what else was I going to do? Run screaming into the woods? One of those beasts would pick me up.

"Are there a lot of those giant mosquitos?" I asked.

He had a puzzled look on his face, but he did seem to understand what I meant. "Too many. We call them Orkain."

"What do they call themselves?"

"I don't know. The interaction you saw is pretty much all of the exchange we've had." His mouth formed into a sneer. His lip quivered. But his anger wasn't directed at me.

"I'm sorry."

"It wasn't always like this. The Orkain showed up several years ago and have destroyed basically everything we've known." He said it quickly, resigned.

"Is that why women were sent here?" I asked. I probably didn't need to be so polite after being sex-trafficked, but Vance seemed so chivalrous. I doubt he was involved.

Vance scoffed. "We need a solution to the Orkain. We need safety. Not more people. I am sorry we agreed to bring you here."

"Well, you didn't have anything to do with it, I'm sure."

"That's not true at all. I sat at the negotiations table as adviser to the prince."

"Oh," was all that slipped out. Okay. He *had* had something to do with it.

"We had no idea that you would not be willing volunteers. That program will now be ended. We would never force anyone into something they didn't want."

That was encouraging.

He stopped his long strides momentarily and met my eyes. "Why did you come here?"

"I like to travel," I said dumbly. "I want to experience a bunch of different places and cultures. Xavia was the strangest and most exotic destination I was offered."

"You did not come to aid in our hardship?"

"No, I'm sorry. I didn't know you were in trouble here. We weren't told about the Orkain. I thought this was going to be a…vacation." I finished lamely.

"What's a vacation?"

Wow, I was really feeling dumb. "It's a trip away from usual work to enjoy oneself and have fun."

"It seems the Xavians are the ones who need the vacation." I searched his face and realized he was saying it lightly, maybe even as a joke.

I giggled. "I guess you're right about that."

"Is there much suffering on Earth?"

"Some. There is suffering everywhere, I think. I'm sorry for yours though."

"And I'm sorry for yours."

I hoped I had handled that okay. It may not have been all correct, but at least my interaction with Vance had been salvaged. He was a very gentle and nice man. Perhaps it was the culture differences, but I was used to people jumping all over me when I said the incorrect thing. I didn't mean to be disrespectful of his world. I mean, honestly though, I hadn't really thought about it. This was supposed to be a vacation for me, but people lived here, and I needed to be respectful of that. This wasn't an amusement park built for my entertainment and leisure. I had been welcomed onto this planet, but that didn't mean that I owned it or that my expectations should drive events. I was a visitor.

Man, I had a lot to learn about traveling. I hoped I would get to do more of it. The government said they would be back in a year—that was twice as long as they had previously told us. I tried not to think how long that was. I had hoped to return to Earth and plan a trip backpacking through Europe in that time span. Instead, I was going to be here.

The tropical beauty of the planet was lost on me. We had been walking for a while now, and although my spacesuit was very protective, it was also very hot. It was a one-piece jumper with long sleeves and pants, and the fabric did not breathe at all. More appropriately, Vance had on loose linen-like material which hinted at the muscles wrapping his tall and broad frame. I held onto his tree-trunk of an arm. It was also clear the man had never skipped leg-day in his life. However even when he was fighting the Orkain, I didn't see any hardness in his face. His gentle demeanor was in stark contrast to his massive body.

"This is my home," he said, abruptly.

We weren't near any sort of village or town like I had seen in the photos with storefronts and streets—*the perfect combination of shopping and tropics.* Instead, he had taken me to what I now saw was a mound of dirt with a door underneath a porch roof.

The look of horror on my face must have been evident.

"It's okay," he assured me. He opened the door and let it swing open, then backed off so I could investigate on my own.

"Where is the town?" I asked.

"We had to abandon the town. It wasn't safe there. I'm sorry. This vacation isn't what you thought it would be at all."

No, it wasn't.

His face fell, and I once again had another perspective shift. This wasn't a vacation. I had been dropped off on this random planet, and I needed to be grateful for any sort of shelter.

"Thank you," I said, and I stepped inside.

I was determined not to be rude again. As far as I knew, Vance was offering me all that he could. He was adviser to the prince. He had rescued me and had escorted me to safety and provided me shelter. He could have passed me off to someone else, but instead, he had taken responsibility for me and my safety. He had provided me some sort of security in this chaos.

Thankfully, I didn't have a chance to be rude. While the outside hadn't been much to look at, the inside was meticulously decorated. For a place that was supposed to be underground, it was bright and cheery. He had plants everywhere and lots of light—although, having seen the outside, much of it had to be artificial. He grinned broadly as I took in the humble escape, a secret hideaway he had clearly spent a lot of time on. I instantly felt safe and nearly comfortable. I was glad he had allowed me inside to see how beautiful it was.

He opened the door to one of several rooms off of a hallway. "I am supposed to be hosting one of you, so this can be your room for the night," he said awkwardly.

He opened the door from the hallway to a bedroom which looked strangely American but not quite. I stepped inside, grateful but also a little confused.

Was I not going to be with him tomorrow? The fear that I felt when I saw the video on the ship returned— that fear of the unknown and loss of control. Perhaps they had some sort of procedure where they were going to match us up with those who would be most compatible.

"I can't stay here?" I squeaked. I didn't know for sure that I wanted to stay here, but it wasn't like the grass seemed greener somewhere else. I had no idea what anything else would be like.

"You want to stay here?" Perhaps he was remembering my previous hesitation.

"I…think so. I'd rather stay here than somewhere else. I don't know anybody." I finished pretty lamely, but at least I was being honest.

"I think I'd like that too," he said.

I felt relieved. With renewed interest in the room, I walked around. It was likely going to be mine for a while.

There was a bed that looked comfy and super long. That made sense if all the Xavians were as tall as Vance and the others. There were way too many pillows. They took up easily half of the bed. Were all Xavian beds like this, or had they pulled their information from the cover of some *American Housekeeping* magazine?

There were a couple of windows which were more like the end of tunnels to the outside. There were a few fake windows as well, which glowed with the same intensity as the real ones. It was really very clever, and I wished that some of the apartments I had lived in had had the same technology and care. I loved sunshine, fake or not. He had also decorated the room with plenty of plants. I didn't know what kind they were. They were as alien as he was to me, but they were still lovely.

There was also a dresser. In an attempt to change the subject, he opened the drawers and showed me what was inside. There was a lot of clothing made of the same cool linen fabric as his own clothes. "These are all for you, but only some of them will fit. We provided a wide range of sizes in the bedrooms, as we didn't know who would be staying where."

"So my sister is in a similar place right now?" I asked.

"She is. She is with the prince—Drex."

I laughed. "I'm sure she will have plenty to say to him regarding our situation."

"He can handle it. We will do everything we can to help you."

I shook my head. This really was a strange planet. I wasn't used to being treated like…a human. Like an equal. "Thank you."

Everything we can to help you. I still didn't know what that would actually entail.

"Do you think our government is coming back for us?" I asked.

He gave it a few moments of thought. "I think so. We had already given them the holmium prior to your, um…delivery," he stammered. "Why would they have bothered to drop you off, if they didn't want to continue the, um…partnership…business deal?"

So, there was some hope that we would see the Earth ship again. Possibly even sooner than the year, if they were in such critical need of the metal. Hopefully, they wouldn't find an alternative to it or another easier place to get it, because then we would be abandoned.

"I can stay here?" I asked again. And it wasn't just about staying here versus another host's home but the fact that I could easily be set out into the jungle. Would he want me here next week? In six months? A year? Longer? I wasn't about to ask those clarifying questions, but just hearing this answer about now, maybe that would help calm me down.

"You can stay here as long as you want," he said firmly. I didn't know if he could read my mind, the worry on my face, but he did say exactly what I needed to hear.

A musical tone played from nowhere. The lights in the hallway and living area flickered. Vance wasn't alarmed.

"That's a communication. Probably the prince. Your sister will be with him," he said as he gestured toward the door.

Chapter Ten
Communications

Vance

Sara followed me into the living room. As I suspected, Drex and a much shorter human woman showed on the settit's surface. I answered the communication. It relayed video and audio.

Sara peeked from behind me and jumped in front of the settit's surface, surprised to see her sister. "Oh my gosh!" she shouted.

"Are you okay?" asked the woman with similar features—Katy. She eyed me suspiciously.

I backed away from the screen so I wouldn't take up as much room. It wasn't the first time my large presence had caused looks of concern or worry. It was my body though. There wasn't much I could do to diminish its size or assure people of my harmlessness. No quick movements.

"Yes! Vance saved me. You've got one too!"

I smiled sheepishly. At least Sara was sticking up for me. Although I didn't deserve it.

Katy asked Drex if she could come visit us. Thankfully, Drex told her *no*. I wanted the women to feel comfortable and be reassured of the others' health and safety, but it was too dangerous to go out when the Orkain were hunting. While they seemed to hunt solo, it was possible that they communicated with each other. The successful one could have told them about a new group of women arriving on the planet.

Katy pleaded with Sara to be safe.

"Of course! I'm safe here with Vance," she reassured her sister.

I felt a mixture of pride and pain. I was beyond pleased she felt safe with me. However, I'd been able to provide all of the security she needed in the last few hours.

We disconnected the call. The settit immediately began ringing again.

"I'm going to put on something more comfortable," Sara said, dismissing herself, when she realized I needed to take the call.

It was Davian. I'm sure we'd be connecting with Drex as well. There would be much to discuss. Any time the Orkain attacked made for a hectic and depressing day. This was truly the worse timing for one though. It was right in front of all of our new visitors.

When we connected with Drex, Katy was no longer in the background. With the women out of the room, Drex slumped in his chair behind his desk. "What have I done?" he asked.

I didn't have an answer for him, but he couldn't be blamed. I was his adviser and I hadn't considered it either. None of us had ever expected that the Earth government would pull something like this. It was…unimaginable to us.

"We really don't think like other aliens, do we?" I commented.

It was true. The Earthlings had taken advantage of their own people for the benefit of a few…Something we would never think to do. And the Orkain swooped down and picked us off without any regard to our lives. There was so much inconsideration in the galaxy.

"It was unforeseeable," assured Davian. Davian was older than both me and Drex. His hair was silvering, and his horns were graying. Even his skin color seemed to be muting in age. It made him look sage. He had served in the government since we were wee kids. There were few of the elders left. Davian and Bolin were two of my favorites. "We must figure out what to do from here though."

"We first have to ensure that everyone is safe, especially our newcomers. And we have to share our regrets for their loss of life." Drex's voice was a low grumble. Sadness blanketed him.

But me? I was angry. Safety was such a temporary thing here on Xavia. This wasn't the time to express it though. Davian was correct—what had been done had been done. And safety, even temporary safety, was paramount.

"I will contact all of the hosts and confirm all the guests have some place to stay and provide any reassurance," said Davian.

"Starting with us… Sara is with me. And, Drex, how is Katy handling it?"

"She was worried about her sister. Hopefully their conversation quelled her fears for the moment. I told her that if you did anything disrespectful that I'd tear your head off."

I laughed. I was OK with that. I wasn't planning on doing anything disrespectful, at least, not on purpose. Drex knew that as well. It seemed strange to have to hold ourselves accountable like this, but having seen the issues that the human women had faced, it was necessary.

I thought about how Katy had eyed me suspiciously. "Davian, be sure to speak with the women without their hosts present. They shouldn't feel uncomfortable discussing their needs."

"That's a good idea," he agreed.

"And what happens after?" asked Drex. I could see the doubt shadowing his face. He didn't want to know the answer we were going to give him.

"Obviously, some sort of official reproduction program is no longer viable, but the women *are* here, and we still need them," started Davian. We wouldn't take advantage of these women, but that didn't change our situation.

"We have to host them and provide them the best home we can. Hopefully, we can convince them to take a chance on us," I said. I thought about Sara's beautiful eyes and her petite and curvy frame. I was definitely willing to take a chance on her.

Drex, as usual, didn't seem very convinced. It would make it even more difficult for him to woo the woman he'd brought home.

"We need to stay the course," said Davian. "Keep them with our program hosts when possible, and hope that something good comes from something so awful."

Drex nodded. He tried on a face of determination.

"I'll interview Katy first. Will call you and Sara back," Davian decided.

I closed out the conversation. The settit returned to its reflective mirror state. I pictured Sara by my side and felt a streak of pride and a pang of fear. Would this work?

I honestly didn't know.

Chapter Eleven
A Wild Moyuki

Sara

I found the room that Vance had provided me. I planned to examine the clothing and find something more comfortable than the government space suit. I shut the door and sat down on the bed. It had been a very long day for only having been a few hours. I tried to take stock of my body. Was I tired? Hungry?

My thoughts were interrupted by a strange noise from under the bed.

Rewr.

It wasn't particularly loud, but it alarmed me all the same. It sounded organic, like an animal. Did Vance have a pet? I rushed out and found him having finished his call at the moment.

"There's…something…under my bed," I claimed, feeling a bit immature. Although having a giant man to protect me felt pretty good.

"Ah…I forgot. That probably upset her," he said, getting up and heading to my bedroom.

I followed after a pause. I still didn't know what it was, and now he'd said that it was upset.

Vance got his lumbering body down on all-fours and peeked his head under the bed. His ass was a pretty fine sight. "There she is. Usually, she meets me at the door."

I shook myself out of my daze. I guessed it was some sort of pet, and smallish if it fit under the bed, but I remained on guard. I *was* on an alien planet.

Meanwhile, he was trying to coax it out. "She won't come out."

"What is it?" I asked, suddenly not sure if I wanted to stay in this room if it was going to have a little monster under the bed.

Vance peeked over the bed to find me at the door's threshold for quick escape. "A saf. A furry pet. It won't hurt you."

"Does it have a name?"

"Moyuki."

I carefully got down on my hands and knees and bowed my head so I could also look under the bed. Two bright green eyes flashed at me in the darkness. My instincts told me to back off, but instead I blinked to feign my trust and called its name, "Moyuki."

It continued to stare at me, so I did back off slowly and then got up so it hopefully wouldn't feel threatened. I didn't want it scheming to kill me in my sleep. I still couldn't really tell what it looked like, crouched underneath there, but at least it did fit under there. And how awful could something named "Moyuki" be? That was a really cute name. Still, if it wasn't going to come out and properly introduce itself to me, I hoped Vance would be able to extricate it from my room before I had to go to sleep.

"How long have you had…Moyuki?"

"Not long."

Well, that wasn't really reassuring.

"She was my neighbor's in Frustnerdd. I took her in when…" he trailed off. "We built homes, underground, away from each other for our safety. The Orkain hunt by heat-seeking. Our villages were too warm."

"Will you ever move back to Frustnerdd?"

He had a pained look on his face. I had unintentionally hit a nerve. "I guess we will see. I don't see an end to the Orkain any time soon, but others are more hopeful."

I nodded. I could tell he was choosing his words carefully. Maybe he didn't want to scare me, but I had seen an Orkain. They were super scary and freaking powerful.

At least I felt safe in here. That was enough for now. I couldn't do anything—I didn't have a way back to Earth. I'd been dropped off here by my own awful government. He could have a sour opinion about his own as well…even though he seemed to be an important part of it.

"What about the saf?" I asked with a weak smile on my face.

"She'll warm up to you," he said.

On cue, the settit-thing rang again.

"That will be Davian. He is independently checking on the safety of every guest. Your presence is requested."

Oh, I hadn't thought of that. That was nice of them.

I let Vance escort me to the communicator. I made sure to leave the door open. I wanted to make sure the saf…whatever it was…would be able to make its exit if it wanted. I could really only see that saf-thing going two ways—it was either some disgusting and frightening monster, or it was an adorable fluffy-fluffer I could kiss between its two green eyes. Either way, I noted Vance's propensity for taking on orphaned pets. It was sweet, but I wasn't going to be his captive thing. I wasn't here to be his pet, and definitely not the bearer of his offspring. I'd be sure to tell this Davian-dude that.

#

I liked Davian the Xavian immediately. He was older, more silvered than Vance and the others I had met on the ship's platform. He was regretful we had arrived under these circumstances and immediately apologized for the situation in which I was victimized and trafficked. He was adamant that our poor treatment would not continue on Xavia.

"You are visitors with all the rights of our civilians," Davian declared. His smile sort of reminded me of my grandfather's smile.

He asked Vance to leave the room so I could answer his questions freely. I thought that was smart. And I realized I must already feel comfortable to not have that cross my mind.

"Do you feel safe?" He didn't look down at a clipboard of questions. He was looking into the screen, into my face.

"Yes, definitely."

"Vance is going to be your host. I'm sorry we are using the same prospects as from our…previous…program, but you understand, logistically, this is what we can provide. Is this acceptable?"

"Of course… I was going to say, it just sort of works out, right?" Another one of my jokes. He ignored it. Wise choice.

"Is Vance being a good host? Has he provided you everything you need?"

"Yes." I went back to simple answers.

"Has he asked for anything in return?"

"No, of course not." I was almost starting to feel defensive for Vance. He had been nothing but kind.

The questions disturbed me. And I realized my government could have dropped me off anywhere. They didn't care. We were damned lucky. The Xavians seemed respectful as an entire species, not just in this situation. We could have ended up with humans or worse.

"You understand that you are under no obligation to pay for any of the things provided to you? You are a guest. You are, if anything, a refugee. There's to be no payment, monetarily, labor-wise, sexually, or anything of that nature. That was *never* the program here."

"Okay…good to know, but we can do…things…if it's our choice, right?" I heard my awkward laugh follow. I didn't even know what I was asking. He had me thinking about trading sexual favors with Vance. It made me kind of hot.

"What you choose to do is your business. We do not condone any sort of trafficking of people without their consent. Transparency is important for us here. We hate that you were dropped off here under such despicable consideration and pretense. You are visitors given all the rights of Xavians."

I thanked him for his professional answer to my stupid question. I mean, now that I knew it wasn't a vacation, I didn't necessarily want to be waited on hand-and-foot either. Sex wasn't out of the question either. I mean, being a womb, obviously not. But Davian the Xavian was right. It sucks how I got here, but hey, now I was going to do what I wanted.

"I heard you spoke to your sister. Is she all right?" he asked. I guessed Vance had told him about my sister.

"I think so," I said honestly. She would've told me if she wasn't, right? Although, I hadn't gotten her alone in the room, like Davian had done with me.

He thanked me for answering but didn't say any more about it. Maybe I should check on my sister sooner rather than later.

I thanked him once again and reassured him that I was really enjoying my morning in Xavia, despite all the ick that brought me here.

The wrinkles around his horns relaxed a bit. "I can't believe I have to ask these questions…" he said, trailing off. I appreciated that it disturbed him as much as me that people could conduct themselves in such a way. Maybe my time here would be OK.

Chapter Twelve
Missing

Vance

Sara retired to her room, and I heard her fall asleep not long after. Moyuki had migrated from under Sara's bed to somewhere else, out of sight. She was the smallest of my problems when Drex called me.

Drex's body, visible from his full-length settit, was in full alert. Though powerful and ready to spring, his face betrayed his panic. The spirals in his dark eyes swirled quickly and his nostrils flared.

Something was wrong.

"Have you seen Katy?" he asked without greeting.

Had I seen Katy? Why would I have possibly seen Katy?

My confusion must have sufficed as an answer: I hadn't seen Katy.

"She's gone. She's left!" he nearly shouted, looking this way and that from the settit as if he might be searching her out in the corners of his own office.

"Where would she have gone?" I asked.

"To see Sara, I imagine," he said.

I couldn't think of a better answer, but Katy had no idea where her sister was. It was getting dark outside, and she would get lost. And worst, she would easily get picked up from the Orkain. She had seen the dangers with her own eyes. Why would she risk it?

"Should I tell Sara?" I asked. Would she know where her sister would try to go?

"I don't know... Please, just be on the lookout. I'm going to go out and search. Hopefully she isn't far."

I decided not to give Sara a reason to leave the safety of my home. I wouldn't tell her if I could help it. I donned shoes and stepped outside, being sure to close the door firmly behind me so I would hear it open if Sara followed. I walked the perimeter of the house. I wasn't really expecting to see Katy, but I had promised the panicked Drex.

The sky was beginning to take on an orange glow. I set my jaw. The Orkain might gain another win before the night's end, and I wasn't doing enough on my front stoop.

I stepped back inside and called quietly into Sara's room. "I have to step out. Will you be all right?"

She muttered what sounded like some sort of OK before falling right back to sleep. I couldn't be sure she'd remember the interaction, but I was also fairly confident she wasn't about to get up and go wandering off while I was gone.

Then I set off searching for a woman I had barely met, making my way slowly to Drex's place. We would be very lucky to find her before the Orkain did. They were better hunters than we were. They had the domain of the sky and could find their prey by their heat signature. These human women were cooler in temperature than even Xavian men, which would be to their benefit, but they weren't invisible. The human woman on the ship had been proof of that.

A snarl trembled from my lips. We still didn't know what they were doing with the people they carried off. Were they killing them for sport? Eating them? Enslaving them? If we had the tunnel system like I had been pushing, we wouldn't have this issue. Katy would have run away and been lost, sure, but safe in our tunnels. She'd just be an idiot rather than a dead idiot.

I was being harsh. Katy and her sister had gone through more than one traumatic experience today. I didn't know how I would have handled such a thing, being tossed onto a planet under pretense, being separated from my family, and witnessing someone of my species being abducted right in front of me. If I was in Katy's position, I might have done the same. I'd only met her today and I could see why Katy would risk her life if they were separated. Perhaps she thought Sara was in danger. Perhaps she thought I would hurt Sara.

I would never. I couldn't even consider it. That's what made me angry about this whole thing. I hated that Sara and Katy and the other women were in this position. We may not have known what would happen, but we played a part in it and thus had a responsibility for the outcome. We didn't consider how other planets might treat their own people. And on top of that, we had encouraged their relocation here, knowing that this place was a dangerous place. We asked for them to be brought here, and we couldn't even manage to keep them safe for one day.

Tunnels were the start. We needed to build a new village and create a community that people would want to live in. Not this. Who would want to live in this? Until we had created the tunnels or shown gains against the Orkain, we should never have invited anyone to come. We had to solve the problems that we had on our planet before we asked others to suffer with us. I allowed them to be in this position. We had only brought more prey for the Orkain to hunt.

What good was building up our genetic lines if it was all for fodder? If we couldn't keep our families safe, we didn't deserve families. And who was I to ask someone as special as Sara to live here with me? The argument had previously felt academic, but now she was here. Real people were now in real danger. She deserved to be someplace safe. I wasn't sure if this place would ever be that.

It was getting dark. I watched the sky as much as I watched the tree line and the paths. There was no one else out, because everyone else was smart. Everyone was in their underground homes, where I should be. I did not see any Orkain gliding in the fading sky. Perhaps they had been satisfied with the one woman, I thought, disgusted.

As I wandered farther, my chest felt tight. I wanted to check on Sara. I chalked it up to nerves— we'd gone through so much today. My body was stressed. But another thought crossed my mind—rotha pains. Sara was my destined mate, and I could be feeling the effects of that.

I decided to return home. There was a chance I was out here for naught. Drex could have found Katy just down the path from his house, and I could be the only one wandering around in the dangerous dusk. With each step toward the house, I felt lighter. Maybe I was just happy to not be out in the hunting grounds of my superior enemy and to be in the same home as a beautiful woman. Yes, it could be that.

When I stepped inside, I found nothing amiss. I put my ear to Sara's bedroom door and listened. I could hear her sleeping heavily, and a heavy burden lifted.

I paced in front of the settit. No word from Drex about Katy. Should I call Davian and initiate a full search? Drex had hesitated, but if she hadn't been immediately located… And Sara deserved to know.

I answered immediately when Drex called. He looked disheveled. He told me about the Orkain he encountered and how he'd saved Katy.

My muscles tightened and my breathing quickened. There'd been an Orkain out there and I hadn't a clue? I hardly registered what Drex was trying to tell me. He'd been passed on because he was a male. They wanted the females for something.

And we'd just brought them more.

With the urgency gone, we agreed to discuss in the morning, and Drex signed off—most likely to watch Katy for the rest of the night.

Sister like sister? It was an irrational fear, but I worried that Sara would wake up and try to pull the same stunt in the middle of the night. Who knew how human sisters were bonded? I couldn't risk it. I slept for part of the night in the living room on the urish. If caught, I'd say I'd fallen asleep, but really, I was guarding the door, from anything that might come between us—whether that be her leaving to foolishly find her sister or an Orkain attacking. I wasn't going to let anything happen to her.

I woke up in the wee hours of the morning and went to my bedroom. I was glad that she hadn't found me out there. I didn't want her to think that I was keeping her hostage. I wanted to be around if she wandered or if she needed anything.

My bedroom was quiet and cool. I slipped under the blankets and stretched out in a way the urish didn't allow. And even though I was the only one in the bed—Moyuki was hiding elsewhere—I didn't feel quite so lonely knowing that Sara was sleeping peacefully in the other room. The whole place felt warmer with her here.

And that troubled me as much as excited me.

#

I only slept a few hours before waking with more energy than I had felt in a long time. I jumped out of bed and began to preen in the bathing room. I took a long shower and didn't rush the body dryer. I lowered the temperature of the plunge pool in case Sara wanted to use it and put fresh towels beside it.

I had tried to ignore the feeling—the buzzing—yesterday. Too much was going on—the attack, meeting Sara for the first time, Drex's encounter. All of that was settling like a heavy stone on my chest, but something else was even heavier.

Was this rotha? Or was this me being stupid, obsessing over a beautiful woman merely because she was in my proximity? She was indeed magical, mesmerizing, and exciting, but there was more than a fluttering of my heart and nervousness. There was something solid and staunch inside of me that hadn't been there before. This was my purpose. This was my fate. I'd never heard of it being so immediate—at first sight, at first touch. But I also couldn't imagine not knowing at this point. My life belonged to this woman. No matter what I became to her, I knew in this moment that all of me had led to this.

Sara was my mate.

It was like all my cells lined up with her cells. Those pains yesterday were rotha pains. I'd be able to hone in on my mate by tuning into that feeling. I didn't know Xavians could experience rotha with other species, but I guess I didn't know other species existed until a few years ago.

Anyway, I was determined to keep this information to myself for now. What was I going to say. "Hey, I'm Vance. Despite my population's desperate need for women and your delivery by your government…I also happen to know we are destined to be lifelong mates?"

There was no way that I was going to be able to pull that off. Maybe if I was a prince. Maybe if this place was *anything* like they had told her it was… Dining and shopping, caves, waterfalls? A vacation.

It wasn't like that here. And I hated that she was here.

And at the same time, she was my rotha mate.

I heard her noisy sleeping and smiled. I could get used to her presence in the house. I'd love to be closer to her. The thought of holding her as she slept even now put a deep warmth in my chest that I let linger as I walked into the kitchen.

I would make her mine. Somehow. Someway.

Starting with a perfectly crafted mug of fah.

I had probably…several hours…to make it.

Chapter Thirteen
Morning

Sara

I didn't know if it was a crash from the adrenaline of yesterday's events, or if stasis-sleep was exhausting, but I woke from a thick, foggy sleep. I stretched long on the giant bed, shifting under the heavy quilted blankets. I remembered stirring in the dark before falling back into irresistible sleep, so the light in the windows meant morning.

I found a thick kimono-type robe and tied it tight before stepping across the hallway to the bathing room. I was going to need more than a swipe of my hand to wipe the evidence of sleep from my face.

The bathing room had as much natural light as my bedroom. Now rested and feeling more comfortable, I was able to notice more about my surroundings. He had placed a lot of plants in the bathing room as well. It made it look fresh. I adored the vines growing along the windowsill that slipped down and traveled along the sink. These weren't plants he'd recently bought to spruce things up before I got here. He'd been tending these for years. Or someone had. I wasn't sure if they'd been adopted just as his animal had. Hand-me-downs. Either way, he was taking good care of them. Better than I would be able to. I didn't have a green thumb. I had one plant that seemed to tolerate my cycle of forgetting about it until it was yellow and brown and then drowning it in water for a week. It wouldn't surprise me if it was still alive when I got back. It had suffered poorer care.

I washed my face with water I swear smelled like mint, so I also rinsed out my mouth with it too. I would have to ask about dental hygiene here. I'd actually have liked my stuff from the ship. I hadn't brought anything with me. We had scattered to the wind. I hoped everyone else was doing OK. My sister was probably still freaking out.

I checked myself out in the mirror. There was still some tiny disconnect from what I looked like and what I thought I looked like. Was that frown line always that pronounced? Did the fat under my chin always look like that? I guessed that was what happened when you didn't look at yourself in the mirror for three months. Things changed. I wiggled my unkempt eyebrows. I had trimmed them, but this wasn't my usual look. I wondered if aliens had tweezers. Something else to research.

I laughed at myself. Maybe my coping skills of distraction and denial weren't the best survival skills, but at least I wasn't freaking out. I could worry about my eyebrows instead of how I was millions of miles from home. I could pretend that this hot, sexy Xavian man was at all interested in me.

I didn't shower, but I dallied in the bathing room all the same. I sat on the edge of the plunge pool and dangled my feet and legs in. It kept the bathing room warm and humid with its heated water. It didn't have any bubbles, but it vaguely smelled of mint and eucalyptus.

Eventually my hunger and curiosity won out. I dried off my legs with another fluffy towel which had been folded thoughtfully next to the plunge pool, replaced my robe on my shoulders, and slipped through the door into the hall.

"Good morning, Sara."

I jumped. I knew he was in the house, but I hadn't expected him to be right there. Vance took up much of the hallway with his expansive frame. How long had he been standing there? He had a cup with some sort of steaming liquid which he thrust into my hands. It was really hot. Still, I wasn't sure what to do. I was planning on going into my room and putting on clothes, and now I'd been given a hot mug of…something. And he stood there, waiting expectantly, but I wasn't sure what for. Did he want me to drink this scalding liquid in front of him? It smelled like some sort of tea, jasmine maybe. Or did he want me to follow him to the living room dressed like this? And the tea was growing even hotter in my hands.

I shuffled it around in my hands so that it wouldn't burn me. "Uh, thank you. Good morning."

"Good morning," he repeated, a little slower, speaking carefully over the syllables. Still trying out our language.

In that way that things become too hot to handle very quickly, I reached my capacity for holding the cup and attempted to return it to him as gingerly as I could.

"It's hot!" I squeaked as I nearly tossed the cup back to him.

His eyes grew wide, and he made his own noises as he reacted to my sudden refusal to hold it anymore. He took it back before he realized what had happened. Apparently, he had no problems holding it. It was too hot for me though.

"It just needs to cool," I said lamely.

He gave a nervous chuckle, which abruptly ended as his gaze lowered to my chest. I remembered again I was in only a robe.

"Let me change, and I'll be right back out." I motioned to the door to my room. I wasn't about to accept that hot mug again.

He jumped out of the way, like he realized that I might have been on my way to do something and this hadn't been some planned rendezvous in the hallway. It was really cute the way he was trying to be host. Maybe he just needed some practice.

In the bedroom, I searched through the drawers. I had no intention of putting on the space suit again. It felt more foreign than the clothes provided to me by the Xavians. There weren't any bras though. I picked out a tighter fitting shirt so that I would be covered through the flowy openings of the other upper garments. Then I picked some extra-flowy pants. I hoped I looked like a comfortable but cute hippie and not like someone wearing clown pants.

I already felt like I had spent too much time in the bedroom picking out clothes. He was out there waiting for me with some painfully hot beverage, but nothing of this was routine. I was trying to figure everything out, even things as simple as clothing. Anyway, being halfway-OK with my appearance, and the less-OK half knowing I needed to reappear out there, I stepped quietly into the hallway.

Thankfully, he wasn't waiting outside the door to scare the crap out of me again.

He had settled for the living room, sitting on the very edge of the couch. He jumped up when he spotted me in the hallway. On a short table there were two mugs—one appeared mostly emptied and cooled. The other was still steaming like heck.

Vance was as gorgeous as I remembered. I took in his large frame with impossibly wide shoulders. I could tell by the way the fabric draped on him that his torso was equally toned. His strong neck peeked from behind shoulder-length dark hair and his shirt collar. A chiseled jaw propped up his almost silly, joyful smile.

"Your drink." He motioned to the mug he seemed resolute on having me drink.

I joined him on the couch, politely picked up the drink and blew on the surface of the liquid. The steam smelled of jasmine and anise. I performed the task mostly to acknowledge the drink's presence. It was still much too hot for me to drink. Xavians must enjoy higher temperatures. The shower and the bathing room sink ran hot too.

"Moyuki was just out here…" His voice trailed off as he looked toward the kitchen where I assumed the animal had wandered.

It hadn't attacked me in my sleep last night, so I assumed we were on relatively good terms. I was becoming much more curious about it. It was probably watching and judging me right now. Hopefully I'd pass the test. I loved animals. While dogs loved everyone, a hard-earned friendship from a cat felt more rewarding—a saf doubly so.

"Are you hungry?" He looked again at the mug, as if realizing it might not be sufficient for me.

"Oh, no. Not really. I don't really eat breakfast. Do you?"

"Break fast? Eventually, but not in the morning."

I shook my head, not completely understanding, but we seemed to be getting by. It was fine for me. I picked up the mug and gave it the tiniest sip. It was still a little too warm to really get a good taste of it, but it didn't taste bad. It wasn't bitter or super strong tasting. Maybe it was tea. And I hoped it had caffeine in it as well. Did Xavia have caffeine?

"And *is* there anything else I can do to help you feel more comfortable here? Are the clothes satisfactory?"

"Oh, they are! Thank you." I had forgotten to thank him for that. I had so much stuff I was grateful for. He had provided for my needs and was treating me well. Things could be a lot worse. Strangely, I wasn't sure if things could be much better either. I was nervous but happy to be sitting here with him.

"So what happens now?" I asked.

"As long as Davian is satisfied, you are welcome to stay with me."

"I'd really like that," I said. And I meant it.

I cradled the drink in my hands and sat farther back onto the couch, cozying up with it. I pointed to different pieces of furniture and asked what they were called in his language. We had been doing really well communicating. I hadn't been offered any language-learning aids before leaving. I hadn't thought about it then, but now that felt pretty suspect and dirty on their part.

The couch was a urish. I was drinking fah, which had some sort of leaf that melted in hot water. I wasn't sure if it was caffeinated, and I couldn't figure out how to communicate my question, but I did feel more alert after drinking it, whether it be the effect of a heated liquid, caffeine, or placebo, I was unsure.

"What are we doing today?" I asked.

"I have to go out for work today. I apologize. You will stay here and relax."

"Uh, no," I said. "I'm not going to just sit inside by myself!"

"Of course. I want to be a good host. I can have my friend, Bolin, come over and entertain you while I'm gone."

While that suggestion seemed considerate…and prepared, it worried me that he wanted me to stay inside. "I'd love to meet Bolin. Could we do it somewhere else though? I'd like to see more of Xavia."

"I cannot implore you to stay inside today?" he asked in a strained voice. He frowned.

"No, not today."

While there was a language barrier, it was an odd word choice. He wanted me inside…as in, not outside. I understand the Orkain were out there somewhere, but he still went outside. There was no way that I was going to stay inside my entire time here.

Thankfully, he acquiesced. "I can escort you there, do my business, then return for you. I will contact Bolin now."

I wasn't being held captive in the house. Good.

Chapter Fourteen
Meeting Bolin

Sara

Vance made me wait while he checked for those freaky Orkain. *No problem.* He was gone so long, though I realized after he must have checked the entire route to Bolin's house. That was OK with me as long as he didn't keep me confined. I hadn't flown all the way out here to hide underground. This was my adventure. I wasn't going to arrive back on Earth and have no experiences to show for it.

That was the whole point of this trip.

Vance did not seem to think so. He rushed me through winding, jewel green paths, blind to the beautiful mossy boulders, except to help me over them. Though his large hand holding mine and his chiseled arm attached to that… Maybe I didn't appreciate the background scenery either.

Bolin lived with a few other unattached men in a nearby underground home. There was new vegetation growth on top of the house, but it was attached to a natural hill with older flora. Bolin opened the door before we had even reached it, ready to greet us. I was surprised by his age. He was much older than the Xavian men that had met the ship. His physique was still straight and fit, but he had much less body mass. His green skin was faded and leathery, and liver spots lined his forehead and framed his face.

"Haellea," I said, like Vance had taught me. I gave a little bow of my head and immediately felt stupid.

Bolin looked at Vance in confusion. His hand extended in what he'd probably been taught about my American culture. Instead, I was bowing. He bowed back.

I took his hand and shook it. I couldn't believe I had done that. I was nervous and bowed! And now he thinks that's, like, my custom.

"Haellea," recited Bolin.

The interior dimensions were familiar, but it seemed much more cramped with the belongings of several people instead of only Vance's things. A room off to the side had piles of fabrics alongside several sewing machines. That had to be Bolin's area, as Vance had told me he was a loabnos or, a seamster or clothier…was my guess at a translation. I walked over to admire the fabrics. There were many rich, jewel colors.

"I will be back shortly for you," said Vance.

I smiled at the words. I liked that he was coming back *for me*.

"My Earth-language is not good yet," said Bolin apologetically.

"It's okay. Earth has a lot of languages. I don't even know them all!"

Bolin picked up a dress and offered it to me. It had elegant lines. Very fancy. "Wow, this is gorgeous."

He pushed it farther into my hands and motioned me to the hallway. He wanted me to try it on. Maybe I should have felt a little more weirded out, but Bolin didn't give me any creepy vibes. He made this dress, and I was honored to try it on.

The dress was much too big for me, as I believe it was made for a Xavian. Bolin was beyond excited when I came out. He chattered in his language and began pinning it up in all the necessary places, like he was finally excited to have a human model.

After he was done pinning, he pushed me back toward the bathing room to change back out. I did as he requested, and he immediately began sewing the dress.

I shook my head. "I don't need this. I don't need such a fancy dress."

My only clue that Bolin understood my request was that he was completely ignoring it. However, he didn't ignore other questions. We were able to communicate enough for me to learn he was Vance's neighbor in Frustnerdd and that's how they met. Bolin and his wife, Hano, had had a daughter Vance's age. Her name was Harla. He showed me a photo of his family, with Harla forever as a pre-teen. Bolin's eyes misted when he showed them to me. The daughter was very pretty, and I wondered if Bolin's and Vance's connection had actually been Harla. Both Harla and Hano were gone.

I tried to tell him about my family, how my mom had died, about my sister who came with me, but I'm not sure he understood. All the time, he worked deftly with his hands, expertly contouring new seams on the dress. I didn't know how I was going to repay him for his work. I guessed I would have to ask Vance to help me translate when he got back. Or perhaps he could pay for the work, and I'd pay Vance back.

"You like Vance?" Bolin looked over his haggard nose which made me think he'd been in more than a few fights before settling down in front of a sewing machine.

"Yes," I said, not exactly knowing what he meant by the question, but it was definitely not a '*no.*' He was a nice host. Also, I was very attracted to him.

"Good. He likes you too." He returned to his work like that matter was now settled.

I watched Bolin work. I couldn't compare it to Earth sewing because I'd never seen that either. I'd always thrown stuff out if it tore or whatever. To me, *Dry Clean Only* meant *Never Clean Ever,* so I was mesmerized by his fine craftsmanship. I'd never seen someone iron a piece of clothing so frequently before. Eventually, he had me ironing the pieces before he sewed them, and we formed a bit of a team. Me, an apprentice. Or copy girl. Iron girl. Even if it was glorified alien-ironing, I enjoyed helping Bolin. He was clearly skilled, and I enjoyed watching him and his craft.

"You like Vance?" Bolin's question echoed in my head as I thought about my alien protector. Vance was wickedly hot—way hotter than Chad—which meant he had to be more trouble, right? At the same time, wasn't that why I was here?

Chapter Fifteen
Frustnerdd

Vance

I left Sara in the capable hands of Bolin and made my way to Frustnerdd. Drex often returned to the town when he was in deep contemplation, so I wasn't surprised we were meeting in person there for such a heavy subject. Although I would remind him that we both needed to be home in order to fulfill our obligations as hosts.

Rather than meet in any sort of government building, Drex preferred to be in a more common place, like in one of the stores off of the primary street. It reminded him who he was helping and what we were working back toward. It was good he was able to keep that in focus. I'm not sure that I was. But that didn't change my job as the prince's adviser and my duty to Xavia, and that meant bolstering the prince in these circumstances.

We met in the general store, sitting cross-legged on the thick glass counters.

"Katy is OK? Are *you* OK?" I asked. I had mentioned to Sara about last night's events, and she seemed concerned but not too surprised. She said she would reassure her sister when she next talked to her.

"We're OK. I wanted to give her some space and privacy. I'm not sure if she's scared of me."

Ugh. I needed to cheer him up. He couldn't continue on like this, avoiding her.

"Even so, this is the best idea you've ever had. Sara is gorgeous. I can't stop staring at her."

"Remember they didn't come here to have sex with us," he reprimanded.

"Uh, the thing is—I think Sara might have." She was single, came here on vacation, to have *fun*. I knew she had seen photos of us. That part was as-advertised. "You're not getting that impression from Katy?"

His look told me how stupid he thought I was, but he said, "I think I need to help her feel more comfortable."

"And you're not going to do that by leaving her alone. We should be working from home instead of sitting on this uncomfortable counter." I adjusted my position.

"I guess I've gotten used to being by myself," he admitted.

"You're here with me. I think maybe you need to be more comfortable *with her*."

He didn't argue with me. I didn't want to give him a hard time, because he'd had a rough night. He had briefed me on the attack, but it seemed to be impacting him more than his simple recounting suggested.

"Has Davian submitted further reports on the guest situation?" Drex asked, having not the time to check.

"While the attack was unfortunate, I think it's scared a lot of the women into staying put."

"And they're satisfied with their rooms and hosts?"

"Yes. They're anxious to stay with someone who speaks English with them, as all our hosts do. They hadn't been given any lessons in Xavian. It was another good decision on your part," I admitted. Learning their language had been difficult, but the ability to communicate during our emergency situation allowed us to save as many women from the ship as we did. More delay would have cost lives. I appreciated being able to communicate with Sara in particular.

#

When I returned to retrieve Sara, Bolin had her working over an ironing board. I scolded him in our language, but I was thankful that he had helped her pass the time.

"The dress isn't ready. He can drop it off later," I translated.

"I didn't mean to have him make me a dress! I just thought I was trying it on!" she said excitedly, finally able to explain her predicament.

It was a beautiful garment. I wasn't really sure what Sara would use it for though. Whatever Bolin's intentions, I knew better than to go against his wishes. "You are getting a dress. He wants to give you a dress."

Sara reluctantly agreed. Bolin loaded me up with a bunch of other clothes that he was also giving Sara that didn't need to be altered. Sara promised to come back soon. It made me happy that my friends enjoyed each other's company.

It was hot in the jungle as we walked back. Sara excused herself to clean up as we got home. I set immediately to preparing a meal. I had scolded Bolin for not providing any refreshments for her. Instead, the old man had set her to work. Sara was concerned about Bolin giving her a dress, but really, he probably owed her much more for her hours she had put in. She was supposed to be our guest.

But I supposed he had entertained her, and she was quite happy when I got back to her. I hated having left her. I would make sure it wouldn't happen tomorrow. Why set up a program to match men and women if they did not get time to get to know each other? Honestly, I was going to need all the time I could get. I needed to learn about her and her needs. How else would I be able to present myself as a suitable mate, especially if she didn't have rotha to guide her?

And I needed her to have me. Her heart and body were intoxicating. I was drawn to it.

"Vance?"

Sara was no longer in clothing. Instead, a towel was wrapped around her torso, secured under her bare arms which bore the faintest freckling and were as smooth as her face. Her long hair, bluntly cut, obscured her soft shoulders. My eyes drew to her soft lips, then to her eyes which were wide with amusement and expectation.

Right.

She stepped out into the room. Her calves and feet were bare as well. She was literally in my kitchen with just a towel around her.

Fryyre.

My body tensed with anticipation. What was she doing out here like this? I struggled to ignore my body's reactions, addressing her as nonchalantly as I could. "Of course. What do you need help with?"

"I can't figure out your shower!" she laughed nervously.

It was then I realized while I had heard the water running, she was not wet. Her hair and the rest of her—of what I could see—appeared dry. I gave her a willing nod and followed her into the bathing room. Her hips swayed with each step of her small feet.

While the shower was quite large—big enough for both of us if there was ever a need and circumstance for it—the entrance to the shower was narrow. I struggled to stay outside the shower and show her how the buttons and levers worked in a way that was appropriately distant from her but also so that she could see. She, however, didn't seem uncomfortable with it. She politely ignored the movement below the waistband of my thin linen pants.

With her help, I adjusted the water to her liking both in temperature and which faucets she wanted on, as there were several. I then pressed a button or two to program it. Now she would just have to push a single button to get the same settings again. She was delighted by that. I stepped aside.

Partially obscured by the shower door, she slipped inside, tossing the towel away. I could not see any details of her body through the foggy glass, but I loved the curves I could distinguish, especially the roundness of her ass and the thickness of her thighs which tapered to her thin calves and ankles. She giggled, and I took that as my signal to leave. As I neared the door, I gave one quick glance backward and saw that she had taken her hand and cleared a small meandering path along the shower stall which allowed me to see her tantalizing skin and the water dripping off of her body.

I jolted in my pants again, a curse falling from my lips. I left the bathing room and closed the door before I made a fool of myself.

Was this what it was like to have a woman in the house? Were they all like this?

I tried to take a deep breath, but it only served to get caught in my chest. My pants were becoming increasingly uncomfortable. I meant to only adjust myself, but my hand wandered in a stroking motion over the cloth. I hadn't felt such a need to relieve myself since I was a horny teenager. I refused to be a creep outside her door, even though the sound of the water splashing was enticing. I struggled to my bedroom and pulled my pants to my ankles.

I grabbed my lower cock while my right hand worked the other two cocks stiffly together. I had only seen hints of her body, but that was more than enough. I could think of nothing else as I furiously stroked. I closed my eyes and imagined kissing her shoulders, neck, and sucking on the point of her clavicle. I pictured the foggy shower and her wiping easy strokes along the wall to reveal hints of sweet goodness to me.

I clenched my jaw as my relief came violently and quick. All three cocks spurted my seed, and my body shuddered as I wrung myself out. I pulled my pants off completely and used them to clean myself up. They had been ruined anyway having not taken them off. I cleaned up quickly and changed, trying not to think about Sara finishing her shower. If I did, this would all be for naught. I already wasn't softening as much as I usually would.

I sighed. Hosting was going to be a more difficult government job than I had given expected. I tossed the ruined pants into the hamper. Maybe she wouldn't notice I had to change. I found my thickest pair of pants and hoped that would be enough to keep me contained when I saw her wet-haired and damp skinned.

Fryyre, it wouldn't be enough.

Chapter Sixteen
Flirt

Sara

I heard the door shut, and my heart fluttered at the thought that he might still be on this side of it. Damn, I was naughty. On a day where I had no power at all, it felt secretly, wickedly good to sway my hips for him.

This place was dangerous. And the Orkain weren't the half of it.

The U.S. government had spent so much time running tests and taking our blood. I had thought it was to make sure we were compatible with space travel and with the planet we'd be visiting. But that hadn't been it. I guessed it had been to see if were compatible with the Xavian men. I didn't necessarily need their answer. Vance was the most attractive being I had ever seen, and I imagined we could figure out ways to please each other. Biological compatibility came second to the chemistry that fired inside my brain every time I thought about his skin on mine.

I focused on collecting some sort of soap-like substance from the dispenser attached to the shower wall. It smelled like sandalwood and maybe citrus…something I couldn't quite place.

My fingers slipped distractingly lower as I washed my body. My fingertips brushed the side of my stomach, swooping below my naval and teasing the triangle of curls. It was something else that had grown wild in my months in stasis. I had trimmed, because I felt better that way, but it still felt wild and unkempt. I was wet too. Even in my confusing circumstances, I had gotten aroused by my interactions with Vance. It didn't surprise me. The undercurrent was intense, even as my mind slipped from thoughts of terror, complicated shower settings, to how close my lips had been from Vance's broad chest. Did their shirts even have buttons up to the neck? Why would they? They all had these amazing, taut, emerald green chests to show off.

Paradise.

I pressed my fingers lower and let the warmth start deep and radiate slowly through my body—enough soft pleasure to distract me. I basked in it as I rinsed off my body and prepared to exit the shower.

I wrapped myself up in the same towel I'd tossed. The towel was still soft and fluffy, and I dried myself, though I didn't feel much cleaner than I had been before. But I did feel fresher, a bit more grounded, and what sexual appetite had sprung forth was now a steady thrum—containable but intriguing.

Vance

After cleaning up, I rushed back to the kitchen to finish preparing the meal. I had decided on light, fresh fare so there'd perhaps be something that Sara would like. I cut up the fruits and vegetables and was setting the food on the table when Sara arrived in some flowing linen pants and a tight-fitting top. I hadn't been lying to Drex when I told him I couldn't stop staring at Sara. I gathered myself again and offered her a seat at the table.

She took it rather demurely. Maybe she regretted flirting with me. I was very appreciative of the peek she had given me, but I wasn't going to take her on this table…well, unless she asked for it. She didn't have to worry.

I introduced her to all the food on the plates. I was thankful to have something to talk about. She still made me pretty nervous. She was very gracious and tried everything, although I could tell she didn't like all of it. I took mental notes so I'd only serve her favorite foods. I wasn't sure about the long-term effects of stasis on the body. I would provide her good food to fortify her against any damage.

"What are we doing tomorrow?" she asked. She poked the fyg suspiciously with her utensil. "Am I going to Bolin's again?"

"Only if you wish. I will be here tomorrow."

"Will you take me sight-seeing?" she asked.

"What's sight-seeing?" I asked, unfamiliar with the term.

"Uh, take me out to see Xavia. I love nature!"

I bit the inside of my lip. She wanted to spend an extended amount of time outside. Part of me wanted her to understand how dangerous that was, and the other part of me didn't want her to know the full extent. I couldn't keep her locked inside. She had already seen one of the beasts. She knew they existed. "The Orkain are really…"

"Dangerous? I know, but they're not out all the time, are they?"

"No," I admitted. "We can check tomorrow. I do have some work to do outside. You could accompany me."

She seemed satisfied with that answer. She nibbled on a brack and seemed satisfied with that too. She ate the rest of it in two crunchy bites.

"That's good with fyg on it." I pointed to the fruit.

Sara tried out my suggestion. "I like that."

I cleaned up after our meal, and even though it wasn't exactly late in the evening, Sara's eyelids began to droop in her tiredness. I encouraged her to go rest, and she didn't argue.

It wasn't until she'd retired to her room that I realized I hadn't seen Moyuki this evening. The saf was either mad at me for letting someone new into the house or was too caught up in observing her to remember I existed. I didn't blame her. Sara had an enchanting presence, and I was intoxicated by it too. For the first time in a long time, she had displaced my obsession with the Orkain.

I struggled to say 'no' to her. She made me want to change reality to serve her better. She was the first thing I thought of in the morning, and I kept her in my thoughts throughout the day, and I knew her image would accompany me as I drifted off to sleep tonight.

It was time for me to check the heshiev plots and I had some seedlings that needed planting. Sara could come with me. I examined the thin scar on my forearm, a reminder of the time that Orkain had attacked Lian and me—that same Orkain from the other day. We wouldn't be going back to that plot. It had been abandoned since the rainy season.

I gritted my teeth. I didn't really have much choice in it. I couldn't keep Sara locked in the house. She wasn't my prisoner. If she wanted to go out, I'd have to do my best to keep her safe.

Sara

I found a long sleeveless shirt which I guess could have been a dress, but for now I was deeming it my night shirt. I slipped it on. The fabric was a little rough, but it was loose and I immediately felt at home in it. The air was much cooler in my room, so I was drawn to the bed. I slipped under the surprisingly thick blankets, my legs and feet crunched at the end of the bed where the covers were tucked. Still, it was surprisingly comfortable, and I felt my eyes grow impossibly heavy, as if my body had only been on emergency power and now having laid down, I was shutting down without any higher cognitive functions telling me to do so.

I closed my eyes and felt my body relax onto the bed in a way that I hadn't felt it relax in a while. In a way that told me I had been much stiffer and holding much more tension than I'd had any idea I was carrying. I think I heard myself snoring even as I was falling asleep.

I thought that, and my eyes popped wide open. I had forgotten about the saf, the strange animal underneath my bed. I gave a little curse, suddenly feeling vulnerable in only a linen shirt despite being under the blankets. I leaped from the bed so that there was clearance between the edge of the bed and my feet and ankles. Giving enough room so that I *might* have a chance of escaping. I knelt and pressed my face against the cool floor where there was no carpet or rug.

I didn't see any green eyes flashing back at me. I didn't see a giant lump of fur which could encase such eyes and what I assumed were even bigger fangs. It wasn't anywhere to be found. And the tiny shot of *fight-or-flight* escaped my body. I didn't even know my body had any left. It quickly dissipated, and I decided it had been cleared out of my room or had left while I was in the shower. My door was closed. There wasn't much else to do when I'd been reassured it was friendly. I didn't have the energy to seek it out. The bed was calling my name again.

If I started snoring before I hit the pillow, I didn't hear it.

Chapter Seventeen
Checking In

Sara

Stasis sleep hadn't been enough, apparently.

I groaned when I thought about my parting actions with Vance yesterday, flirting and practically stripping in front of him. What had I been thinking? Nothing. That's what I had been thinking. Vance was probably begging on the other side of the door, thinking I'm going to throw myself at him. The scary thing was, part of me—a very particular part of me—was not against doing that. In fact, I wasn't sure if I could trust myself around the hunky man.

Vance was *definitely* as advertised in the government pamphlets: tall, strong, and green. He was a prime choice of an already exquisite species. I wasn't one to complain about current conditions—I worked to change them when possible. So I wasn't going to complain about Vance landing in my lap. I was going to take full advantage of it. I didn't have a ship to fly away to a planet with less sky-demons, so here I was... And here he was. And I was really curious about him. *Really curious.*

Because it was right by the bed, I used the reflection from the handheld settit. I was not Sleeping Beauty. Drool caked around my lips in the same color as the gunk around my eyes. I wondered dumbly if someone was watching me pull crumbs from my eyelid creases. Vance had given me the settit so that I could talk to my sister after she pulled that stunt and tried to run off.

Obviously, she was having more trouble adjusting to this than I was. I was sorry for it—this hadn't been her idea, and now she was here for a lot longer than either of us had anticipated. I had to keep reassuring her that our ship would be back. I didn't want her panicking that this might be our lives. I had faith it wouldn't be. I never really knew how to explain it, but I had a lot of intuitions about things, about futures. I knew that this wouldn't be all there was.

Speak of the devil, the settit began to flash in my hands.

"Hi, Katy." I laid back down on the bed and held the settit parallel to it. My face was partially obscured by the pillow. Most of the other pillows had been tossed into a corner of the bedroom. I could tell from the occasional rearrangement of the discarded pillows that Moyuki had spent some time in the soft fortress. I still hadn't gotten a good full view of the animal. From what I could tell, it was like a cat, but at least twice the size.

I was just calling to check on you. "I was just calling to check on you," Katy said. She was already dressed. She had a cup of fah steaming in the foreground. It was a good sign. She had already ventured out of her bedroom this morning.

"I'm just waking up," I said needlessly.

A pillow shifted. I saw a green eye staring at me from within the pile. I blinked to let it know that I wasn't scared and was trusting of it. Then I rolled over, bringing the settit with me. I didn't want to intimidate it. I was going to get it to trust me and love me if it was the only thing I accomplished on this planet... Okay, no, I'd be pretty upset if I didn't accomplish *Vance* while on this planet too. The cat-thing was a close second though.

The U.S. government may be filled with a bunch of assholes, but that didn't mean they didn't sometimes know what they were doing. If I'd been specially selected for this mission, as they said, then they hit the nail on the head. I was already planning on having some good sex on this vacation. Heck, I almost wished they'd just been honest with me. I might have still joined up. I probably would not have invited my sister though. That was a little much.

"But everything is OK over there?" she pressed.

I tried to glare at her with my sleepy eyes. It was all right. It had been all right yesterday, and last night, and I assumed right now, but I had just woken up.

"Okay, I'm sorry. I'm just nervous," she said. "I hate that we are apart."

We had never vacationed together as adults. And while I couldn't be completely blamed for what had transpired so far, I began to think this would be the last time. I wouldn't have even answered the call this morning, but I didn't want her running off to 'rescue' me again.

"Look, you need to chill," I said. It probably wasn't the right time to have this conversation, but I couldn't go to sleep and wake up to worried calls from her for the rest of the year. "We aren't going anywhere. Things are OK here. Why don't you…I don't know…try to have some fun? Don't you think that Drex is cute?"

It was Katy's turn to widen her eyes and pin me with a sisterly glare. She stammered. I took that as my opportunity to further my point, the cross to my jab.

"Methinks she doth protest too much."

She shook her head and rolled her eyes, but couldn't argue with me. I knew she was attracted to him by the way she talked about him. I also knew that it would take a minor miracle for her to act on it. I was all for fun during vacation. My sister was more…calculating? Less fun. Decidedly less fun.

"Aren't you concerned that that's exactly what our government wants us to do…*mate* with them?"

"You're going to deny something you actually want because of what our government did to us? I'm not about to make decisions based on *them*." I used her word but directed it at the ones who really deserved the 'otherness'…the men who had betrayed us.

Katy's bottom lip twitched to the left as she worked out what to say. I lessened my pressure on her; she wasn't wrong to think those things. "I'm saying that you should start thinking about *you*. Don't do things or not do things to spite our government. They aren't here. They are millions of lightyears away. Your past is millions of lightyears away." I touched on her previous relationship trouble. I hoped that flying here would help her see a different path.

She paused. "Government aside, these men do want to mate us."

"That's what I'm counting on." I giggled.

"Seriously though. I don't want you to jump into something you don't understand. We don't know their culture."

"I'm not going to marry anyone!"

Pain shot through Katy's face. I had mentioned the M-word.

"Sorry. I'm just saying that even though we were brought here under pretense, it doesn't mean we can't forge our own path."

"A path of sex?" she said flippantly.

"Possibly. I plan to have fun and experience…cultural exchange… It seems pretty clear that they don't want to force us into domestication. I'm not going to be domesticated. And I'm not going to be tamed either."

She laughed. I had gotten silly, but I think I had made my point. The point was that we were doing okay. "I'm okay. Are you okay?" I asked, bringing it back to the crux of the conversation.

"I am," she said quietly. "Thanks. I'll call you this evening?"

I waited until she was sipping her fah. "Definitely, but if I don't answer it's cause I'm riding that giant green penis."

Katy almost choked. "SARA!" she yelled after recovering. Then, in a much quieter voice. "Have you seen it? Are they big?" Her face was a mixture of amusement and curiosity.

"It's gotta be big, right?"

"We don't know. Could be anything down there," she warned.

"Well, I'll find out and report back to you," I said.

She guffawed, but then stopped to scold me.

I turned off the settit in fake-casual ignorance before she could get the chance. I rolled onto my back and stared up at the ceiling. Yes, I was definitely going to find out about that enormous bulge in Vance's pants.

My arms were at my sides, and I felt a gentle pat on my right hand. I looked down to see nothing. The saf had disappeared. I made no motion or acknowledgment toward it, but I was glad to be making friends.

It was time to make another one.

Chapter Eighteen
Playing in the Dirt

Vance

When I heard her stirring in her room, I began making her fah. She wouldn't be out yet for some time, and it would give it time to cool. Humans had a lower body temperature, so it made sense their preferred temperature range for beverages would also be lower. But it also seemed that Sara liked hers disproportionately cooler. I assumed that part was personal preference. I enjoyed figuring out our differences and what she liked. She liked the fah and fage. Made from the same plant, they complimented and complemented each other well.

Just as hers barely steamed, she shuffled into the living space. She shook her arms and hands to stop me from standing up to greet her. She didn't seem to like that formality this early in the morning.

She wore a long silky robe, open. Underneath were the clothes she'd clearly slept in—a tight but disheveled tank top and a loose pair of shorts. Her sumptuous legs folded underneath her as she settled into the urish next to me. She cupped the fah with both hands and inhaled the thin wisp of steam.

"Yes, fahhh," she drew out the word. "Did I wake up early? I thought you'd be glued to that settit doing work-stuff."

I chuckled at the idea that maybe she had woken up early. She'd actually slept in. "No, I have today off…mostly…to help you settle in." I crossed one leg over my knee and put an arm up on the back of the urish, trying to match her relaxed posture. I was actually pretty nervous as to what we would do to fill the day. I didn't really know her.

"It's not like I have a lot to unpack," she said. It was true. We were coordinating for the humans to get items from the ship, but it wasn't Sara's turn. "Will you still take me out?"

Any hope that she'd forgotten her desire was smashed. We would have to go with my plan. "You can help me with…farming? Is that the right word?" I asked.

"Maybe. That's a word. What are we going to do?" she asked politely for more information.

"Taking care of plants to eat… Farming," I tried the word again.

She nodded, "Or *gardening*, possibly. I don't know the exact difference… Maybe scale? Or the intended consumer… Sorry, I'm rambling. I like thinking about languages. What would you call it in Xavian?"

"Heshiev"

"Heshiev," she repeated to both of our satisfaction. "Is it going to be hard work?"

"No, I'm not going to put you to work like Bolin," I laughed.

"Yeah, I'm not much of a hard laborer, but I do love all your plants. You'll have to show me your green thumb."

I showed her both of them.

She burst out laughing. "I'm so sorry," she crooned. "I didn't mean… It's a figure of speech, but it works. It means you're good at growing things."

"Humans don't have 'green thumbs,' but I do," I said, finally understanding her unintentional joke.

We finished our mugs of fah in good humor. My nervousness turned to excitement to get to know Sara more. Every bit I learned about her, every time I heard her laugh, brought a giant grin to my face. I wanted to learn all about her, and I wanted to make her laugh, every day, even at my expense and my own green thumbs.

Sara

I changed out of my sleeping clothes and tied my hair up with an excessive amount of ribbon in lieu of elastic bands. By now everyone had put those high on their wish list, I bet. By the time I'd get to the ship, the few there, if any, would be swiped. I also didn't have any sunscreen. I hoped the sun wasn't too bad here. I didn't really know. Probably something our government should have prepared us for. The longevity of the program and its participants wasn't a high priority, I guessed.

Gardening ended up being the correct term. I thought we were going to go out into a field and deal with long rows of vegetables…but, like Vance reminded me, that would prove to be picking grounds for their enemy as well. Food for everyone had to be grown in small plots where sun could reach them but where cover was always nearby. I might have had a different opinion of his proposal had I known we were merely playing in the dirt by his lanai, but I couldn't find it in my heart to complain when Vance presented me a large tray of sprouts as if I would find them impressive. I guessed I should. It would later feed the Xavian people…if I didn't mess it up. Vance was, by far, the largest man I knew in person, which made his puppy-dog awkwardness all the cuter. But there was also something else about him—maybe it was the broad shoulders or the mischievous smile—which made me want to do crazy things.

"Is it…spring? The time to plant?" I asked. If so, summer might be warmer than I was anticipating.

"We can plant many times before the rains, then after. Nele far from rain, likes dry." He explained nele was a root vegetable, and I'd be eating mature ones for dinner tonight.

I liked dry too. I wondered how rainy 'the rains' were. Seasons were less distinct close to Earth's equator, and the weather was a bit like this. Nice, balmy. The only storm-like swirls I saw were in Vance's alien eyes. Intense, their centers churned hypnotically, digging into my soul even though the rest of his face and body were at ease.

It was too much. I blinked them away and looked at the small dirt estate between us. I troweled, creating spaces for the small plants, moving rocks so they'd have room for their roots to grow to edible size. He mounded dirt above the poor sprout, but he explained that it ensured that the roots would stay in cool ground.

After Vance stopped constantly looking at the sky for those flying beasts and found a steady gardening rhythm, he ventured into small talk. "So, is your sister your only family?"

"She is. Our mom passed away six years ago. Cancer." I spent the next couple of minutes explaining the illness.

"Was your mother a traveler?"

I spaded some dirt as I turned the thought over in my head. "No, maybe that's why I am. She settled down immediately with my dad. He had us both and then left. I don't have any communication with him. Then she was sort of stuck where she was, caring for two daughters. She raised us by herself. I don't want that. I don't want to get…stuck." The ironic word caught in my throat.

"Your sister is a traveler too?"

I laughed. "I can't say '*no*,' right? She took the ultimate trip, but I doubt she'd do it by herself. If anything, she takes more risks with the promise of fewer rewards." I knew he wasn't catching all that I said, but it was still freeing to speak my mind. He listened intently, and I really enjoyed the attention. I'd never expect such a burly, strong beast of a man to show interest in me.

I wasn't an idiot. I knew it was really more about supply and demand. I didn't mind being in demand. I relished in this new power. For example, typically I'd feel self-conscious around someone so fit. While not a part of him had an ounce of fat, no part of me didn't have at least one. Sporadically repeating positive affirmations in the mirror had nothing on the way Vance couldn't keep his eyes off me. Even as he kept his hands to himself, his gaze constantly hugged my body's curves and rolls. The way he watched me and hungered for me. The way he responded to simple movements, like my own hand placed upon on my body or the lilt of my hips… I was in control. And that left no room for my self-consciousness. Maybe it wasn't rude in their culture to stare. We were well past rudeness. His eyes pored over me.

"That's enough here. Let's plant more—" He gestured to another spot over my shoulder.

Or maybe he was monitoring his future food supply. I'd gotten lost in my thoughts. Heat rose on my cheeks as I jerked my head to see where he indicated. At the same time, he stood. I nearly fell into his crotch. Recovering, I panicked again when the bulge in his pants leaped toward my retreat.

Okay, I wasn't the only one feeling it right now. We awkwardly separated and gathered the items to take to the next location. If Xavians could blush, I bet the skin on his cheeks would've glowed beet red against blue-green skin. He had nothing to blush about. I wasn't sure what was under there—he was an alien, after all—but I knew it was large and very…active. I tore my eyes off of it and back onto his tremendous chest. His muscles rippled under my gaze. I was sure it was on purpose.

Despite his condition, he managed to walk to the other small hillside. His hair was probably the same shade of brown mine was, but it was shinier and silkier. I hoped a few weeks of his soap…or maybe it was the water…would get me looking as good as him. Beyond his hair, monster arms bulked from either side of his body. His muscles had muscles. I wondered if humans even had some of them, because I'd never seen them before.

He balanced the tray of sprouts on a decaying log, preparing to plant near its former base. I had the spade, so he'd have to wait. He realized a moment later, and was soon looking back to see if I'd follow.

I could decide to keep my distance. I could toss in the trowel after that…disturbance in the force. I worried morbid curiosity would outweigh my libido and I'd end up in a situation that I wouldn't be able to finish. Besides the outrageous physique and horns, there hadn't been a lot of anatomical differences, but to be honest, the way it moved scared me.

It also excited me.

Silkiness between my legs came unbidden. I squeezed my inner thighs as if to brace myself for his next inadvertent panty-wetting gesture. I thought of my soft-thick thighs laying on his meaty muscles. No, one step at a time. And each step was to him. I was willing to see where this led me.

I encroached into his space before dropping to my knees suggestively. His giant goofy smile disappeared from his lips as his jaw flexed and rocked.

He wasted no time. He lowered to the ground, his breath warm on my face. For a moment, I wondered if Xavians kissed, but I couldn't imagine being this close without our mouths finding each other. When our lips touched, a turbulent rush of spices and adrenaline flooded my system. I had no doubt of our chemistry now, our lips crashing and twining together. I pulled away and felt him give chase, capturing my mouth with his again.

Our bodies aligned, tantalizingly close. The crook of his elbow hugged my waist, his bulky forearm crossing my back, his fingers tickling the hairs at the nape of my neck. I craned my neck to reach his lips as electricity ping-ponged between our bodies. I played my tongue at his lips, flirting at the edge of the next interaction. I moved my body into his.

He moved his tongue…s into me.

Christ.

I slipped my head back. Suddenly the sounds of his language made a lot more sense. His tongue was shaped different than mine. I laughed, stuck out my tongue. His glassy eyes blinked, and he stuck out his. He had three, or three tips at least, with the widest one in the middle. That explained a lot, and I really didn't care, I wanted to play more.

I dove back in, my tongue lost in a space that it had never been before, amongst three twisting tongues. It was like its own orgy. It caressed my tongue, and it all tumbled into my mouth. It felt uncomfortably full for a moment but undeniably hot. He pulled back slightly, probably to give me room to breathe in the back of my throat. Something crossed my mind, and I pulled back. "That's all you have three of, right?" I joked.

A slow grin crept up his face.

Oh shit.

Vance

"Are you being serious?" Sara asked, her eyes growing wider and then smaller as she tried to decide whether to believe me or not. She pulled farther from me.

The smile she left on my face with her kiss began to disappear. Her touch had been electric—her lips exciting—her single tongue was my single desire. I would not let her worry. Another smile took the place of the love-drunk one.

Xavians had three dicks.

"Do earthling men not have…?" I began.

"Let's get this straight. They've got one. One cock and two balls. What do you have?"

That did surprise me. "I thought they'd at least have two, since you have…" The human men hadn't discussed any differences in our anatomy. They must have felt one was insufficient.

"No, no, stop. What do you have?" She spoke so quickly, then changed her mind. "No, that's rude. You don't have to…"

"No problem," I said, standing to unbutton my pants.

"—No! Don't show me… I mean, not right now," she laughed.

I was confused. "I have three cocks."

I didn't show her.

"Okay. Yeah, cool. Cool," she stammered.

"Is that a problem?" I asked.

"I can't think of any problems… No… Not at the moment. I'll get back to you on it." She smiled weakly and giggled.

I, myself, was confused. I thought things had been going all right with the kiss. We were getting ahead of ourselves. I wanted her back in my arms. How would I make that happen again? Despite saying there were no problems, she made no motion to return to me. Rotha meant we were compatible in all ways, but I wasn't sure how to get us both there. She didn't even know what rotha was.

Until then, we heshiev nele. I reached for the spade which Sara had abandoned. It would save us this awkward moment. I tilled, mixing rotting leaves and adjacent sunlit green, loosening the packed dirt. Sara bent over and began separating a seedling from its first mobile home, taking over each other's jobs. It seemed heshiev was not that different from Earth, which was hopefully okay, because I enjoyed it. At least I used to enjoy it. It was difficult to think about anything but the curves of my mate.

We planted the nele, both absorbed in thought. I had one more potential plot in mind for nele. I balanced the spade on the tray of remaining plants in one arm and helped Sara up with the other. Her hand was small and cool. I felt protective of it. And the woman attached to it. Every time I touched her, a new wave of desire pulled me desperately deeper into her, like an ocean I could drown in. I wanted to pull her into a tight embrace, but instead I led her to the next location.

The next plot was out of sight of the house but still in my domain. I would take care of these plants and harvest them when ready. We all took care of the heshiev now that we could not have dedicated fields. I was growing nele, but others were growing other vegetables. Food was plentiful now, but Drex and I had spoken about preparing for leaner times—a delayed or prolonged rainy season could hurt us, especially if our numbers began growing.

"Is that all we're planting today?" Sara wiped her brow with her tiny arm. I forgot the weather was comparatively warmer to her own.

"Today, yes. There are companion plants, but those seedlings are not ready yet."

She cast her eyes down. She had trouble keeping eye contact with me. Me, I couldn't keep my eyes off of her. It might have been stupid, but I didn't want us to go inside without kissing again. It felt like our moment might pass. Rotha be damned, if she got a bad impression of me, she'd never get to know me.

I brushed a smudge of dirt off her arm, wrapping my fingers around the diameter and pulling her in over the newly planted nele. I ignored the small look of doubt that might have reflected my own and planted my lips back on her.

The sparks were still there. I hoped she felt the same. I wondered if I was a fool, seeing rotha when it could not exist, when her lips parted and her tongue pressed until my mouth opened for her.

No, this was it. We might be different species. We might have been pushed together by ignorant assholes, but this was rotha. I no longer trusted the human men's instruction. I would discover what would please Sara on my own. I would learn all her desires, and then I would satisfy them daily.

I might have crushed the nele as I climbed over them and on top of my love. We made out, tongues twisting, lips pressing. I was getting hard. I couldn't help it. My dicks had already interrupted this once. I wasn't going to let them get in the way this time. I adjusted. I thought I might lose it though when Sara lifted her hips off the ground and rubbed on my erection. Fryyre, I wanted her.

I placed my leg at her clothed apex. I dragged a tongue against the roof of her mouth as she ground against my leg. Her breath escaped in huffs between our kisses as her legs tightened and clenched around mine. Could I get her off like this? Was that possible?

She began to sound and move in a needy way. It excited me to watch and sense her progress. Her lips pulled on mine. She grabbed my wrist and yanked my hand below her waist, squished between my leg and hers. I curled my fingers around her, cupping her. Her pants were damp. I imagined how wet she was underneath them and my cocks jumped.

She moaned against my mouth as her legs squeezed my hand. Her whole body tightened. What it would like to be inside of her when that happened… With an exhale, her body softened. She released my mouth, and I kissed her face and the top of her head as she relaxed. She gave me a sly grin and wiggled from underneath me. I wasn't sure who was more out of breath, her or me.

Then she skipped off back to the house, leaving me hard as a rock with the heshiev to finish. Her fine ass bounced up and down. I looked forward to having it do that on my cock. I chewed on my lip as I gathered up the spade and tried to tidy up what I had ruined. I flexed my legs to pull blood away from my cocks to be more presentable. I pulled my mind away from it too. Damn, this girl was fun. I couldn't wait to play more.

Sara

Fuck. Did he make me cum?

I felt a release against his hard, thick leg. The intense need was gone, leaving the duller, simmering want for more. I wriggled from underneath him. I didn't trust myself. Before I could make a bigger fool of myself, I sauntered away. I hoped it was the way back to the house. I was a little out of it. He didn't correct me though, so I must have gotten lucky.

Back inside, I felt sticky from heshiev and whatever *that* had been. I thought about my custom settings in the shower. This would be a good time to clean up. I hummed a song while I slipped out of my clothes and into the steaming shower scented with lavender and sandalwood. Katy would recognize it later as the theme to *My Favorite Martian*.

Chapter Nineteen
Dinner and Dessert

Vance

By the time I reached the house, Sara was in the bathing room. While I was tempted to knock and request a partners' shower, I decided instead to impress her in other ways. Letting her be, I went into the kitchen and prepared a meal for us. I assumed after our activities, she would be hungry. I had a different hunger I was contending with, but at least cooking would distract me.

I seasoned and cut up vegetables, including nele, as the oven and the roasting pan heated up. I wanted to get them smoky and charred to bring out their best flavors. While those roasted, I prepared a first course salad with fruit I had dried from my gardens some time earlier. I set the salads on the table. I flipped the vegetables, pleased that I hadn't crowded the pan and they were roasting as opposed to steaming. The impatient could cook…sometimes. It helped that I wanted to impress Sara. Xavian plants weren't just beautiful to walk through. They were abundant, delicious, and versatile. I wanted to show her all the planet had to offer, and also how much I had to offer.

It sounded like she was getting out of the shower, so there was still some time. I mixed up a dessert, a sweet pudding with fruit, and then put it in the cooler to set. It would be ready later in the evening, probably after our after-meal aperitif. Speaking of which, I poured us two big glasses of fage. I put the glass of fage on the dresser in her room, and lit a couple of candles in the living room. She would be able to relax while I got cleaned up.

Moyuki weaved between my legs as I walked down the hall.

"You're going to have to make an appearance, eventually," I said to her.

She looked up at me slyly, like she knew exactly what I was talking about. She had been sulking around the house for days now, hiding away from our guest. It had taken Moyuki awhile to warm up to me. I had no idea how long it was going to take Sara. She came out at every chance to remind me that she still existed. Maybe she was jealous.

Sara had told me that they had small animals as pets on Earth. Still, I didn't know what sort of animals those were. I didn't know if Sara would be frightened once she saw Moyuki out in the open. I had to admit that her bright green eyes in the darkness were a little disturbing—they'd spooked me more than once in the night. I hoped my guests would eventually be able to befriend each other.

Moyuki disappeared in the middle of our conversation without a trace. The reason why became clear when I heard Sara's melodic voice behind me.

"You should call it 'fade.' That's what it feels like." She leaned against the threshold of the door, her hand lazily cradling the glass of fage. She had cleaned and had figured out the dryer. Her hair was dry, and she stood in silky clothes with a long, open robe for warmth. She looked delicious and delightful, ready for an easy evening. She had an easy smile on her face as she looked in on me in the kitchen. "Anything I can do to help with the meal?"

"Will you take dinner out of the oven in ten minutes?" I asked. I didn't want to leave Sara to entertain herself for too long, but I did want to clean up. I wanted to be as presentable as the meal.

I showed her how the timer worked and how to turn it off, as well as the oven. With a lingering hand on my bicep, she told me she could manage it, and I rushed off to clean up. Cooking had distracted me, but her touch instantly had my body buzzing again. Her sweet smile and the way she touched me at any opportunity instantly perked me up.

My erection was back with a vengeance. I replayed her orgasm in my head—it rushed over me like the water against my body. I recalled how she'd gotten wet from my touch. I cursed under my breath as I touched myself, unable to do otherwise. I had never felt like this before. It was a desperate need inside of me. It wasn't just attraction and lust. Maybe it was some genetic need to survive. I wanted to spill my seed inside of her. I needed her to be mine.

My cocks convulsed one by one as I sprayed the shower. The absolute ache that had settled in my balls calmed and soothed as they pumped themselves dry with the pressure that had built up over the course of the day. I caught my breath, but even in this moment after release, I knew my body still wanted more, needed more. There was something about Sara that I needed, and until I had her, I was never going to be content again. She was my unreachable desire.

I milked my cocks dry and finished up with my shower, refreshed and with a clearer mind. But I knew as soon as I was in the same room with Sara that I would go cloudy again with desire. She had me in a haze, and I wasn't sure how I was going to navigate within it. I didn't want her to be waiting on me or for dinner to get cold. I dressed and stepped out into the fog that was Sara's mesmerizing and disorienting presence.

Sara

It probably wasn't fair to compare Vance to the men of my planet. He could be doing the bare minimum compared to his peers, but personally, I'd never been treated so well. He put together a multi-course meal while I was in the shower. All I had to do was take the vegetables out of the oven when the timer went off. I pulled out the perfectly roasted vegetables—mine always turned out soggy—and let them cool. I was impressed by anyone who could cook. I came from a long line of non-cookers, which was difficult given that everyone has to eat. My genetic line would have died out a long time ago if 'take-out' hadn't been invented.

I'd done a fairly decent job of plating the food and putting it on the table when Vance reappeared in the kitchen. He had spent some time in the dryer-stall, I could see—a fabulous invention Earth needed. It dried your body and hair with warm air. It also had dispensers for misting lotion and hair products. I was in love.

The ends of his hair were still damp. It gathered in large locks around his massive shoulders. He had hardly bothered to button up his loose white linen shirt, showing off his chest and the muscles gathering around his collarbone. He wore leather pants which showed off his bulky legs and the mass above it. He wasn't dressed for comfort after a long hike. He was dressed to impress.

"Come see the dinner I made you," I joked as I poured us glasses of fage.

The vegetables melted in my mouth, and soon I was trying not to shovel the food in. I eyed Vance out of the corner of my eye. He had to be as hungry as I was, but he had the self-control to not inhale his food. He was eating with a polite slowness.

"It is so good," I said, only putting my fork down when my plate was empty.

Vance grinned appreciatively and got us both seconds. This time he drizzled a bit of oil on them, and it set off a whole different profile of flavors in the food. I continued to be impressed. All the meals had been light and delightful. I wasn't sure if they weren't a heavy meat-eating society, or if it was just Vance. There were a lot of vegetables and fruit. I never felt exhausted or hungover after a meal, so I guess he had something figured out.

The food gave me new life. I didn't feel heavy. I felt energized. We cleared the table together. Then moved toward the couch with the remainder of our fage. Fage was another delightful invention I'd love to take back with me to Earth. It was everything we wished alcohol actually was with none of the hangover.

He sat a respectable distance from me, but I wasn't here for gardening and polite conversation. Before an awkward silence could set in, I stood up and leaned over him. I placed my hand on his bare chest where his shirt had been left unbuttoned for that very purpose, I was sure. I kissed his lips.

His hand came to my face, his fingers brushing the shell of my ear. My knees met his and guided him to spread his legs. I knelt lower and let my lips travel down his chin, his neck, and onto his chest where my mouth replaced my grazing hand. His skin glimmered where I left moisture, sparkling green like emeralds. The breath in his chest moved thickly, his hard pectoral muscles rising to meet the softness of my cheeks and my gently foraging lips.

At the first row of ridged abdominals, I also reached the first button of two that had been assigned to hold his shirt on. I let my lips play on it for a moment and with a flick of my fingers, I revealed two rows of firm abdominals. I ran my fingertips along the bars of muscle. I'd never touched anything like them, and with each slow breath, they rippled beneath my fingers.

I dropped to my knees to gain access to the next button on his shirt. This one I unfastened with my hands and pulled the shirt apart to either side, exposing the rest of his stomach. My hands grasped his obliques like rigid handles. The heat emanating from his washboard abs and from the bulge that had been so far ignored by me underneath my chin felt like the glow of a campfire, warming my chest and neck. My breasts pressed against the inside of his legs as I brought my face close to his stomach and pressed haunting kisses between his abs to the waistband of his pants, the front of which was pulled taut by its contents.

I popped the top button of his pants, and for the first time since I had started this march down his body,

I looked at Vance's face. His mouth had fallen open in a stunned silence, as if any action on his part besides the gentle caressing of my hair would halt things. The galaxies in his eyes swirled intensely, a subtle difference that somehow felt stranger than his horns or skin.

"May I?" I asked.

He choked out a surprised noise, eyes wide. "Whatever you'd like," he managed with the formal politeness that he'd used during dinner. This wasn't necessary to host a guest at one's table, but I was ready to eat.

Several buttons kept the flaps of his pants together, which I could already tell would open wide. Despite the pants being tight on him, he wasn't going to have to shimmy out of them for me to have good access to his front. I slowly yanked at the buttons. I wanted to make use of the anticipation, but I was also a bit nervous. He claimed there were three down there. He was so human and yet the differences made me nervous.

With each button undone, the covered mass pulled tighter on the fabric. I ran my hand across the fabric, and it jerked underneath. Vance grunted above me. It was definitely a penis. Sooner than I was ready, there were no more buttons to undo. I put my hand on the flap of fabric to turn it over and reveal his situation.

There was…more fabric.

Dude wore underwear.

My shoulders slumped, and I looked up at him in part humor at myself and part desperation.

His face broke into a large grin. and he erupted in his joyful laugh. He had let me get all worked up, and there wasn't anything yet to see. I sat on my feet between his legs and pretended to pout.

He stood up and crowded me on the floor as he leaned over to undress. He pushed his pants below his knees and sat, bare-ass, back on the cushion.

I pulled back, if only to gain some perspective. Between his legs was the largest and strangest peen I'd ever seen. A singular, wide base with two shafts that appeared to wrap around a third, slotting together with smooth ridges. The thickest and longest had a thick mushroom cap of a head.

He slowly moved it as one unit, but not like any haphazard flexing. They were like elephant trunks, multidirectional, twisting, pivoting, bending, and lengthening. Vance continued the slow demonstration of its range of motion, like it was a high-tech rabbit toy with all the buttons and settings.

Holy shit.

I was a mixture of amazed and curious. Any fear was matched with slickness between my legs. It was unusual—I could see the benefits.

"Sara?" he asked, peeking his head around.

I nodded weakly. I couldn't imagine the acrobatics to get any of that inside of me.

Independent of each other, the two smaller penises uncoiled from the main one whose divots and ridges did not quite fill out. A 'training-wheels' thickness, it would seem. The smallest was three or four inches, rooted closer to his naval. The other could probably reach my butt hole…damn. I had a feeling that "vanilla" sex for Xavians was a lot more Neapolitan.

"May I?" I asked, reaching for him.

"Sure," he breathed. His stomach tightened as I wrapped my hand around his thickness. Clear liquid leaked from the top, and I spread it down his length as I explored the ridges of his shafts with my hand.

The dicks were stiffer than I expected, despite their continued mobility. Thick and green…and kind of complicated. Not unlike Xavian showers, there were lots of features. I was sure we'd find something that benefited us both. The more I played with them and watched them, the more excited I grew. This configuration of flesh could be mine in all sorts of ways.

His hands came up under my arms, and he put me on my feet, prying me off his cocks. Under his watchful gaze, I flung my shirt off. I didn't wear any underthings for this very purpose.

Vance

I pulled her off my cocks.

If I hadn't cum before dinner, I don't think I would have had the willpower. But this woman wasn't here to please me, as much as she did. This woman was my fated mate and I existed to please her.

Sara was relentless. With a grand sweep of her arm, her shirt was on the ground. She stepped back so I could take her in. The line of her neck dropped gracefully to her collar bone. My tongues flicked, like my eyes over her luscious, pink-tipped breasts. They hung partly over a curvy belly.

"You are…amazing. Stars," I mumbled. Pants continued to cover the bottom half of the body that I would worship for the rest of my life. I would start here.

Encasing her comparatively tiny wrists, I drew her close. Her hands worked on the fasteners of her pants as I swept my tongues against the delicious curves of her flesh. Despite my preemptive attempt, my erections were no smaller between us. They reached mindlessly for her, threatening to distract her hands' clumsy motions. I pulled her nipple into my mouth with my tongues and sucked, devouring her breast.

She cut off a noise in her throat, as if she didn't want to give me the satisfaction. She wanted me. She no longer stumbled over the button on her pants. She yanked them down, stomping them off her ankles and feet while I ardently sucked her breasts. I traveled between them, twirling a tongue or two around her naval before dipping to the tuft of curls.

I wrapped my hands around her waist, pulling her onto the couch, and dipped low. She stepped in between the cushions. We met somewhere in the middle.

My nose was in her curls. I breathed hot and hard, flicking my tongue and nibbling against her skin. She must have thought me to be teasing, because she grabbed a handful of my hair and rolled my chin down at the apex of her legs.

Before reaching her entrance, my tongue rolled over a small mound. The way her hips swayed in my grip revealed its sensitivity. I couldn't ignore that. My tongue darted back to it, twisting around it. Sara nearly kicked away from me. I held her body tight against me and eased off on the pressure of the precious button.

"What is that?" I asked, my cheek against her belly.

"*That*, that's my clit."

Xavians did not have a *clit*. I liked it. I grazed all sides of it as my tongues dipped deeper—one on either side, another atop her swelling entrance. I fought the urge to sink my tongue into her channel. Instead, I swept her clit with the broadness of my tongue. Her body shuddered. I swirled a tip over the clit, over, under, across, writing little messages of pleasure and desire.

The scent of her priming fluid filled my nostrils. I could no longer resist the tastes and hints of my partner. I thrust a tongue into her opening.

Her pussy tightened around the base of my tongue before it traveled deeper into her core. The wash of fluid only encouraged my grip on her ass. I squeezed her cheeks tight, sucking her clit, and lapping up her pleasure. Her groan turned to a grunt, and I realized she was fighting me for space. My hands loosened, her hands still on my head. She had changed tactics, pulling my face tight into her soaking pussy.

I dove tongues against her clit, pulsating above and pressing from below, inside her. Her hands grabbed fistfuls of the urish as she fought for some balance and leverage.

Fryyre, she rode my tongues.

She wrenched at my hair, unaware of how painfully tight as her body writhed against my tongues and jaw. Her body quaked. I heard her gasp before she found a real breath of air. Her first after several moments of pleasure I had provided for her. She sighed again when my tongue slipped heavily out of her.

I pressed my cheek against her inner thigh, fighting the urge to dive in again immediately. I breathed in deep, moving curls with my inhale. She tasted delicious, and I wanted more of it. I listened to her breath, her stomach moving raggedly. She wasn't ready for more. I was simultaneously proud of myself and upset with myself for pushing her over the edge so quickly. I couldn't stop licking her. Her nectar tasted divine, and the more I licked, the more she gave. When she recovered, and I got another chance, I would have to take my time.

Chapter Twenty
Sister, Sister

Sara

I woke up in my bed, stretching out and avoiding the cool spots in the sheets. The lower half of my body still felt heavy and content from Vance's attention yesterday. *Finally.* I was really getting tired of flicking my own bean like a peasant. I was *still* mad at whoever took that out of my bag. They planned to desert me on this planet and didn't give me the decency of my vibrator.

While I sort of hoped I had been reaching the age when I'd have to stop teaching partners how to do oral on a woman, Vance was a fast learner. Not only was he eager to please me, he didn't have to unlearn years of Earth pornography. Yes, of course, the fact that he had three tongues shortened his learning curve, but I knew guys that still wouldn't have been able to find a clit if their whole mouth were tongues.

I got up lazily. I didn't know what we were doing today. It could be more of the same for all I cared. Maybe I'd let him put one of those green dicks into me…*one*. At a time. I daydreamed about it in the shower as I freshened the dessert buffet for him. Who knew what he'd like for breakfast. Possibly brunch at this point.

My handsome, pussy-eating hunk was waiting at the end of the hall with a mug of what was going to be insanely hot liquid.

Before he could thrust it into my hands again, I scooted by him. "Could I have some water instead?"

I was thirsty from yesterday's kissing and oral sessions, but I wasn't going to admit that. He rushed into the kitchen so that he could set down the wickedly hot fah—I was right—and pour me water.

I was thankful for the room temperature water. It went down easy.

"Good. You'll stay hydrated," he said.

I laughed before I could figure out if he meant it as a joke or not. Had he known how thirsty he had made me? And how thirsty I was?

I went for it. This was shaping up to be a fantastic vacation. "Don't worry, I'm still wet for you."

"Wetness isn't enough. You will need more work before you can take me." He licked his frosty blue lips.

Wetness might not be enough, but it was a start. My mind started doing somersaults.

"Unfortunately, your sister and the prince of Xavia are at the door."

What?

Sure enough, when I walked to the front door, I heard voices on the other side. I silently shot Vance all the expressions he probably didn't understand.

Did he know how much of a tease he was? Or was this some weird culture or language barrier thing?

"Are you guys going to knock or what?" I shouted as I opened the door, channeling my enthusiasm into something new.

It was instant. I hadn't realized how much I missed her until I laid my eyes on my sister. I pulled Katy into a giant hug, pulling her tight. We'd traveled across space and time—I was so glad she was safe.

She looked me over with concern. She didn't have Mom's eyes or my eyes. I assumed Katy had our dad's. I didn't have any memory of him, but in my mind, he had several of my sister's features. And none of mine. When I hit my last growth spurt, I had grown taller than Katy by a couple of inches, but her caution and bossiness ensured she remained my big sister.

"Isn't this place amazing?" I asked her, pulling her into the house so she could see how not-scary this place was. I didn't want her to worry about me, even though I knew she did.

"This is Vance!" I let go of Katy and put my arms around him.

Drex followed in and closed the door. "It seems you two are getting along well." He was already commenting on us. He wasn't as formal as I thought he'd be for a prince. I liked him already.

Drex was darker than Vance. He was a turquoise green and his horns were a dark brown. My arm still high on Vance's neck, I mindlessly traced Vance's horns. They were sleek and almost black. I loved his horns and *all* the things that made him different from the other men and women I had been with.

Katy plucked at her hair. I could tell she was anxious. I invited her to drink fah on the porch. Vance had pre-mixed it. He brought it out for us, and then tended to Drex.

"Who knew that big guy likes flowers?" I laughed about Vance as we settled onto the big, fluffy covered-porch chairs. He liked lots of soft things.

"They're beautiful," she said, which was basically the first words she had said since she arrived. Maybe I hadn't given her enough time, but she wasn't exactly bubbling to express herself.

"He has a very delicate touch," I offered.

She rolled her eyes. She knew what I was getting at. I figured if she wasn't going to lead the conversation, then I would, and she wouldn't like it.

"Have you had sex with yours?" I asked.

She swallowed her fah hard, having almost spit it out. "That's not what they're here for," she said in a hushed voice, like we weren't supposed to be talking about it. We were the only ones who hadn't. Two entire governments had met and planned it out—PowerPoint presentations over the pros, cons, and all the logistics. And she wanted *me* to hush.

"It's kind of what they're here for," I joked with her, but I also wanted to know what she thought. I was seriously considering smashing mine when she left.

"We are not staying here, Sara." She gave a warning look that reminded me of our mother.

I wasn't thinking about staying here at all. I wanted to enjoy my time. "Okay, but think of it as an extended vacation. Don't waste time here. Have some fun. Seriously…sex that dude up. You are *not* going to regret it. They have—" I decided not to spoil the surprise for her.

It was perfect timing. She didn't have an opportunity to ask for clarification as the men came out. Vance moved me so he could sit in the chair with me on his lap.

"Don't let us interrupt," he said, but they had, because Drex and Katy were not about to share the same seat.

I opened my mouth to tell him so, but Katy stood up.

"No, it's okay. We'd better be on our way. It's my turn to get my stuff off the ship."

I wasn't even going back for my stuff. Vance had given me plenty of clothes and accessories to wear. I had everything I needed right here.

I wiggled on his lap. Sitting on him was making me very warm. I remembered his promise and really couldn't find a reason to argue with my sister to stay. She could head out if she wanted.

Vance

I wasn't usually bothered by Drex's requests, and this one was a reasonable one. He thought it would help Katy to be able to visit her sister in real life. I hoped he was right. She certainly didn't stay here very long. I gave him a *good luck* look as he was rushed out the door by whatever sister dynamics were at play.

"What did you say to me?" Her index finger poked the middle of my chest as I turned around.

My grin formed around my teeth. She remembered.

"You need more work." I stared into her eyes, daring to put my hands around her hips where I planned to work.

She didn't back down. The finger on my chest turned to a grazing, traveling touch up to the collar of my shirt and my neck. She grabbed my neck reflexively as I picked her up and carried her out of the foyer. She squealed but made no effort to fight me.

She wore a loose tunic, and I pulled away her underthings with the hook of my finger as I set her on the back of the urish. I pushed the folds of the dress into bunches around her waist and pulled her legs apart. Her scent was lost from the shower, but I would soon awaken her. I kissed her ankles, nibbled her calves, worshipping her legs.

She warmed and wetted for me. I obeyed the guidance of her hands when she was ready for me to lick her. Slow and soft, my tongues entangled in her entrance, wrapped around her nub, and dove into that slick, tight channel. I needed all three of my tongues with their length and control to properly explore her. Stars, I wished I had more. She swelled and squirted for me.

But she was not to be deterred, nor was she willing to accept more 'work.' She rolled me over on the urish and slid down, kissing her wetness off of my lips before becoming sloppy and eager. Her breasts grazed my chest, and her legs squeezed tight around mine.

I didn't realize I could get harder, but I did. My cocks slapped gratuitously on her round butt, as if knocking for permission to enter. She lifted up onto her knees, and I thought for a moment that she was leaving, but she was merely positioning me underneath her. She reached down with one hand and grabbed my main trunk and guided me to her entrance.

My head found slickness and the smoothest skin possible. I felt her heat. She dragged me across her lips, coating me with her priming juices as I released mine. Doubly wet, she pushed me into her narrow space. Her eyes rolled back into her head for a moment before she refocused, looking me directly in the eyes as she slowly eased down on me. I fought to remain still. She felt amazing sliding onto my cock, and I didn't want to jerk and hurt her.

She didn't have the opening that our women had, but I didn't miss it. Her clit wasn't internal. It was out and easy to touch and play with. I ground against her clit with my hard front cock. It was perfect. My back penis nestled between ass cheeks, enjoying its home against this perfect woman. Her eyes rolled back and her hips clenched.

"Holy…" she cursed as she finally reached her full seat. Her pussy convulsed and fluttered before relaxing around me.

Sara

"Holy…" I cursed, exhaling deeply and willing my body to relax around his giant stem. I appreciated how still he was. I'd seen him gyrate them like a dizzying state fair ride with no guarantee that you wouldn't fall off. Falling off was the least of my worries at this point. There was no room for that back penis, because even though it was a different entrance, there was simply no room. It was uncomfortable, bordering on painful.

He put his hand on my chin and tilted my head up so that we were looking at each other. He had his lower lip between his teeth. I guessed he was trying to hold back—thankfully, because I couldn't handle any more—or he wasn't sure if I was enjoying myself.

Honestly, I wasn't sure if I was enjoying myself, but I didn't give away any indication of pain, because I also didn't want this to stop. The swirling glitter constellations in his eyes drew me in, mesmerizing me. We locked stares, and I felt myself melting like warm butter. My body stopped fighting, and my cavern melted over his thickness. I sighed and felt myself drop another inch over his member.

It wasn't until my lips were on his and he was kissing me gently that I began to feel at ease. My space adjusted to him. I felt him moving inside of me despite the fact that he wasn't thrusting his hips. His penis lengthened and retracted inside me slowly.

The gentle stretching of my space was no longer too intense. It was sensual, and I felt my channel being probed in ways I'd never experienced. He filled and rubbed, slick with a deep heat inside of me. He opened his eyes and searched mine as he intimately explored me, observant of my reactions and repeating and focusing on spots that lit my eyes up.

He soon found my g-spot, right behind my clit, and that's when the soft gyration starting from the root of his cock began. He pressed in on it with each passing as his cock rotated incredibly slowly inside of me. The ridges and bumps where his smaller cocks would typically nestle felt pleasant. I moaned with each passing over my g-spot, and I couldn't help but pump with my legs. I was building up and suddenly wanted more.

Vance grabbed my hips, his fingers digging into my flesh, and pressed me forcefully down. I cried out in pleasure and attempted to rise up again, but his strong hands and arms stopped me. He kept me tight down on him, and moved his cock up my channel in the same motion that I was attempting.

I didn't need to bounce up and down. It felt strange and wonderful all at the same time. I could now focus on my building passion, and he was in control of it. He began pumping up and down and kept the pressure thick on my g-spot. I bit my lip, then moaned anyway.

He stared into my face, determined to watch while he built me up. Everything I liked must have shown on my face because it was quickly repeated and added to a growing repertoire of movements occurring inside of my softness.

And as I pulled close to my orgasm, my hands grabbed onto his shoulders to brace myself. He planted his mouth against mine and suddenly pulled back on his cock, lightening the pressure on my clit, on my g-spot, against my limits.

I felt my body sigh, not having reached the climax that it had wanted. He held me back at the last possible moment, and at first, I wasn't sure why. He hadn't misread a single sign since the start. He hadn't stopped stroking, just not as hard. I gave him a confused look, and he took that as a signal, I guessed.

He stroked deep again inside me, slow, steady, and harder than previously. By the second stroke, I was back to the edge. The third deep strike inside of me pulled me past that edge into some unknown territory I did not know. I felt the peak pleasure of the orgasm, but my muscles weren't clenching yet.

My eyes widened, soaking in the intensity. I was floating. Another gyrating thrust sent my eyes back and my core clenching. The apex of the orgasm. It rippled through me, like waves of electricity buzzing through my body, and the entire time we were lap-to-lap, basically motionless. His upper cock pressed hard on my clit as a wave broke, and my ass clenched tight onto his lower dick as another thrill smashed through me.

The thrill must have passed through to him too, as I felt his back dick and his front dick shudder at the same time. His main trunk pulsed into me, and for the first time, he stopped watching me intently. He arched his neck and made a growling noise that reverberated through his chest and jiggled my breasts.

I grabbed his hands from my hips—they didn't need to be there. I wasn't going anywhere. I put one on each breast, and he clamped on and pinched my nipples, sending me for another ride as he orgasmed inside of my body with deep shuddering pulses.

"Oh, Sara," he moaned as I grabbed his horns and brought his face back to mine. We were face-to-face, damp noses touching as he finished pumping into me.

"You came?" I asked softly. For such a large member, I hadn't felt his cum inside of me. I had expected a powerful jet.

"I orgasmed. I didn't ejaculate…I didn't know if you wanted me to—do you?" He looked at me with a worried look on his face.

I looked at him in amazement. "You can control that?"

"Yes, I'm not an overexcited teenager." His brows furrowed. "How else do you have sex without procreation?"

"Yeah, how else…" I said with a giggle. That was different. Also, freaking fantastic. Definitely a plus one for the aliens.

He was still inside me. Our damp foreheads against each other. He wrapped his long arms around my waist, his hands settled around my butt. Dang, I could stay like this forever. That sex was like a freaking spiritual experience. It was nothing like I had ever had before. Human sex was crude, jerky, and forceful compared to this intense closeness. In its intoxication, I wondered what it would be like to experience it every night.

Vance

I let my dick marinate in her pussy until it softened. Then I pulled her close. It surprised me that Sara thought I would ejaculate inside of her without her permission. Apparently human men did not have control of that function and most sex was synonymous with the risk of pregnancy.

I tried to wrap my mind around it. Sara thought she was chancing pregnancy to be with me. What did that mean? I appreciated her choice to be with me even more. It also worried me.

"You are more than a womb to me," I said, looking her in the eye. That's not why I'd had sex with her. I had sex with her because she was my fated mate…I couldn't tell her that though.

She giggled. "Good to know it wasn't just your government duty." Her cheeks were still pink from the exertion.

I hoped I had impressed her. I hoped she was learning to love me, because I already loved her. Everything about her.

"That was amazing. I'm having so much fun," she sighed.

She was right. The sex was amazing. I knew it would be, because it was with her. Rotha did not lie. Sara was the one for me. I would continue to get to know her, take care of her, and maybe she'd decide to stay here and continue her vacation indefinitely. I could only hope. But until then, I would enjoy caring for my sexy goddess from across the stars.

Chapter Twenty-One
A Dream

Vance

I dreamed I was in between Sara's soft legs. I breathed in her scent. My tongues reached out to taste her delicious cunt. As I pushed inside her, her legs transformed into Orkain wings on either side of me, and she flew away. I heard Sara's screams of terror as her legs carried her away across a spacious clear sky.

My eyes popped open in the darkness. Beads of sweat slid down my forehead. Sara was curled against me. I told myself she was OK. With a deep breath, I sank farther into the bed. I felt hollowed out. I hadn't imagined her scream—I *remembered* her scream. And I was terrified it wouldn't be the last time.

I turned my face and buried it in her hair. She used the same soaff as I did, and yet it smelled different on her, a synergy of spices that tickled my nose, warming me. Her softness felt like home. I hoped she was starting to feel the same. I'd gone from panicked to in danger of falling back to sleep.

The amount of light in the room indicated I needed to rise for work. Every bone in my body detested leaving the bed and this beloved creature next to me. I had never hated my complete obligation to the Xavian people and the government until now.

I gently uncoiled my arm from around her. She made an adorable snorting noise but otherwise did not wake. I was glad she would be able to sleep in, especially after tiring her out—I couldn't get enough of her gorgeous body. Sara joked she hadn't seen me sleep yet, but I might have last night. Another wonderful day and night of consuming her and being consumed by her. It's possible I had fallen asleep first. She sucked the thick cum from my third cock, and all of my limbs had felt heavy when I pulled her into a cuddle.

Morning now, I rinsed the sex off in the shower. Heat and passion replaced with sterile, minty steam. After a blast from the dryer-stall, I slipped on some slacks and padded into the kitchen to start my morning ritual of fah. Sometimes I didn't even have time to drink it or forgot about it, but I always *made* it.

As I put the kettle on, I heard a small growl from the shadows beside the stove.

"Moyuki," I said, acknowledging her presence.

I wasn't surprised by her sulking. She had been hiding since Sara started falling asleep in my bed, be it for bedtime or power-naps between sex sessions. Moyuki absconded with hardly a look in my direction. I frowned. I didn't know much about safs. While she was hesitant toward strangers, I thought she'd warm up to Sara quicker than she had. Her previous owner was a young woman too—Sangin.

Drex used to joke that Sangin was going to be my rotha-mate. I met her when we were young, too young for such things to happen. After the invasion, things became hectic. After Drex's parents' deaths, everything was in chaos. I was hardly home. We lost Sangin as part of a mass casualty. I didn't even think about her saf until she got hungry and made enough noise in the apartment. Poor Moyuki. She had been in my care ever since.

"I'm sorry, Mo," I said to the empty kitchen.

We'd lost so many people. Maybe she was right to not get attached to one more. I set out fresh food for her, knowing she'd probably hold out for another day. She was strong like that.

#

The sky was clear and the day already beautiful as the dew dried along the path. I was glad I had to be out today. In between sex sessions, Sara had been asking about "sight-seeing" again, and it would have been impossible to keep her inside for another beautiful day. No matter how good the weather (and it was good much of the year), I'd much rather Sara be inside and safe.

I was meeting Drex and others for a glor mine inspection. Perhaps now with the truth of the women out, Drex would see things differently. It was a contentious situation, because we were only mining glor for the humans who had proved to be untrustworthy in some ways. All of the Xavians, time, and resources could be used elsewhere. The equipment used in mining could create tunnels that would directly benefit the Xavians.

Personally, after knowing they lied to Sara, I didn't care if we held up our end of the deal. I wasn't worried about Sara being taken away from me by humans. If she didn't want to go back to Earth with them, it would not be so. I could promise that.

I was about halfway there when I felt a hard twinge in my chest like I'd absorbed the impact of an invisible rock. I stopped and instinctively checked the skies, despite knowing I was alone. I tested the expansion of my chest. The pain hadn't disappeared, but it had dulled. It was a constriction, like a bad feeling I couldn't shake. The nightmare from this morning flashed in my mind.

Orkain wings and her scream.

My heart raced, and I raced back.

By the time I arrived, the pain no longer rattled in my chest. I was quite sure she was all right. I didn't know what had gotten into my head. I opened the door to my place, feeling like an idiot. Hopefully she wouldn't even know that I had come to check on her. It would be fine. I stepped inside to find nothing disturbed. Opening the door to my bedroom, there was Sara, sitting straight up in the bed, her hand to her own chest. She heard me enter and looked at me with brown and black eyes.

Something had been wrong. I had been called back to her. "Are you OK?" I rushed to her.

She accepted my embrace, leaning against me, but her eyes returned to the end of the bed, although her gaze reached farther. "I feel okay now," she said but still sounded lost.

Actually, I felt okay too.

Besides my confusion, all of the pain that had brought me here was no longer present.

"Must have been bad heartburn or something," she laughed dismissively.

"Pain in your chest?" I questioned. It couldn't be the same experience I had. That would mean…

"Yeah, but I'm OK. Woke me up, that's all. Where were you?"

"Rotha," I muttered as it skittered across my mind.

"Rotha? Where's that?" she asked.

While I knew Sara was my fated mate, I didn't think it was possible for her to undergo such a transformation. Sara was a human. We had talked to her government about mating rituals. While there remained some communication barriers, the humans didn't seem to have anything like rotha. Their bodies didn't change physically with time spent with their mates. No rotha marks. Their connections seemed more tenuous than our lifetime changes, their biological need more generic. We didn't need rotha for procreation, so after initial consideration, we didn't discuss it further.

Suddenly, it was very important. Maybe we hadn't understood.

"Let me ask. How do couples form between humans?" I started.

She shook her head at what seemed like a change in subject, but after a moment she answered. "I guess they're attracted to each other and get to know each other. And if they continue to like each other, they incorporate the other into their life. Eventually they might get married, have babies, and grow old together."

"What's married?"

"It's a ceremony and a legal condition in which the two people are united, promising to stay together and remain loyal for the rest of their lives."

That didn't quite sound like rotha. "How do they decide to do that?"

"Uh, I've never been *close* to that situation, so I don't know. Katy was, but Mike ditched her before they got married."

That wasn't rotha. No one would leave their mate. I couldn't confirm its existence in her world, and I struggled to find the words for it. It seemed safer to talk about her sister.

"Did she ever feel pain when she wasn't with him?"

"Well, when he didn't show up for their wedding, yeah, she felt a lot of pain…but that's not what you're talking about, is it?" she pulled away from me so that she could watch me.

I was quiet, so she tried me again.

"I woke up because I felt a pain in my chest, and then a few minutes later, you ran in here. How did you know I was in pain?"

"Because I was in pain too."

"Why would that be? Something we both ate last night?" Her eyes ran across the room as she internally searched her memories for what they had done last night which might have caused this. She settled back on the same question. "What is rotha?"

"That's how Xavian couples form. It's a connection on all levels—spiritually, emotionally, and…physically."

"I'm physically connected to you?" Her eyebrows rose skeptically. "What? I'm going to feel that pain if you're away? How far away? How long? All the time? What the…?"

I opened my mouth, but words did not come out. This was supposed to be good news. And I felt really nervous, because she was only taking it as bad news.

Worse, I had known and didn't warn her. I hadn't realized this was even a possibility. Apparently, even my people didn't have a full understanding of rotha. She jumped off the bed. I reached for her, but she only pulled away.

"What did you do to me?"

"I didn't do it," I said, panicked by the betrayal and fear I saw in her eyes. I'd seen the same the first day she had arrived.

I wouldn't have done this, or anything to her, without her permission. I didn't even know for sure what was going on. And, as stupid as it was, it had been the first time I had reached out and been denied her touch. She was fully in her right to do that, and intellectually I understood it, but fryyre. It also hurt. Was this rotha? And would it continue to be this much trouble?

"And it's because I had sex with you?"

"No, no," I said, finally finding the words. "It can happen before couples have sex. It's not some effect of sex. It's how my species finds their true, life-long companion with whom they're fated to be."

"Like...forever?" She looked at me suspiciously.

My heart caught in my throat. "Yes."

"This hasn't happened to you before?"

"No. It's a once-in-a-lifetime chance for a Xavian. There are no others—you are mine."

She was quiet.

I'd aways dreamed my rotha would be a wonderful moment of discovery and celebration. And this moment was difficult to tolerate. She didn't know anything about rotha. Still, it was difficult to not take her reactions and emotions personally. Did she not feel the same?

"Besides heartburn, what else do I have to look forward to? Am I going to grow horns?"

"No…I don't think. But there are rotha marks. They appear on couples, like on their arms or legs."

"Oh god, are you serious?" Her lips curled back in disgust. "Don't touch me anymore."

The words bit but not as severely as when she backed away from me fearfully. Her eyes swept over her limbs in cursory examination before she rushed to the bathing room. I didn't know what to do. I considered following her, but maybe she needed some time to herself. My own head was spinning. I'd answer more questions when she was ready. Hopefully my heart could take them.

Chapter Twenty-Two
Confusion

Sara

I rushed to the bathing room and only saw my idiocy staring back at me in the mirror. I had no marks on my body. Was he messing with me? Maybe I had talked about the heartburn in my sleep, and he recited it back to me. Unfortunately, it wouldn't be the first time a guy would go to such lengths, but…I was having trouble reading him. His fear and confusion seemed as genuine as mine…nothing like the previous happy-go-lucky vibes.

I thought it was just good chemistry. Vance and I made really good sex. I didn't think it was going to manifest itself into some fated miracle shit. I've made mistakes when jumping into bed with others, but none of it ever led to some weird vicinity-based couples-arrest. (Well, except that time Chad came into my store, discreetly handcuffed me to a mannequin, and felt me up while I pretended to fold clothes. We didn't get caught, so I don't know if I'd count that as a mistake.)

And let's say for a moment this rotha-thing was real. It happens between two Xavians, not one Xavian and one human woman from Earth. He could be jumping to conclusions. He could be mistaken. Because, me? Yikes. There were better candidates. My sister, first of all. She was the one who wanted to settle down and get married. I'm sure that children were going to come after that. Why not attach himself to her?

I turned on the shower and undressed, although I couldn't bring myself to get in yet. I set the steam feature to fill the bathing room with stupid fancy aromatics and marched back and forth across the floor naked.

I needed to learn more about this rotha-thing. I had a lot of questions. Could it wear off or reverse? Could he get another fated? I was too angry to listen right now. I could barely listen when I was relaxed in a normal environment. For now, I settled on angry. And I had a right to be. I stepped into the shower and wished I knew how to make it hotter if just to distract myself with discomfort. It was unfortunately preset, and I was not in any state to try to find the right buttons.

I scrubbed roughly as if I might be able to wash off Vance's lingering touch and this weird complication. I thought of that South Pacific song as I washed my hair. Mom had liked that musical. *I'm gonna wash that man right out of my hair.* Although, in this case, it was a turquoise, horned man whose touch had sent me off into the stars. And might keep me here.

I hadn't come to make a life here.

I did love his touch though.

I towel dried. I couldn't bring myself to use his fancy technology hair and body dryer. I knew it was a bit irrational, but there were very few outlets for my anger. My face felt hot and flushed, the cool rush of air from the hallway hitting it as I crossed to my room.

In the dresser, I found the least sexy clothes I had left myself, a loose top and a maxi-like skirt that went to my ankles. I would put on a sweater over my arms, but I was still too hot from the shower. I sort of hoped Vance had left for work. And then I realized I'd know if he had left. I was ready to stop killing time. I suddenly wanted answers.

What was this rotha thing?

And how do we stop it?

#

In the kitchen, the man I was upset with sat with two steaming mugs of fah. He jumped up to get my chair for me. When he caught my glare, he settled with pulling the chair out and backing away.

I sat down curtly, not touching the fah. If I wasn't so angry, I'd ask him who taught him that—currently frustrating—Earth custom. I hated he was being so gentlemanly. I had been okay with all of his actions and his flirting up until now because I didn't really think there was anything at stake to enjoy it. That apparently wasn't the case.

"Tell me more about this rotha," I said, ready to analyze and cut down any bullshit.

He fidgeted in his seat. "It's a relationship bond. Especially at first, there can be some pain when you are separate from your mate. It's supposed—"

"—Your *what?*" I butted in indignantly.

His pained look made me immediately regret it. He was trying to answer my difficult question in a second language. I sounded harsh. He didn't say anything, and I apologized. "I'm sorry. Why is it painful?"

"To uh, encourage mating and facilitate reproduction… I'm sorry it startled you. It startled me."

"But I'm not Xavian. Humans don't have anything like this. I mean, they call it head-over-heels in love, but…"

"Head over heels?" it was his turn to ask.

Language barriers were hard. "It's a figure of speech for when someone falls in love. It's like they do flips or go upside down."

"But they don't really…?" he requested confirmation.

"No, they don't really."

"Thus, it's head-over-heels, which is the correct order."

"Um, sure. I don't know. But my point is, we don't have rotha. So how do I *feel* it?"

"I…I don't know," he said.

How would he? It would be hard to feign the confusion we shared. "How do you make it stop?"

"You don't make it stop. It's fate. We're mates."

"What does that mean? What happens to your rotha couples?" I tried again, this time more delicately. He couldn't know what that would mean for us.

"They immediately bond. Live out their lives. They have increased fertility over other pairings. They even die around the same time."

"You've got to be kidding me. This locks our lives together? If you die, I die? What if you fall off a cliff or something?" Or I push you off said-cliff.

"I'm sorry," was all he said, and again, I wasn't really sure how much was translating.

I should be the one apologizing. I'd likely be the one to die prematurely. Vance was strong, high in his government, and a fighter. I'd been trafficked, flown across the galaxy, and deserted on a planet with predators who preferred to take off with women like me. I'd be our weakest link.

"What happens if I leave and go back to Earth?"

Vance frowned. I hoped he hadn't thought I was staying here.

He lowered his head. "Couples have lived apart before. Perhaps the pain fades."

I momentarily felt bad for him. If he was telling the truth, he hadn't made any conscious decision for this to happen. It wasn't his fault. And my flippant attitude probably wasn't helping as Katy was always quick to tell me. I was sorry about this mess, but seriously, it also wasn't my problem.

I stayed quiet for a moment, watching the steam dance over my mug of fah.

"Should I stay with someone else? Can we reverse this?" I was here for vacation, not for the long haul. Of course, I also knew I wouldn't be able to deny myself Vance if he was going to be across the hall the whole time.

He was careful with how he answered. "I don't think that will matter. Rotha has set. It's forever as far as I understand it."

"So we might as well enjoy ourselves?" I asked, finding his answer convenient and suspicious. I smiled for his sake, but seriously, it seemed like a bad idea to blindly accept *forever*. I could *consider* it.

I guess he didn't blindly accept it either. He didn't brighten. He stared into his untouched fah, mulling over something he hadn't said yet. "I'm sorry. I didn't warn you because I didn't think it was possible for you to feel the physical effects of rotha."

It took me a moment to process it. Warn me? How could he have warned me? Unless…he had already known.

"How long have you known?"

He swallowed, looked up at me with those strange eyes. "I guess since I've met you in some amount of awareness. I…didn't know how to tell you…and I didn't think it would matter."

It wouldn't…*matter?* How could that not matter? "What do you mean?"

"I didn't think you would experience us as fate. I didn't want to take that choice from you. The truth is, you would probably be better off going home. Safer."

"Wow." Yeah, there was no way this guy was messing with me. What a gem. Ugh. "I, uh, OK. I understand. It's a lot for both of us to process." I wouldn't know how to handle his end either. "You'd better get to work…if you can get that far. Do I have to go with you?"

He laughed. "I don't think so. I'm hoping that was partly the shock and confusion. Perhaps now that we're aware, we can convince our zaratas we won't be far."

"Zaratas?"

"Mm, the stuff that makes you a Xavian, or, I'm sorry, a person or being. Personality and uniqueness and how we connect to each other."

"Heart…soul," I offered.

"I'll only go if you're OK," he said. He placed his arm across the table in my direction, but he made no attempt to actually touch me.

I brought my arm across and broke my no-touch statement. "I really am OK," I assured him. I was scared and angry. "We will figure it out."

I hoped we would figure it out anyway. At least, there was nothing else to do now. I stood up so that he would do the same and consider leaving. I wanted some private time to think things over. I was also curious to feel that pain again. That was love? That was mine?

After Vance left, I took both mugs of fah to the lanai. I sat on his curated comfortable furniture, wrapped in a light, soft blanket, surrounded by beautifully manicured plants. I sipped, deep in thought, and braced myself for the pain that stung my chest.

Maybe this wasn't anything. Or, was it? We didn't know anything about alien-human compatibility. Perhaps we weren't supposed to have sex with them, like Katy had said. The Xavians didn't have a lot to lose, did they? But the situation I was in was not okay, either. I hadn't come here to be Vance's lifelong mate. So what was this pain settling dully in my sternum?

Chapter Twenty-Three
Inspection

Vance

Sara had panicked, and I didn't blame her. I had felt panicked myself. But she'd convinced me she was OK, and my next priority lay with the prince. So I left for the glor mine to be inspected. I was late—very late—but I waited until I was out of sight of the house before I picked up into a run. My feet stomped the ground. My breathing picked up.

I had only accepted that *I* was experiencing rotha. I hadn't even told Drex. Now, Sara was experiencing rotha…as a human. I should be astounded and ecstatic. Instead, I felt inexplicably angry. I didn't know why, except that rotha had always been discussed as this wonderful, romantic thing. I held it in high regard, but now it felt like a cruel joke.

I was supposed to care for this alien woman for the rest of my life. I had no idea how to even discuss that with her, much less do it. What did I have to offer her? Because of me, she had been trafficked to my world. I couldn't even keep her safe. In an instant, she could be plucked from my life by the Orkain.

Meanwhile, the rotha started as sharp needles in my lungs, as if I was running too hard. Then it settled as a burning pain, rising into my throat—something I couldn't quite swallow and relieve. While the physical pain didn't disturb me—it was the fact that Sara felt the same. I couldn't bear that. I ran harder.

Still, even I wasn't dumb enough to think that Sara feeling some chest pains would be enough to keep her with me forever. Just because the stars had declared us life-mates, she'd be an idiot to live out a short and pointless life with me. The tunnels would extend our lives. Unfortunately, the machines and men that would be used to build the tunnels were currently being used for mining glor. And I was arriving late to the inspection.

I stopped at the mine's entrance to catch my breath. I was not alone for long. Drex climbed out, followed by Zade and Lian.

"You've missed it," Drex said plainly. He gave me no insight into the results.

"Hopefully doing his civic duty," smirked Lian, noting my state.

I was not in the mood. "Haellea. Sorry," I apologized to the prince, then glared at Lian. "You are only here as a recruit. The adults are talking."

"At least I was here…" mumbled Lian.

I let it go because he was right. I'd missed the entire inspection and my chance to influence the process. Lian's motives were obvious. The humans were likely the only way he would have a chance at a relationship with a female. He needed the glor to keep flowing.

"Are you going to continue the mines?"

"Continue and expand."

"Why? Why should we give the Earthlings any more glor? They are unethical." I had missed everyone's arguments, but I had to throw in my own.

"I don't trust them either, but I'd like to have something they want if they do return. We can be specific that any other women are fully informed and consenting of what is happening. I will not accept another drop-off like this one." Drex's horns pulled closer together as his forehead wrinkled.

"This has to be a long-term operation. Some resources should be moved to building safe infrastructure."

"The tunnels again!" Zade threw his arms up. "Not at the expense of our mining operations. We decided this when we brokered the deal with the Earthlings."

"That was before we knew! These women were tricked, and it's not exactly paradise here, is it?"

And, according to Drex, the Orkain were taking women preferentially over men. What they were doing with them was anyone's guess.

"Say Sara wants to stay with you when the ship comes back, but we don't have the glor they wanted. Do you think *they* will want her to stay?"

"No, but I also wouldn't let them take her." Even though I wasn't quite sure how I felt about Sara, my rotha roared—anger boiling at the thought of the human men taking away my mate. I would fight them, and I was pretty sure human men would prove a lot more vulnerable than the Orkain we were training to fight against. I might not be able to protect Sara from the Orkain, but she was not going to be forced anywhere else by humans. She was at least safe from that.

"Then what are you three arguing about? Don't you have more important things to do?" Lian asked, making a crude gesture.

His sentence was hardly finished before I stepped in front of him and grabbed him by one of the small horns on his head. I jerked it down so he was forced to double over. "Do *not* talk to your prince like that."

"Sorry," he stammered.

"You are lucky that we need your seed," said Drex. He put his hand on my shoulder.

I pushed down one more time before releasing him. It was difficult to keep our young males in line. Most of them had lost their mothers, their sisters, their friends. He was angry and disenfranchised.

I didn't have answers for him. I had Sara, and I didn't even have answers for me. The yearning in my chest wasn't just for Sara, but also for a solution that would allow us to stay together and build a family. I didn't know how anything like that would be possible in a world like ours.

"I volunteered you for tomorrow's scouting trip," stated Drex.

I groaned, forgetting "not to talk to your prince like that." It was Drex's way of encouraging me to find other solutions to the tunnels vs. mining argument, but I didn't have time to deal with that. At the same time, I hoped my walk home would be long enough for me to think over what Sara and I were going to do. It was difficult when I had no answers for either of us.

Chapter Twenty-Four
Apart

Sara

Dinner was awkward. I have to admit, things between us were uncomfortable, no matter the distance. Earlier in the day, when he was far from me, it physically hurt. When he was here, it was, well, strange. Before our discussion of rotha over fah this morning, we'd been physically attached for tens of hours. All of the polite gestures that had seemed intimate while naked now felt awkward and formal between two clothed strangers. I was eager to return it to the status quo. Now that he had explained rotha to me, I didn't think he was creating any sort of ploy to get me to be his 'mate.' And I didn't really see the difference in having more sex or not. As long as I trusted Vance's word and ability to control insemination.

I know Vance was being respectful, but I also truly missed his hands roving my body. My sister interrupted the thought with a settit-ring.

"Hey, that's your room, right?" asked Katy. Her eyes darted around, scoping out my background. "You're alone."

"Yep, answering on the personal settit from Drex. I wonder why he felt the need to give me that," I said warningly.

No matter how I felt about Vance right now, I did not want to give Katy another reason to go wandering off into the jungle by herself. I had to save her from herself. And that included pretending I wasn't in trouble and didn't need rescuing.

Easy-peasy.

Actually, my sister was pretty distracted.

"You did not tell me," she had waited to say. Even now, she said it in a conspiratorial tone.

"Didn't tell you what?" I asked innocently. There was a lot I hadn't told her. I sat crisscross-applesauce and busied myself by gathering the skirt around my hips.

"Their penis*es*," she drew out the plural generously.

Oh yeah, that one. Or, those three.

I couldn't help it. I cracked into a giant grin. So, she had seen! Good for her. Maybe she could do well even if I had managed to get into trouble. I really did want her to be happy.

She was starting to trust Drex. Her settit call with me was relatively short. I guess she had *longer* things to attend to. Mm.

Halfway through dinner, I had realized it was a mistake to tell him not to touch me. He was so damn respectful, he didn't come anywhere near me, and that made me want him more. I was the only thing stopping us, and that gave me some secret sexy power. I remembered his broad shoulders, large pecs, and washboard abs. I imagined my fingers grabbing to find purchase as his cocks played inside me. My fingers instead found my clit, already swelling, and the slightest bit of moisture through my panties.

The sex with Vance had been amazing, but it didn't fully satisfy. I had only grown ultimately hornier with each of our sexual acts. I hated that they'd taken my vibrator away from me. How did they expect me to get satisfaction with men like Vance around? Stupid, overly respectful men who wouldn't touch me unless I asked for it. I brushed circles around my clit and imagined his tongues. When I opened my eyes, Vance stood at the doorway to my room. I went deer-in-headlights, my hand frozen between my legs.

"Uh, I'm sorry. It was open." The galaxies in his eyes sparkled.

Yeah, of course it was open. I totally forgot it was open, but he didn't need to be casually leaning in the doorway watching me. I moved the discarded settit in an attempt to block his view of my fingers pulling from beneath my skirt.

"You know, I can help you with that." His voice made my heart skip a beat.

"No. I told you. No touching," I said firmly. I wasn't surprised at all that I had to remind him…

"I know. I still want to help," he repeated. Christ. It took me a moment to realize what he had meant. He still wanted to…participate…in whatever way I would allow. He took one big step to me. "I want to help you cum."

My hand fell immediately back into my lap as I stared into his eyes. It was an impulsive decision fed from the entire meal of not being able touch what I wanted.

"Do you want to help me, or do you want to *watch* me? Because all I see right now is a lot of watching," I bit my lip. I didn't know where he would take it, but he did not disappoint. He flexed for me, unbuttoned and took off his shirt.

Meanwhile, my fingers worked on my clit as my hips moved in lazy circles.

"Take them out," I demanded.

Vance immediately stood up. He yanked off his pants and kicked them away. He put a knee up on my bed to display his freaky creatures to me. I gazed at them, moving in slow motion with pulses and waves. I probably shouldn't have tempted fate, and yet, it felt so good to think this man at my feet really wanted to be with me. *Me.* Forget the forever thing. This man wanted to please every bit of me with every bit of that.

His grunt brought me back to awareness. He wasn't touching himself. He watched my hand pass over damp underwear while his own struggled to stay still on his thick, bare thighs. He was waiting for me to give him…what? Permission? Well, fuck. I had never thought of it that way. I leaned my pelvis into my hand, creating pressure. He watched.

"You know what would help me?"

"What do you want?"

"You can't touch those cocks until I start to cum." I rocked onto my hand again, leaning forward, getting close to him. His cocks fucking reached for me. I leaned back, releasing the pressure. His jaw nearly wagged for me. I bit my lip thinking about my mouth on his cocks. God. I leaned forward again, grinding on my fingers, feeling fold and friction of multiple members.

"You want to touch yourself?" I asked.

"I want to touch you," he said, but I could tell from the strain of his cocks that he was incredibly turned on.

And what would happen if he couldn't have me? It was a dangerous game to play, riling up a man much stronger than me after requesting he not touch me. A game that was fucking turning me on.

"You want to touch me, huh?" It sounded porn star-ish, but what did he know? Heck, the U.S. government officials may have handed off their personal stashes for educational purposes. And I mean, it worked for me too. "How did I make you feel?" I continued to talk dirty until I lost track of what I was saying. "Touch yourself. Imagine my pussy smashing down on that cock. Grab it," I moaned.

A string of curses passed through his lips as he gritted his teeth and pulled his cocks into one pillar. I had no idea I had gotten him so turned on. He seemed to be vibrating green crystal energy as he yanked at his cock, towering over me riding my hand.

"Fucking cum for me!" I shouted even as thick strands of pearls coated my bare legs where my skirt had been hiked up.

All of my core tightened and wouldn't loosen as I felt wave after wave of pleasure hit me. My free hand wiped at the thick wad on my leg. It was hot and sticky on my lips, and salty on my tongue. I squeezed my clit and folds with my hand as the flexibility in my body returned.

He leaned against the foot of the bed and grinned lazily. It was an impish grin that I loved to hate, on men mostly, because they are who I typically found myself mad at…but not this time. He managed to get us both off while following my every rule and request.

Maybe rotha was right. We were sort of a good team.

He swapped out my blanket with a fresh one while I sat there stupidly in that clothed politeness again. But then again, I'd also just orgasmed, so I was feeling not too bad about it either.

"Do you request anything else?" he asked.

I thought about giving him restrictions for the night, but that seemed too mean. We had both been generous to each other. I settled on the current assignment: no touching, sleep in the other room.

He wished me good night, and I missed him the instant he slipped away.

Chapter Twenty-Five
Marked

Sara

When I woke the next morning, I reached for Vance before remembering I had enacted a no-touching rule and thus was alone in my bed. I felt the echo of the rotha pain. Maybe that was its background buzz. It wasn't a heartache. It was a restlessness, perhaps to go find him. Whatever it was, it wasn't going to let me go back to sleep.

I fought to untangle myself from the sheets. I wasn't sure what the plans were for today, but it needed to include going outside. When Vance had gone off to wherever he had, I felt cooped up, and I hadn't quite shaken it.

Yesterday evening had been less awkward than I expected. I couldn't deny we had wicked good chemistry. It was hard to remain standoffish with him. Everything about him made my walls fall down. It was too easy, exhilarating even, to be with him. I mean, that was sort of soul mate, destiny, and fate shit, right?

I laughed at myself, it was just like me to be given a green flag and stop. Chad? All red flags, and I blasted through. This was going well—like, *really* well—and I was putting on the brakes.

Maybe Vance was a drug to me. Rotha, a withdrawal. Surely there was a better explanation than that we were a magical pairing from across the cosmos. Of course, did it matter if my partner believed it to be true?

In the bathing room, I pulled off my night shirt and noticed something strange on my arms—weird shadows. Were the lights different in the room? I raised my arms, and the shadows followed. On my hands and arms were tiny, faint swirls.

Rotha marks.

I rubbed them. Was this an elaborate trick? I couldn't imagine Vance pulling it off, or why he would try. We were doing well. I had hopped into his bed. He had no reason to fuck with me like this. I stared at my body in the mirror, naked, the defeat slumped in my shoulders. So much for slowing this thing down.

I had several tattoos. Small ones. My mom's birthday on the inside of my arm. A flower on my ankle. This felt like waking up with faint tattoo sleeves I never recalled wanting. Would they darken? Continue to spread? How much of me would change? It was difficult to not feel betrayed, not just by Vance but by my own body. Did it know something I didn't? I felt branded. Were the marks permanent? Hide-able by make-up, or could I get it laser removed?

Boy, had I gotten myself in trouble. My sister was right. We shouldn't have signed up for this trip. I should have adventured in my own country, my own world, first. I wasn't ready to come out here and be some sort of ambassador for space tourism. I had no idea how *my* world worked, much less how his worked. And now, I might be this alien's bride or something.

In Vance's culture they were supposed to be a sign of love, but we hardly knew each other. We hadn't grown to love each other yet. Hadn't even had a chance to love each other yet. I didn't want to offend him and his culture, but it wasn't mine. This concept didn't belong to my people, so why was I experiencing it?

I sat bare-ass on the tile, unsure what to do. It wasn't cold. They must have floor heaters. I appreciated the quiet luxury. There were worse places to be. And though I felt angry, I had trouble directing it toward Vance. This was an unexpected event, but it wasn't his fault. While he might have grown up with knowledge of rotha, he had no control over it. I needed to talk to him.

I threw my night shirt back on and left the bathing room, unbathed. Even though I felt like I'd woken up early, Vance was already sitting at the kitchen table. He had both hands on the cup of steaming fah, but he was staring at his arms. I recognized the pattern immediately, despite the color difference. Mine were a faint honey color. His were pale blue.

They were gorgeous.

And something in me clicked. I was doing that to his body, the same as he was doing to mine. This wasn't some trick. This was some sort of transformation neither one of us were ready for. I probably should have been scared, but instead, I felt something else. I desired to touch the glaze of color I'd brushed upon his skin.

I lazily rationalized that I hardly ever knew what was good for me as I approached Vance with my arms outstretched. He accepted me into him, and yeah, there was no way that his hug could be wrong. I soaked him in for a moment. What life was this? What were we becoming? I traveled to explore. Why would I not explore this? That was the point. I wanted to throw as much paint on the wall as it would hold. I wanted to throw spaghetti and see what stuck.

"I'm sorry it had to be me," I joked. Still, it also didn't feel far from the truth. In all the cosmos, he probably deserved better than me. The choices were slim.

"I'm sorry it had to be you too," he said with a large amount of sincerity. And I realized he didn't understand it as a joke.

"What do you mean?"

"I am sorry if this is not what you wanted." He gestured at himself, defeated, at his comically god-like body. He meant the whole situation with my government and the Orkain, but I still had to stifle a giggle. I'd never known a body like his.

"Honestly, I don't know what I want. I really like you. I don't know what's happening, but I don't think it's bad. I travel to try new things—" I traced one of the lines on his arm. "—To see where these rivers flow."

I kissed him.

The tension and fear melted. His embrace was warm and comforting. He kissed me timidly back. This was new to him too. I took the lead and pushed my tongue into his mouth, against his teeth. I closed my eyes as our tongues wrapped together, tickling taste-buds, our breath becoming one.

If I couldn't tell him how I felt, maybe I could show him. I was anxious to get lost in him like I had the first time, to find that connection—a connection that made its mark on me.

I walked Vance backward to his chair and straddled him. If he was having any doubts, his members did not. They hardened underneath me nearly instantly. I arched my back and pressed my ass against the jumble of sex. His mouth, unoccupied, attached to my neck, sucking needfully, lapping lightly against my collarbone, and nibbling with sharp teeth.

Anxious to feel that sensation across all of my skin, I crossed my arms, grabbed my shirt, and yanked it off.

Vance devoured my breasts, mouth open, tongues escaping and squeezing my flesh with their strange, prehensile movement. He pulled a tit up and let it fall, savoring the bounce, flicking my nipple sharply with the tip of one tongue while the others licked my breast, sending electricity through it. He grabbed it gruffly with his hand, watching my eyes widen with surprise as he pinched. Then his mouth was on my other breast, sucking hard, making me rise up, bringing my chest closer to his face. He clenched a handful of ass, holding me to him, enjoying his buffet of boob and booty.

Fuck, he was getting me wet. He buried his face in my breasts the same way I wanted him to do between my legs—deep and with meticulous tongues. He grabbed the other ass cheek and stood. I swung my arms around his neck. I figured we were heading to his bedroom, but he put me on the stone counter. He yanked my panties off, and I shivered against my points of contact on the counter. Before I could complain, he had a hand on each knee, pulling them wide apart, butterflying my legs. My mound presented against the kitchen counter like a meal on a serving dish. I was exposed and excited.

From between my legs, his branded hands explored my body, squeezing breasts, caressing curves, as he breathed hot on my clit and folds. As desperately as his hands roved my body, he was impossibly slow with his mouth, giving soft touches with the tips of his lips against mine. A gentle rolling of his tongue along either side of my clit, separating it from the mound, letting it swell.

When he put my clit into his mouth, I melted on the counter. I slowed my breath, eager to feel every bit for as long as I could before he lost me over the edge. His lips moved, whispering sweet nothings. His tongues danced, sending soft pleasure in enjoyable waves throughout my body. He kept eye contact with me as his tongues glided across like cursive love letters, praising my body and elevating my passion.

I grabbed his horns to push him harder against me, to encourage him to begin sucking me hard, but he did no such thing. He kept his steady gentle stare into my eyes as he slowly—impossibly slowly—marched me to the limits of my pleasure.

I groaned. My channel clenched against nothing. I lifted my ass off the counter, desperate for the pressure I needed against my clit. When I didn't think I could take it any longer and that maybe the chance might pass, he flattened his tongue against my clit, pressing hard, the tips of his tongues slipping in and out of my space. I shattered, my body convulsing against him. His tongue lashed into the hot liquid filling my space. His pace changed as he relished in the reward he had pressed from my body.

The momentum didn't change. He grabbed a leg in each hand and yanked my pussy to the edge of the counter before gently turning me over. My belly was against the cold spot where my lower back hadn't touched the counter, but my tits had a warm spot from my shoulders.

My ass was exposed to him. I felt his hot breath on it, a grazing of his teeth. Tongues slipped between my legs, sliding into my pussy and over it, lapping at my button of pleasure. Meanwhile, his third tongue slowly swirled around my asshole, sending a wonderful sensation up my spine, and settling warmth in my chest.

Hands on my ass, spreading me wide, he rimmed me while I hissed through my orgasms. His play sent my pleasure into overdrive. He had me so turned on, even the tip of his tongue darting in and out of my hole wasn't enough.

"I want you," I huffed, my face smashed against the quickly warming counter. He grunted in reply, his tongues quickly retreating and leaving me empty and aghast. He leaned against me as he worked the buttons and fastens on his pants, letting the fabric and belts brush against the curve of my ass. Soft skin that wasn't his tongues but his cocks pressed between my cheeks. He rubbed the length of himself along my slick entrance. It was so long, and I tensed with anticipation. He leaned over and kissed my neck and shoulders, alternating between kisses and soft bites as he adjusted his dicks.

He grabbed me by the hips and adjusted me underneath him. First, a cock pushed against my clit, stamping over the elegant cursive letters but still had me clenching my jaw. I needed him inside me. Inch by inch, he pressed into my entrance. My skin stuck on the counter, holding me in place as he worked his cock inside me.

"Please, I want it," I pleaded with him as the third dick's head pushed against my tight asshole. I wanted him to fill me.

He pressed and pressed, but I couldn't relax enough, as much as I wanted it. Maybe he should have teased me with his tongue more. I was about to say something, but he grabbed a mouthful of my shoulder and bit down hard. At the same time, he pulsed inside my pussy. The mixed signals of pleasure and pain made me cry out. He popped into my ass while I was distracted.

"Holy fuck," I cursed, but the pain was over. He remained still while I gathered myself. I was so full of cock. With a deep breath, I moved my ass to take more of him in. I wanted to feel him deep inside.

The pressure on my g-spot sent thrills through me, and an orgasm rolled easily through me. The cock on my clit captured pleasure from all sides.

He exhaled, thick and hot in my ear. I could tell it was a lot for him too. I cut my eyes at him and saw his had no focus. He hardly moved his dicks, which were so hard and thick.

"Sara," he groaned in a lengthy rendition of my name.

"Don't you dare cum yet," I said greedily.

He took a moment to compose himself. "I exist to please you," he grinned slyly.

Without the aid of his hips, his dicks pulled back then thrust inside me—long, slow, and deep. He reached my limits, and I moaned, unable to form words. He did it again, backing off before pushing in fast and smooth. My breath caught in my throat, like he had stopped it himself. The third time I came on his cock, my channel pulsing and tightening on him.

He pounded into me right through that orgasm. It only encouraged him to thrust deeper. Above me, his skin was getting hotter and damp. His words became incoherent, and I knew he was close.

"Cum for me, Vance. Pump that cum into my ass," I managed before I gasped.

He yanked my hips, taking my body and using it for his pleasure. The jet of fluid pumping into my ass sent me into my own frenzied orgasm. My channel rippled over his thick trunks. My nails clawed at anything I could reach, and my legs shook underneath me with the rhythmic shocks of pleasure.

Vance collapsed on me, smashing me against the counter, a bundle of damp heat. My wet pussy spasmed when he pulled out of me. After a moment, he peeled me off the counter, scooped me up, and we cuddled on the couch in a puddle of naked pleasure.

I couldn't help but admire our rotha marks. How could a manifestation of our time together be a bad thing? Vance was everything I'd dreamt of. I was honored to carry his passion written on my arms. How long would it last? Vance thought forever.

I wasn't so sure about the cosmos, but it hadn't been wrong yet.

Chapter Twenty-Six
Mine

Vance

I held my naked, spotted mate on the urish. Her pebble eyes gazed at me from that delicate, pale face. Warm swirls on her skin were miniatures of my blue. She was everything I wanted in ways I had never imagined. Sara was my mate from the stars. That's the only thing that could explain this morning…this woman…against my body.

Honestly, I had nothing but doubt when I woke to find rotha marks on my arms. Before the Orkain's arrival, I had taken the concept and journey of rotha for granted. There was a certain amount of confidence it provided. It didn't happen to everyone, but if it happened to you—well, it was difficult to get it wrong after that. Now it seemed there was a whole lot to get wrong. Sara enacted a no-touching rule in protest of rotha symptoms. She'd done it to avoid these permanent marks of belonging. And here they'd shown up anyway. I had seen them through her eyes— they would frighten her, upset her. She didn't want them, so I did not want them.

But she surprised me by seeing something completely different. Something I had been told to watch for…goodness. The purity and sweetness in her were as alien to me as her anatomy…something I hadn't experienced previously and enjoyed immensely now. She was scared, but she was optimistic. I couldn't have asked for anything better.

Sara lazily raised a hand and admired her marks before lightly rubbing the closer horn. "Will you take me out today? I want to explore your world," she asked sweetly.

It's not the first time I had heard that request. I regretted missing the tour of the glor mine. It had been a missed chance to argue for a different life where I could happily comply to Sara's request.

"Maybe," I hedged.

It wasn't rational to keep her inside indefinitely. No one else in Xavia lived like that. We were cautious though. Drex had taken Katy to Frustnerdd, but that was different. He probably had to, or else Katy would have gone by herself. She was stubborn. And Drex hadn't been risking his rotha mate. That's what I would be doing. "Once in a lifetime" was a very real threat that frightened me.

Drex had told me about his encounter with the Orkain that night. It had been hunting Katy, a female. It did not take Drex. Orkain were preferentially taking the women of our world. They had taken one of the humans already. No, I felt safest with Sara inside. I'd distracted her by introducing her to new people and projects near the house. I would continue to do so until I had created safe passages for her, even if I had to dig them with my own hands.

Sara never gave up easily. "I just need to get out of the house, you know? Do you ever get cabin fever?"

"Are you feeling ill?" I asked. I hadn't heard of that human ailment. I pulled her closer to make sure she was warm enough. Her body was so small and so much cooler.

"No, I'm feeling quite well," she laughed. "Just…antsy? Jittery?" she wiggled. "I need space!" She reached her arms out and shook them above her head.

"We can do more heshiev—"

"No, take me up a mountain! Or show me the ocean!" She smiled as she tried to get her point across.

I wasn't sure how much longer she'd smile when she realized that I wasn't being obtuse, but that she'd been dropped off on a planet where she could not freely and safely walk around like she could on hers.

Sara

"I wish I could," Vance said. I noted the sadness in his voice. He rubbed his arm in a motion I recognized.

From this vantage point, I could see his target—a faint scar, now lost among rotha marks. My fingertips danced over the slightly raised surface. "Where did this happen?"

"Not far from here," he chuckled darkly. "At one of the heshiev plots we've tended."

"What happened?"

"An Orkain attack. That's *what happened,*" he spit back. His muscles tensed around me like a cage.

I hesitated, stared down the lines on his arms— larger versions of mine, waiting for him to calm. "It's dangerous out there—" I started.

"How many times do you have to see it? Your sister just ran out there. This place? It used to be booming with people."

I bit my tongue. I wouldn't know half of that because he hadn't let me see much of anything. Not even counting the time Katy had run off, she'd been out much more than I had. Vance went out regularly. I had a feeling most people did. Except me.

"You're mine. I want to keep you safe," he concluded.

You're mine… my eyes returned to our rotha marks. As much delight as I found in them—I only knew what Vance told me. Rotha, the Orkain… Maybe Vance wasn't letting on all that he knew. I worried at how much Vance wanted to keep me inside. The episode with the Orkain and that woman? Terrifying. But nothing terrified me more than thinking I'd die isolated and "safe" in this tomb.

"I don't wish to see *it* anymore," I addressed the violence at the hands of the Orkain. "But I do want to know *more* about it—what it was like for you, how we can keep safe."

"I shouldn't have brought up the past. It doesn't matter. To stay safe? Stay indoors."

I slumped against him. He wasn't going to budge. I didn't feel like I had enough evidence to argue with him. Perhaps we shouldn't be going outside at all, but that didn't seem to stop others. He'd argue that I'd been outside plenty—heshiev, visiting Bolin. I'd declined the trip to the ship…oh.

"There is a reason I need to go out though."

"What?" He remained quick to want to please.

"I thought of something I wanted from the ship. Can we go get it?"

"I can have Lian get it for you."

"Actually, I don't—I don't think I'll be able to explain how to find it. It'll be easier if I go." I craned my neck to meet his gaze.

He studied me. Was I testing him? Maybe. But if he wasn't going to let me in or discuss it, what other option did I have? And he didn't have a good reason to say no.

"Is this that 'cabin fever' thing?" he asked.

I hoped so, and nothing more. "Yes, maybe," I admitted.

"OK, we can go." His broad smile made my legs go all noodle-y despite not bearing weight.

"Thank you." I gave him a squeeze before wiggling out of his arms.

"You mean now?" he asked in surprise.

I didn't want him to change his mind. "I mean, could we go today, at least? Is there a time that's safer than others?"

"Midday. Yes, if I don't get any reports of Orkain in the area, we can go then."

I gave him a quick peck on the cheek and flashed him a smile. "I'm going to go get ready."

I nearly skipped to my room, giggling. Yes, perhaps, it was just cabin fever.

Chapter Twenty-Seven
The Drop Pod

Vance

For all the outdoor adventures Sara could have demanded, visiting the drop ship was relatively simple. I regarded it safer than visiting Frustnerdd. I at least managed to make her wait until midday before we headed out. The sun had warmed the day and the ground, disguising our movements. And there'd been no reports of Orkain.

Even with my instincts to keep Sara safe were on high alert, I couldn't help but enjoy her company. I was hyper aware every time she touched me, and she did so often. I, too, constantly felt a need to close the distance. I was undeniably uplifted near her. Everything felt elevated to a higher level—even walking through the woods.

The skies were clear. We were not in danger. Sara nearly danced around the path, picking up rocks and leaves and asking me to identify them. She enjoyed telling me about any similar plant life and geology on her world and what they were called. I delighted that she appreciated the textures and appearances of nature.

I felt the same and worked hard to pull those details into the apartment.

Drex had laughed at me for how soft and green I had made my apartment, but nature made us naturally happy. It made sense to surround oneself in it, especially if otherwise it was dingy, dark, and underground. I appreciated the simplicity in the modern lines that Drex and many Xavians adopted, but the warmer lines of nature were more welcoming to me. A home should be welcoming. I hoped I had done enough to attract my mate, because I wanted more than anything for Sara to enjoy my place and want to stay.

Our trek through the lovely forest was not long enough. Even Sara was able to spot the shiny metal pod in the clearing.

"Oh, there it is!" she said. She quickened her step, but I grabbed her arm. Momentarily, her eyes shot daggers, but then she paused to hear me out.

"There's no guard there. Stay here and let me check that it's empty."

She agreed and moved back from the clearing. I checked the skies one more time before leaving her at the jungle's edge. There had been no sign of the Orkain. Lian had checked and cleared the ship earlier, but we'd stop constant guard of it. We did not have the people to spare, and the Orkain had shown no interest in it.

The drop pod had the same color scheme as the parts of the ship I had spent time in with the awkward seafoam green accents. I realized we had been given a tour of one of these halls but hadn't been told they were detachable from the ship. I quickly swept through the first half of the rooms. They were all the same.

Hardly any room to hide—a cot, sink, stasis pod, and its accompanying machinery.

"Vance?" I heard behind me as I left one of the rooms.

I turned to see the stasis pod door open. Lian stepped out. "I'm so glad to see you. I thought you were—"

I didn't hear the rest. My head smashed into the door frame. The ringing in my ears didn't stop. Instead, it tuned into the killing screech of the Orkain behind me. My hand searched wildly at my hip for my knife while I attempted to find my feet, falling forward into the room.

Lian grabbed the cot which was no longer secured to the floor. He swung at the massive being in the entry behind me. The metal frames clanged against each other, preventing the Orkain's entrance into the small room. Unfortunately, we were trapped inside.

"What are you doing here?" I asked, more out of surprise than looking for an answer. I readied my knife in my hand, wishing I had brought my spear instead. I thought of Sara outside.

"I spotted it as I was leaving. I dropped my communicator outside."

The Orkain took a moment to duck through the door. It sized us both up with menacing red eyes as it rose to its full dimensions. Lian had dropped the cot. A giant hocked foot sent the frame spiraling into the lower half of the stasis pod Lian had been hiding in.

With a snarl, the Orkain extended the claws on its otherwise Xavian-appearing hands. They doubled in size and became deadly sharp. I had seen Xavians fall from swipes to their neck or the arteries in their arms and legs. I felt exposed without armor, but even more so knowing that Sara was outside at the jungle's edge.

The ship was not built for this creature. It unfurled its wings, puffed out its chest, mouth agape and baring its fangs as it towered over Lian and me.

It screeched, but the startling noise was cut off mid-squawk as it lost its balance and stumbled toward us. Lian and I jumped out of the way.

As it scrambled past, I saw its source of misbalance upon its back. The tiny body of Sara had caught him by surprise. I did not waste a moment. I picked her up by her waist and tucked her under my arm.

"Come on, Lian!" I yelled.

He didn't need any more encouragement. He managed to grab the cot again and threw it onto the beast. We both climbed out of the room, peeled out of the drop-ship, and launched ourselves across the field and into the safety of the jungle.

Sara

I was surprised there was another Xavian, a younger man in there with Vance. Vance grabbed me and ran out while the other Xavian followed on Vance's heels.

Vance had me in a death grip on his hip, carrying me like a hog, ass first. We barreled out of the ship. The Orkain had recovered and made its exit as well. From my vantage point, the Orkain emerged from the ship and shot straight up into the air. I lost sight of it from there.

Vance carried me into the jungle where hopefully we wouldn't be found either. He shouted something to the other Xavian who barked an affirmative and ran off. I got the impression he was younger than Vance, both in appearance—his horns were shorter and his skin brighter—and how he responded to Vance's command. There wasn't supposed to be anyone in the ship, so that Orkain must have trapped him in there. And then it followed Vance inside. Vance had told me to stay. He would have wanted me to stay outside and safe, but that wasn't going to happen.

Only two thoughts passed through my mind when I watched the Orkain creep onto the ramp and disappear into the ship after Vance. The first was what Vance had asked me: *How many times do you have to see it?*

The second? It was my fault we were out there. So I snuck inside and then charged the beast full force from behind as it entered one of the rooms. I was thankful he'd extricated me after that. However, now I wanted to be let down.

I tried to get Vance's attention. I beat on his hip, but I couldn't fight out of his grip. He was so much stronger than me. He was racing through the jungle, like Tarzan with his Jane.

"Put me down!"

"We're almost there," he huffed. He was running so fast. He must have thought I couldn't keep up, but I was sure he was panicking.

"I don't see anyone!" I yelled. "Put me down!"

"No, we're almost there."

Maybe I was the one panicking. I took a deep breath, assessing the situation. I was safe. Vance wasn't listening to me, but he was taking me home. I craned my neck to see the sky, and I was thankful I wasn't someplace worse. I was uncomfortable, but he was right. We were almost there.

Still, by the time I finally fought free of his grasp, we were in the foyer of his home. Inside his freaking house. I was fucking livid.

"Are you OK?" he asked. His arms hovered over me as if they could further guard me, even inside.

"What do you mean 'Am I OK'? Didn't you hear me yelling?"

"I'm sorry. I needed to make sure you were safe." He led me to the couch and sat down next to me. I climbed into his arms, shaking. Wow, the adrenaline was really flowing. I wasn't sure if it was because of our encounter or the way Vance had treated me.

I didn't like that he hadn't listened to me. But I needed some perspective. We were attacked by one of those beasts. I attacked it! And we were safe. That was the most important thing. We were safe.

He held me as we both tried to catch our breath.

"That other guy?" I asked.

"Lian. I sent him to Vjann. I will check. Are you sure you're all right?" He pressed closed lips to my forehead. "You should not have come into the ship like that."

I separated myself from him so he could access the settit. "Yeah, I will have a weapon next time. I saw him follow you in."

"No, you should have stayed where I said."

His words surprised me. He expected me to not help, to not even warn him? "I wasn't going to leave you in there like that."

"You shouldn't have been out there at all." He turned to the settit as if that was an appropriate conclusion to the conversation.

That made me mad—mostly because I'd had the same thought. "Or how about… It was a good thing I was there because I helped you?"

He returned to me. Looked me in the eyes intently. "You did help me, but I must keep you safe. You are my fated. You are my rotha."

I looked him right back into his eyes. "I didn't ask to be that. And aren't you *my* rotha too? From what I gathered, it's a partnership, not an excuse to hide me away. I deserve a life."

"Well, if it's a life you want, you shouldn't have come here," he said bitterly.

Wow, clearly wouldn't translate. I had nothing else. Before I opened my mouth and said something stupid, I retired to my room.

Had I given away all my independence when I fell asleep on that ship on Earth? Was there any way to recapture it? And I had made my usual mistake; I trusted someone who, back against the wall, became overprotective and controlling. Yeah, the Orkain were scary, but I felt like if Vance had it his way, I wouldn't ever leave his home. What would that make me? Just his simple sex pet? The bearer of his children? And while I would stay inside 'for my own safety,' he would travel and work as he pleased.

I rubbed at the marks on my wrists. I swear they itched. They were like handcuffs to this new life. I had come here for adventure, and I had found more than I was allowed. I couldn't stay if it was like this. There was more adventure to be had, and if Vance wasn't going to let me share equally, I'd take the next ship out of here.

Chapter Twenty-Eight
Trapped

Vance

I stared at the closed door from the living room urish.

She didn't get it.

We had been moments from death. First, it would have ripped Lian and me apart. Then, it would have taken her. To do what? We didn't even know, but we knew they were taking females preferentially. I didn't want to think about it, but it was our reality. She had been so close to a horrible fate. I couldn't seem to make her understand that. Instead, she was mad at me.

Whatever. She could be mad at me as long as she was safe here in this house.

I felt like I was underwater and still sinking. The whole incident had taken so much from me. I had faced an Orkain, sprinted with Sara underarm, and now we had argued. I had hardly thanked her—hadn't thanked her—for her help. At the same time, I couldn't get her to understand the danger she was in. I couldn't even begin to untangle the emotions I was feeling about it all either.

Maybe she was mad because, deep down, she knew I couldn't keep her safe. She was doomed—fated to a man who was weak and losing a war. Was that how rotha relationships worked now? Keep each other alive to keep oneself alive? I wouldn't fool myself. We were both young and healthy—we would survive a separation, not like those who spent lifetimes in each other's rotha-marked arms and died of heartbreak at a frail and elderly age.

But the point of the connection was to have a partner for the rest of your *long* life. Sara would be better off leaving. This part of rotha didn't make sense to me. The more I cared about her, the more I wanted her safety and happiness over mine. I didn't want her to live this life with me. I needed to send her away.

I also didn't want to suffer this heartbreak.

I received a message on my settit from Vjann and Lian. So Lian was OK. They were attempting to track the Orkain. It was a good idea. When it finished searching for us, Vjann might be able to track it home. Not that we'd ever been successful at it before, but it was still a good idea.

I returned to the urish, and realized Moyuki hadn't greeted me, which would have been her routine after Sara went to her room. Perhaps she had sensed the tension and had decided to avoid the situation entirely. I glanced at Sara's closed door. It was possible the saf was in there and hadn't escaped in time.

I partly hoped that was the case. First, I didn't like the thought that Moyuki was still purposefully avoiding me. And second, perhaps Moyuki could convince Sara it wasn't so bad here. Moyuki enjoyed it here. I could keep them both safe if they'd stay underground where the Orkain couldn't reach them. What was so wrong with living here? I had originally balked at living underground too, but I had done a lot to make the space like any space aboveground. There were lots of lights, countless plants, and so many soft things to sit and lie on. Even before I knew she was arriving, I had made the space comfortable for myself, Moyuki, and for another. I had dreamed about having someone like Sara in my life. However, this life didn't agree with Sara. How do you keep an adventurer underground?

I couldn't, so what was I going to do? The adrenaline from dealing with Sara had completely drained from me. I felt anchored to the urish, my body and brain overworked. I sank into a thick, deep sleep that I knew I would not be stirring from anytime soon.

That was OK. Sara probably needed her space. At least she was safe inside.

Sara

It was the next morning when I ignored the call from my sister. I knew she'd be there for me, but I hated using her for that. It was my fault that she and I were in this mess in the first place. I was the one that was so desperate to travel, I didn't care I was basically dragging her along. Her worst nightmare came true— we'd been trafficked and basically deserted by our own people. Then I told her it wouldn't be all that bad, that we could sex up these aliens and that nobody would get hurt, and we'd fly home. Nope. Instead, I'd made a mess on top of the *intergalactic one.*

I wasn't ready to answer the call with these alien markings all over my body, needing her to bail me out again. No, I was going to—I *had* to—figure this out on my own. And if that meant pouting in Vance's bedroom, then so be it.

Unfortunately, while I didn't have to talk to my sister, I could hear Vance at the door. He knew the settit would have woken me up. Did he want to know what I would tell my sister? Or did he want to take the opportunity to——?

"Sara?" he asked through the door.

"Uh, yeah?"

"May I come in?" Dang. I should have pretended to answer the call. I wasn't quick enough.

"Yeah, I guess." I sat up in bed and self-consciously patted my hair down. I'm sure I looked like a mess.

He opened the door, and a blur streaked from my room. Moyuki had been trapped all night. Poor thing. I understood its instinct to run. Maybe Vance did too. He stepped timidly into the room.

"Lian's all right. I have to go out for work today."

I was suddenly alert. "Are you going to hunt that thing? Did you find it yesterday?"

His eyes widened. Maybe he was surprised, or maybe he was judging whether to tell me the truth. "We're going to look for it."

"Why?"

"It poses a danger to us. And to you, so I hope you understand when I ask you to stay inside."

"If it's dangerous, why don't you stay inside too?" I was being difficult. If he was going to treat me like a child, maybe I'd act like one. Really, though, I was scared. Maybe we should all get on the next ship to Earth.

"We need to learn more about them. I have to go out to do that."

"And I have to stay in?" It was easier to pick the fight than to tell him I didn't want him to go out anymore either. Still, the tension in the air was thick.

"I can send someone to get your things from the ship," he tried.

"It's not about the stuff."

It definitely wasn't about the stuff.

"Can I go see Bolin?"

He gave me a pained look. He didn't like telling me no. "I can send Bolin over."

That made me feel bad. If it really was that dangerous, I didn't want Bolin to be out there either. I begrudgingly saw Vance's point.

"No, it's OK. I can speak to him on the settit if I need him."

"Do you promise not to go out?" he asked.

I looked him in the eye. I hadn't taught him that word, *promise*. Or, at least, hadn't used it in this way. It caught me off-guard. The dude did know rotha though. His timeline for promises was long.

Sure, for now. As long as nothing changed. "…I won't go out."

"Thank you. I will be back as soon as possible. I programmed Drex's contact information into your settit."

That tidbit of information worried me. He was preparing me in case he did not return. "Is it really that dangerous?" I asked.

His chest puffed up. "Nothing we can't handle," he chose his words carefully. It put me on edge.

"Promise you will—" I didn't know what to make him promise in return. "Promise you'll come back."

Vance made a small huffing noise. It wasn't something he could promise, but he did as I did. "I'll come back," he said.

Then he left.

I didn't follow him. That was never my go-to. It was times like these that I would run away. I would go back to my apartment, or to a friend's house, or to my sister's apartment. I would absolutely leave. But I couldn't leave. I'd be an Orkain snack for sure. Besides, I had promised.

It wasn't until later that I realized that Vjann and whoever else he met would be seeing his rotha marks for the first time. What would Vance tell them? And would anyone believe me if I said that I didn't want this?

I broke down. Honestly, I'd been avoiding my reflection or looking at my arms. My body had betrayed me. It wasn't mine anymore. I felt disconnected from it. I didn't recognize the markings. It was like I had caught a disease or a cancer that I was ashamed of. I supposed Xavians would be excited to see such a thing—hope for their dying race and all that. I was more selfish than that. I hadn't asked for them. I wasn't their hope. Given my recent decisions, I wasn't even *my* hope. I was creating problem after problem.

I plopped on what was strangely similar to a papasan chair on Earth. I had one in my first apartment. It was incredibly comfortable, and I hated Vance for it a little more. I hoped the chair was as bulky and as cumbersome in this culture as it was in ours. It was nice in the first imagined spot in one's place, but it fit nowhere else and did not traverse well through decoration changes. That's probably why it was in the guest room. It was comfy though. The feathers were a bit much. I liked the eggplant-colored animal print though.

Beside me, something thumped underneath my bed. I had lived with Moyuki long enough to know that she didn't make noise unless she wanted to be heard. What was she doing back in here? She must have wandered back in during our conversation and had gotten trapped again. I could relate.

At the very least, I could solve her problem. I worked my body from the depths of the low-sitting chair…another issue with them. I managed to basically roly-poly out. Before I opened the door halfway, a streak of gray and black darted from under the bed and through it.

Damn, it was huge. It was more like the size of a medium dog, but it moved like a cat. My instincts told me it was a hunter to be feared. Despite the availability of a direct path, it ricocheted off the chair, upending the round part from its foundation, and scaring the life out of me.

However, after it had run off and I had closed the door, I shrank in sadness. I didn't know that Moyuki had been in my room, but now it felt extra empty. It would have been nice to have the company. Now, I was alone with an upturned chair and unturned thoughts.

Chapter Twenty-Nine
Failure

Vance

I had failed.

I kicked over the thought in my head as I hurried to meet Vjann and Chelk. I would not miss my opportunity to tear that fucking Orkain to shreds if Vjann had, in fact, tracked it down. That Orkain had threatened my rotha's life.

And I had failed. There was really no other way to put it. Here I had rotha marks, which I had always considered marks of success on others, scattered up my hands and arms. In the years prior to the Orkain, after the younger years of thinking females were disgusting, I had believed I would gaze lovingly on the rotha marks of my loved one. I would trace them with my fingers, creating invisible lines between them, constellations of my heart, and never, ever doubt that they connected always to mine and me.

Perhaps that rotha existed before. Perhaps it could exist with others. It didn't seem possible with an enemy like this… How could we live our lives like this? How could we love like this?

Maybe we couldn't.

I hated to think what Sara thought of her rotha marks. She seemed disgusted by them. And I couldn't help but project that same disgust onto myself. I understood that she had come from a very traumatic experience… At least, I had thought I understood. Maybe if I truly had, I would have slowed us down. She was only a few days from waking up to the biggest news of her life. Did she have time to process it properly? Probably not.

And in my haste, I had complicated it even more. There was no denying our strong chemistry. It hadn't been just initial attraction or convenience… We kept returning to each other, enjoying each other, and growing even closer. It hadn't been just the curiosity. I had never felt like that before, but I also recognized it as something real and stronger than us—something that had united others through the histories of time, through the worst of adversities. I still couldn't quite deny that.

But it was a space that maybe we would never exist in. Rotha was so real and now, so dangerous. Perhaps we had gotten a taste of it too soon. She was scared. Honestly, I was scared, too.

I could not in my right mind ask her to stay here and be my rotha-mate. Here was nowhere to be. I couldn't keep her safe. I couldn't begin to give her the things she wanted. She wanted adventure. She wanted freedom. She had traveled across the galaxy for vacation. What could I offer a woman like that?

Asking her to be my mate would be asking her to stay forever hidden, and to not do the things that she wanted out of life. I couldn't ask her to do that.

It hurt that our world used to be like that. Even at full population, we had so much that was unexplored and beautiful and everything I think she would have wanted. Sadly, I never saw the world being like that again. It had been ruined by the Orkain. We had yet to kill a single one of them for the thousands of us they had killed.

I had dismissed really thinking about this during the negotiations. I thought perhaps the aliens were different. That whoever came would know what they were getting into. Clearly that was wishful thinking. The earthlings thought so too, else they would have been honest with their volunteers. Instead, they'd basically abducted them. And I expected Sara to live up to my own delusional expectations. I didn't have the means to get her back to Earth now, but that didn't mean that I deserved to keep her.

Now, these rotha marks were a mark of shame to me. Maybe they would fade if she was far from me, a galaxy away. I had never expected rotha to be as complicated as it was. Perhaps that's why I didn't think it could exist in this part of my life…to an alien…on this Orkain-infested world. It turned out, rotha was as complicated as life. And I was used to not getting what I wanted in life, so I guessed that part made sense.

I had failed my only opportunity at that rotha-love. I put my head into my hands. I couldn't hear her at all. Was she sad? Angry? She had every right to be both and more. I had only made things worse.

I was completely unprepared for Sara. I had some sort of romantic notion of rotha and what my mate would be like, but I realized now that I had never thought that person would be her own entity. She had her own desires, needs, annoyances. And some of that was amazing. She was beautiful, creative, and I really appreciated her straightforwardness. However, she seemed to have needs that were incongruous with what I could provide her. Maybe if she had grown up on Xavia, she would understand our world and her limitations. Instead, she had grown up lightyears away in a completely different world.

She might as well be on a completely different world now. She was tucked safely in my home, and yet I felt so distant from her. Not just physically—we had been hip-to-hip and hand-in-hand for days, yes—but a cosmos away in connecting with her like we previously had. I hadn't realized how powerful emotions could be until I got swept up with Sara. She was a whirlwind, which was justified given all that she had been through. It was also true that I had never felt this way before.

Chapter Thirty
Infestation

Vance

If I thought I would feel better having Sara promise she would stay inside, I was wrong. I felt even worse. What sort of mate was I if I couldn't even keep her safe? My rotha marks felt laughable, and that made Vjann's and Chelk's congratulations feel like knives in my gut which already burned with rotha.

Chelk was taller than me, a darker green. We both had wide shoulders and narrow hips, accentuated by our athletic builds. We had been thrust into leadership positions before gaining the necessary experience to lead. Vjann was stocky, with meaty limbs to match. He looked as if he stomped, but he was surprisingly light-footed. Besides my all-purpose knife, I had a spear. Chelk and Vjann carried projectile weapons I had yet to see take down an Orkain. I didn't bother.

I was torn about the scouting mission. I wanted to find the Orkain who had threatened the safety of my rotha. I tensed as I remembered Sara on its back, her hands in its feathers. I wanted to destroy it. However, I'd also been on these expeditions before. They were fruitless and continued to pull resources away from strengthening ourselves underground. I've been considering the difference between enemies and prey. Enemies can attack. Until we learn more about the Orkain, we can't attack. We're the prey. Prey can only defend themselves. Hide.

The tunnels were hiding places.

Vjann led. He had followed the Orkain last night to this vicinity before losing it. We were going to check out the nearby caves. Chelk followed. I brought up the rear. Ahead, Vjann stopped and pointed to something in the distance—a cave entrance. For something canopied in green, the rock outcropping that housed the tomb-like cave looked especially barren. Ivy had died upon it, turning it a dried brown, stayed upon it as the cave was less accessible to that which inhabited the moist ground and devoured decay. One had to crouch to enter—Xavian and Orkain alike—but Vjann insisted that the small entry led to a large cavern, capable of housing a group of menacing Orkain.

I began looking at the land upon which we'd stopped. We would camp out and watch for any activity from the cave when it got dark. Perhaps we could not only confirm their location, but also learn about their behavior and routine. Chelk's eyes also surveyed our surroundings, but after a moment, Vjann moved toward the cave.

"Do you want to get closer?" I asked. Maybe he wanted to adjust our plan.

"Yes, we're going inside," Vjann barked over his shoulder.

That was definitely an adjustment.

Chelk didn't offer an opinion but he did take rear-position so I could continue talking to Vjann.

"Zroso!" I addressed him with a respectful name, which, despite his earning it, I hadn't used since becoming more or less his equal. "What are you doing?"

I'd given Vjann a lot of space and hadn't ever questioned him, but he was trying to operate outside of Drex's immediate control. He should have brought this up before trying to pull it here.

"We will be careful. We need more info from these trips. We're getting nowhere doing what we've been doing. We will approach—slowly, quietly—looking for signs. As soon as we find them, we will leave. We are *scouting*." Vjann drew out the last word.

I had cited formality with my address. He responded in turn. Formally, this was in the realm of 'scouting.'

He'd assumed Drex would say no, but that I might allow it. He wasn't wrong. Could I tolerate the disloyalty to Drex in order to possibly gain new information? And what if Vjann marched us into a nest of murderous Orkain? Chelk had stopped looking for places to camp and seemed set to follow Vjann—us—to the cave.

Maybe this trip would give us the information we needed.

"From here, stay quiet," said Vjann.

We didn't have proof that the Orkain had hearing like ours, but we still did not want to chance waking them up. We moved through the jungle, creeping rather than crossing.

As we continued on, we searched for clues. There was no foot-traffic trample, but there wouldn't necessarily be for a winged species. The outcropping created a natural opening in the canopy to fly out like furang from the cave. There was no sign whether the Orkain were here or not. We had to investigate further.

We still had no answers when we reached the mouth of the cave. I had never visited this one, but I had never needed to take shelter in this area. There was a whole network of caves along this same outcropping, farther out, which were much more attractive for exploration and recreational purposes.

I had been lying to myself if I thought I'd actually stop Vjann from entering. This wasn't the place to argue—the decision had been made. Vjann crouched and disappeared into the entrance. After a delay, I sent Chelk. Then I followed.

Inside, I was immediately able to stand. I crossed the few meters to join the others at the edge of a steep drop off. My eyes adjusted to the low light. It was as Vjann had described. We were in the mouth of a large cavern with sharp rocks below, but he'd not described the Orkain roosting above, appearing like menacing formations—twenty of them. He also hadn't predicted freshly dug openings in the ceiling that I suspected connected to the mountain's cave system.

We finally had information. And it was not good news. There were twenty Orkain, probably more. And they were building a home here. Our infestation was worse than we imagined.

Chapter Thirty-One
My Fear

Sara

I called Katy back so she didn't worry about me. In that same vein, I kept the lights dim. I was paranoid she'd be able to see my spots, but they were faint, and she wasn't looking for anything like them.

She was less worried than I thought she'd be after missing her call. She also seemed less nervous than when she had visited me.

Drex had reignited her love for photography, and she was documenting the Xavian culture for her upcoming showcase. If Katy was starting to feel comfortable on Xavia, I didn't want her to know what trouble I'd made. She seemed happy when we said our goodbyes. At least I had that.

I was still trying to figure myself out.

Actually, I did need some information. And I needed it straight. I called Bolin on my settit.

"Ah, Vance told me you might call," Bolin said, peering at me carefully. Vance must have told him about the rotha markings. I held up my arms for inspection.

"They'll darken," he assured me.

"I don't know if I want them to," I confessed.

Bolin's deep-set eyes traveled from my arms to my own eyes. "Vance is a good mate. Good rotha."

"I'm sure he is. It's just...I don't know if I want to be here or live this life."

"You like Vance," he said simply.

"I do."

"You want to be with him. You are here with him. Everything else will work out."

"He wouldn't let me go see you. He won't let me outside."

"He is scared. He has seen many lost. Taken many onto his shoulders that he should not."

"Drex relies on him."

"Indeed. And have you met Moyuki?"

"She was a neighbor's pet?" Vance had mentioned it.

"Sangin. She died at the claws of the Orkain."

"How awful."

I couldn't imagine what this community had gone through before my arrival. What a mess. I thanked Bolin for sharing with me. Vance was trying to spare me the pain or wasn't ready to share with me.

I shouldered the rotha pain. I hadn't asked Bolin one last question. I didn't want the answer. *Would I know if Vance was killed out there?*

I cried myself to sleep.

Vance

We had finally found the Orkain. Unfortunately, they had already established themselves. This was possibly an extension or outpost, their numbers finally growing past their ability to hide from us, which means there could be more. Many more. After taking note of the number of Orkain and the changes they had made to the caves, we returned to the previously planned campsite to monitor them.

We saw no activity from that cave mouth. Had we not explored farther, we'd have thought it another dead-end. In the early morning, we escaped unnoticed to debrief Drex.

Chelk and Vjann were loud and rambunctious, excited about our discovery. They didn't think about how we still didn't know how to defeat them.

I was silent, because all I could think about was Sara.

She had changed everything.

While I had never said it out loud, I had believed Xavians were on their way out. Our population was minute, fine for our planet and its competition, but on the brink on any cosmic scale. The universe belonged to more populous species—the Orkain, the humans. Their small deposits of people had all but destroyed mine. Sara had told me that her planet, much larger than mine, was so populated that their lights blotted out the stars. I knew it could be true. Lights in our densest towns had done much the same, but one only had to hike a bit away to find the blankets and streaks of celestial bodies. I couldn't imagine not being able to escape it except on the highest mountains, in the deepest canyons, or in the midst of vast crop fields which fed millions. Species that couldn't adapt—didn't have the numbers to adapt—would die.

I argued the solution was to go underground and try to sustain a population down there with humans. Perhaps we would make it, perhaps not.

To claim a mate while dying out was not only futile, but also a needless death for her. Sara should be elsewhere. Her people had obviously grown strong. They had blotted out the night sky with their lights. They were powerful enough to have traded for faster-than-light technology to begin to sweep the galaxy, depositing thirty presumably fertile young females of their species without hurting the main population. She should not have been thrown away like that. We were being used as she was.

Now I had seen the Orkain living underground as I had proposed the Xavians should do. Tunnels were not going to be the answer. I should have felt defeat. However, as much as I feared losing Sara, I also *had* Sara. I hated telling her she couldn't go outside. I wasn't going to tolerate it. She wasn't going to tolerate it. I had to make changes, or I was going to lose her, one way or another. Either she would leave me for the freedoms she loved and that had brought her to me in the first place, like a breathtaking whirlwind in my life; or the Orkain would rip her from my arms. Neither of those options was acceptable.

Sara was my rotha. She was my life—my new life. She gave me a strength to fight the Orkain I did not have before. She was supposed to be with me. We were supposed to be together. Would the cosmos bring us together through the sea of planets and stars and used the bad works of the Orkain and of the humans just to show her to me and then rip her away? Were the stars that cruel? Had I ever known them to be that cruel?

I wasn't sure.

The human men had dropped off thirty fertile women with little regard. Their population didn't need them. Well, they would be treated better by the Xavian.

To us, they were so much more. I didn't realize how much. This was an injection of hope I never anticipated. Only the stars, fate, rotha could bring Sara and I together. Who was I to argue that an Orkain…twenty Orkain…more…could destroy it so quickly? I didn't know how we were going to defeat an undefeated enemy, but I didn't know how I had found my love millions of light years away either. It didn't make it impossible.

I slipped quietly into the house. Only Moyuki noticed and greeted me. I could hear Sara's sweet snores in her room. The dull rotha ache lifted, and I felt many times lighter.

#

Despite having spent most of the nights of my life alone, the bed felt cold and empty in the morning without her presence. It was the first thing I noticed. The second thing I noticed was that at least my body was rested. I hadn't realized I'd been pushing my body to the limits of exhaustion. Hours of vigorous activity with little sleep, water, or food could do that to someone. As much as I hoped that Sara had tossed and turned, missing me, I hoped more that she had gotten good rest too, even if it was without me.

I stumbled into the kitchen to prepare her a mug of fah. And even though she didn't typically eat breakfast, I knew it was possible she hadn't eaten much yesterday, so I prepared a morning meal for her. I cared for her, and I would gladly spend every day we had together taking care of her.

But I also understood that if she felt drawn elsewhere, I wouldn't be able to follow her. I was needed here. There may be millions of people on her planet to take care of things, but here, we were few. I couldn't abandon them for a life of adventure with Sara.

For me, Sara was the adventure. I thought of her crystal-bright laughter. I thought of her smooth, delicate skin and how it felt under my fingertips and against my lips. I could explore her for years. It hurt that that might never be. In fact, I might never touch her again after ordering her to stay inside my home, justified or not. She'd be on the next ship home.

And yet, she wasn't happy on Earth either, right? Instead, something inside of her urged her forward to me. I questioned the odds of rotha occurring between the two of us, but perhaps rotha had been acting far before it ever manifested as a small pain in our chests and as spots on our skin. It had been working to bring us together, an entire galaxy apart.

So why hadn't she experienced that connection between us? Why wasn't she automatically content and excited to be with me forever? Maybe it was the same as me. She was scared. I feared asking her to stay in this dangerous place, unable to move from it. But if rotha had pulled us together, who was I to doubt something so powerful?

I saw my clear path in front of me.

No one would be taking my faith and my fate away from me. It wasn't about my own protective abilities. It wasn't about would-haves, could-have, should-haves. This was my fate to grasp, and I wasn't going to let it go because of the dangerous paths it could take me. I wasn't going to cower from the fear, from the potential pain, from the potential grief. That wasn't living. Was the life I imagined with Sara possible?

Whatever the human women and the Xavians had endured would end with us. It ended with rotha. I observed my rotha marks, my chest puffing with pride. I was marked with love, strength, and hope. I wasn't going to let my fear command our relationship, like it had all my life.

I would convince Sara to be mine. She would see her marks as symbols of strength and love for me. And if not, if she decided to leave, at least I would have these moments with her and know that it was worth it. Fighting was worth it, and that could be enough to change the war.

Did Sara have the same fears? Perhaps it was time to ask her. Perhaps it was time to really get to know my love. I hoped that it wasn't too late.

"Where have you been?" I asked as Moyuki slinked into the kitchen, now investigating the smells of the unusual early morning meal.

Moyuki, of course, didn't answer me. However, I heard the shower turn on in the bathing room.

"Have you been with Sara?" I knelt and rubbed behind her ears. She rubbed appreciatively against my hand and then my shins. "Thanks for keeping her company," I whispered to her.

I made her an identical dish of food and set it by her small water fountain. She nibbled while I cleaned the kitchen that didn't need cleaning… Anything to keep me busy as I worried whether Sara would make an appearance and greet me, or if I would have to seek her out and risk rejection. I was ready for either. I wasn't going to waste the time I had left to convince her to stay.

Sara

The progressive natural and artificial lights alerted me through puffy eyes that it was morning. I hoped it had been several mornings, but alas, likely not. I glanced around the room, which remained annoyingly, delicately curated and simply not mine. The door was shut. The chair remained off kilter; the cushion half-slumped on the ground. For the lack of anything else to do, I shuffled out of bed and set the chair upright… Something I hadn't thought to do at all last night during my pain and self-argument but now seemed perfectly correct to do.

My body, not rested from sleep but instead tired from my crying session, followed the chair's re-positioning with my own butt in it. I slumped into it, not fitting well. It was meant to be a chair one curled into, not to sit in properly. For someone who never sat in a chair properly, why I was attempting to do so now felt more due to grogginess than anything else.

I wiped the crust from my eyes and looked down at my arms. Were the markings fading? Simultaneously, I hoped so and also desperately tried to memorize their positions and shapes. This *something* was mine, ours, no matter what happened next. I suddenly realized the rotha pain had dulled too. I had woken up without it—Vance must be back home. I was grateful and still a little lost.

As I sat there staring at the back of my hands and forearms, a grapefruit-sized ball rolled from under the bed and stopped against my bare feet. It was soft and squishy, similar to a ball of yarn. I realized that Moyuki must be under my bed again. This time, she hadn't signaled that she wanted to leave my room. I guessed she wanted me to play.

I underhand threw it, rolling it back under the bed from whence it came. It shortly thereafter returned to me. My chapped lips cracked into a small smile, and my eyes watered for a completely different reason.

I took a chance and rolled the ball next to the bed. The large cat-like animal gingerly crawled from under the bed and batted at the ball as innocently as a kitten. It was about the size of a medium dog but with longer legs and a sleek pantherlike body. Part of my lizard brain whimpered about prey and predators, but I reminded myself that the Xavians were larger people. They probably tamed larger animals. Still, I believed she could cause damage if she was in the mindset to do so, though she didn't appear to be. Her bright jade eyes glinted at me as she batted the ball back to my legs. Before I could reach down, she jetted over to me, rubbing her chin on my knees.

I guessed I shouldn't have been surprised that Moyuki looked so similar to cats of our world. Aside for some unique features, Xavians and humans were similar. Besides the increased size, Moyuki's ears were larger than a domestic cat's ears. She also, surprisingly—or maybe not—had two tails which seemed to serve similar purposes in balance and communication.

I offered my hand, and Moyuki rubbed on it too, bringing it to the side of her face for me to scratch. Also like domestic cats, Moyuki enjoyed scratches behind her ears. She purred a thick, strong reverberation that shook me. I closed my eyes and soaked it in. It felt like the first sweet touch I had experienced in a long time. That wasn't actually the case. Vance and I had been together two nights ago. The emptiness of it felt vast and wide. I hadn't done anything nice for my body since, either. Little food. Little washing.

I felt empty without him.

I didn't know if I had ever understood that or experienced that until the saf's purr echoed in the space. I felt like a shell.

And honestly, I had never felt that with the absence of a lover. The love had always turned sour. It had always been a relief to run away. Perhaps I hadn't the chance to run away. That might be it in part, but this also wasn't like any of the other flings or even relationships I'd had. I had never known the ending at the beginning. Instead, I made assumptions, had great optimism and blind faith. Why would such a good omen destroy what relationship I had?

That might only be my fear.

Heck, I had often been warned about red flags, bad relationships, and told of potential bad outcomes. People I knew didn't really have faith in my relationships, especially my sister who was always picking up the pieces afterward. And I had pursued those relationships against others' better judgments, against my own better judgment.

This was the one I should have faith in. This is the one that the cosmos had sprinkled proof of fate and a lifetime of love upon me. It was written on our bodies. And I sensed it when our bodies were together. We completed each other.

Yes, my circumstances weren't perfect. This place wasn't perfect. It was possible that I would never get to experience life the way I wanted to… That's what happens when you're trafficked and you end up on a planet covered in deadly, vicious aliens. But that was life, right? I laughed sickly at the idea.

Moyuki paused, sat down, and looked at me quizzically.

"None of this is Vance's fault. Why would I throw away the only good thing I know?" I whispered the question to Moyuki.

She mewed. Possibly questioning why I had stopped petting her. I continued on, because that was the answer. Why stop the good stuff?

I rubbed her other ear until she felt it was evened out, and then she walked to the door, asking to be let out. I wasn't sure if I was ready to go out there, but at least I could wash up. I grabbed a new set of clothes and opened the door for Moyuki and I to the world that we couldn't deny any longer.

The shower was the perfect temperature and smelled a bit like peonies but with some citrus notes. I felt refreshed, relieved Vance was home, and looked forward to seeing him. Still, I would wait for him to come to me.

I settled in my room, doodling in a notebook Vance had given me. I sketched the plants with the pouf chair featuring several times.

My heart skipped a beat when he knocked softly on the door.

"Come in," I shouted at the door, like I was busy with other things. I wasn't.

The door creaked open, and Vance stuck his head inside, as if I would change my mind once I knew who it was. I raised my eyebrows at him to acknowledge him. I let him decide how much more welcome he was.

He timidly walked in, leaving the door open. "Are you hungry?" he asked.

"No," I lied.

"May I sit?" He gestured at the papasan chair, which was shorter than half his height, low to the ground.

I found myself saying 'yes' just to see him attempt to sit in it. I suppressed a giggle when it turned out as I hoped—with his feet on the ground, his knees jutted nearly to his face, and his butt sat super low in the rounded chair. He looked incredibly uncomfortable. I wasn't mean-hearted, but for someone who had been in a lot of awkward positions, recently being on a new planet with a bunch of different customs and being dropped off like a sack of potatoes off the back of a truck, it was nice to be on the opposite side of that. Why did he have this chair?

"It was my mother's," he said as if I had asked the question out loud.

That made sense. His mom had probably given him his preference for soft materials, fibers, and a home overflowing with greenery. It was also why he kept such a cumbersome chair, even though it only fit in his guest room. It was his mother's.

I had to admit, it made my heart ache a little more. I missed my own mother. Heck, I missed my home planet. Everything here was so strange, and I didn't know how to navigate it, including this man. One that had a mother that liked soft things, and so he liked soft things. And who had some sort of weird animal running around his home because his maybe-more-than-a-neighbor had died tragically. Maybe I was an asshole for sleeping with him, not realizing I'd get caught in this biological rotha web. And yet, I didn't exactly regret it either.

He was the most amazing sexual partner I had ever had…and I'd had some good sex partners. Maybe I shouldn't have been surprised that his genetic code or whatever thought we would be good mates. I actually had little doubt that we would.

But that's not why I was here.

I missed my opportunity to say anything about his mother and how sweet that was. Of course, I had gotten distracted by sex. Really, I was happy to see him again.

I couldn't stand it anymore. I climbed out of the bed. My pounding heart drowned out any padding feet on the soft carpet as I crossed to him. I delicately inserted myself into his lap, navigating around his jutting knees. He held me in his arms, wonderstruck.

"I was afraid for you…out there," I admitted. "I felt like you were out there because of me, asking for stupid material things off the ship, or worse—"

"It was a good thing we went. Lian was trapped. It would have been some time before someone checked on him," he assured me. His beaming smile made me wonder if he'd ever see me as doing wrong.

"Even so. You've saved me in two of those encounters. You're always trying to keep me safe. If you say I should stay inside, I'm going to listen."

"I want to take you out," he said to my complete surprise. The scouting mission must have gone well.

"What about the Orkain?" I asked.

"They're still out there. We found more, actually."

I pulled back slightly. That wasn't good news. "What's changed?"

He inhaled deeply. "I don't want to hide you away especially at the cost of losing you." He paused, thinking. "We will be careful, and I'll teach you how to look for them." He nearly recited my words to me.

I smiled at him weakly. Life and rotha were much more complicated and, hell—beautiful—than I anticipated. Adventure, huh? "What should I wear?" I asked.

He wrapped me in a long hug.

Chapter Thirty-Two
Flowing

Sara

It was actually fairly overcast when we set out, even though it was the middle of the day. I really had slept in.

"I prefer traveling at this time anyway. It's the warmest, so it's the safest," Vance explained.

I knew there was some sort of evolutionary benefit to my sleeping in. It was a waste on early-rising Earth where everything started so early in the morning and was closed in the evening.

I appreciated learning from Vance. He pointed out some of the nature he knew the name of. I was sure my sister would have appreciated knowing all the flower names, but it was sort of lost on me. I loved when we ventured off of the clear path and we traveled close together in the brush of the jungle. There was nothing that was painful to walk through, but I was appreciative of the long pants all the same. I followed all his advice and took it to heart. I was quiet when he told me to be quiet. And he taught me how to look out for the signs of the Orkain in the skies, even when it was overcast like this.

A shadowy burden seemed to leave him halfway through the trip. We hadn't seen any signs of the Orkain. He knew that they didn't hunt every day, but knowing and having faith in it were two different things. The air was so fresh and the colors were beautiful and I loved wandering the jungle with such a handsome man. He helped me over mossy boulders, and he pointed out the stream we were to follow. I didn't have huge expectations of the waterfall after he showed me the stream. I didn't think it could be much.

We stopped for a short break at the bottom of a small mountain. Or a big hill. I wasn't sure what the size range was for these things. The planet was relatively small, at least compared to Earth. Vance explained there had been several villages of the Xavian which were separated not really by government differences or property lines but by geography. They were, from what I understood, a pretty homogeneous group, not like Earthlings who had evolved different characteristics based on the land they had lived on. We talked non-stop about our planets, our people, and what we understood of it all.

Instead of going up the hill like I thought we were going to, we separated from the creek and walked around the hill. The trees were older here and grew closer together. It made for dimmer, cooler travel with only the listless sounds of birds and the trickle of the creek. I really liked it. And Vance seemed to enjoy it too. The hill gave us protection from one side, and I had trouble imagining any Orkain being able to swoop in between the trees with their wide wingspan.

I began to tire, but I didn't want Vance to know that after I had made such a big deal of the excursion. It wasn't like I was really big on exercising on Earth either. I mostly stayed on the couch and ate popcorn and drank wine. But I didn't want Vance to think it was a mistake to bring me out here. I didn't want him to think I couldn't handle it. Our conversation slowed a bit. I focused on my breathing.

A gentle pat on my arm stopped me, and he pointed with two fingers to an area we could sit. I was grateful for the break. He put his satchel on his crossed feet and pulled out a handful of fruit. He took a bite from the fruit about the size of a muscadine. He fed me the rest. It was juicy on my lips, and I felt it dribble down my chin. I giggled, but I didn't care. It was really refreshing and what I needed. His thumb wiped the juice from my chin, then my bottom lip, lingering close.

His eyes weren't human. Their intense centers swirled hypnotically, like he was digging into my soul. It was too much. I blinked them away and looked at the small gap left between us. He handed me a full fruit. I popped the entire thing in my mouth.

"There's a seed," he said, eyes wide.

I squinted as my molars brushed something solid. I worked my mouth and teeth around it, pulling the fruit from the pit, then spit out the offending seed.

Vance's eyes were still wide. I think he was impressed by my skills. He didn't have to know that I chomped down on it at first. I wouldn't make that mistake again. He put one in his own mouth and it bulged awkwardly.

I already knew how skilled he was. The seed emerged without fruit between his lips in short demand. I giggled and then bit my lip, thinking about his on mine.

Vance

The overcast skies dulled a lot of the shadows that would have alerted me to danger. I struggled knowing a glut of Orkain were slumbering not far away, but there didn't seem to be any out. Soon, I was wrapped up in walking in the wilderness with Sara, leading her through to one of my favorite waterfalls. It had always been fairly secluded due to its distance from the village. And now it was beautifully desolate. I hadn't seen anyone there in any of my last passings, whether on patrol or hunting.

The jungle had grown a bit in the summer months here, and there were more than a couple of moments that I went on my sense of direction rather than recognizing familiar landmarks. I eventually found it though. It wasn't the most magnificent waterfall as far as waterfalls go, but its seclusion and drop into a small pool with smooth rocks surrounded by greenery made it a pleasant place to spend the day.

"Oh wow!" she exclaimed when the waterfall suddenly came into view. She grabbed my arm and jumped up and down. "It's beautiful."

I couldn't help it. I broke out into a giant grin, as if I had formed the falls and written gravity all for her.

She was right. It was beautiful—calm and serene.

"I can't believe this is in walking distance from your place. Why don't you live here?!" She knelt and brushed the water's surface with her fingertips.

I hadn't considered the idea. It wasn't practical to live even this far from my people, especially if we were going to build a tunnel system. Beauty like this needed to be shared. "So everyone can enjoy it."

"Do lots of people come down here?" she asked.

"No, not really. This one is pretty quiet," I said. Had she hoped to spend time with others? Perhaps that could be our next outing.

That apparently wasn't what she had in mind though. She dropped her pants to her ankles and stepped out of them, revealing a small pair of shorts underneath, her white legs shining against the backdrop of deep forest greens. She giggled, pulling her top off.

"Are you going to join me?" she asked.

I looked up at the sky to see if there were any Orkain. The pool itself wasn't completely covered in green canopy, but its edges were. We hadn't seen the enemy all day. They didn't seem to be out. I tried to rationalize. The water was cool. It would disguise our body temperature. It might actually be safer to swim.

I looked down at Sara who had already dipped in. Her long hair floated around her body, obscuring my view of her body. How could I resist?

I took off my shirt. She smiled appreciatively. I was a lot less graceful with my pants, and almost slipped on the mossy stones trying to get them off. I had chosen a thicker pair of shorts for underneath, because, well, Sara had a way of necessitating coverage of my erection—right now being a prime example. I had taken her out for a hike, and now she was undressed, waiting for me in a pool. Already tight against my shorts, the cold water on my calves helped lessen that. I settled gingerly into the water. It was a greater adjustment for me. When I got waist deep, she floated on her back and used her arms to swim away. Her breasts popped up above the surface and I immediately tightened against my shorts again.

Sara was beautiful.

Her breasts and her stomach floated near the surface of the water. I immediately followed. I wanted to swim up against her body, feel those curves along my stomach. I wanted her arms around my shoulders, her breasts against my chest. And that sly smile on her face, her eyes watching my every move and lingering on my own body's responses...she knew. She was driving me crazy.

She turned away from me so that she could swim more directly to the waterfall, a wink over her soft shoulder beckoning me to follow her. The small of her back and the curves of her ass were obscured by the water's surface as her long legs kicked to propel her. This woman continued to tantalize me.

My toes kicked off of slimy stones as the water deepened. The pull of the water changed. I wasn't sure what would happen when I reached her, but I knew I'd follow her all day without complaint. With one more sexy look over her shoulder and a few strokes of her arms, she disappeared under the waterfall's flow.

Sara

I emerged on the other side of the waterfall in an alcove created by the rock outcropping. The waterfall was much more impressive than I expected when we followed that small creek. The falls weren't wide, but they were tall, probably thirty feet above us, emptying into the round cove-like pool, framed by the beautiful Xavian jungle—a hidden gem that Vance had thought to show me.

I hoped he didn't think I wasn't appreciative because I'd stripped so quickly after arriving and distracted my alien guide. I felt so warm from the hiking and wanted to cool off. Perhaps stasis for months at the same temperature made it difficult for my body to regulate its temperature in varying environments. Sure, that's what it was.

The water was clear and cool. It was probably cold, but it was easy to ignore the chill while Vance watched me move in the water. I invited his eyes with a couple of backstrokes, both to give him a different visual perspective, but also to give him room to join me. I was basically presenting my body (again) to Vance. Something about him—maybe it was the broad shoulders or the mischievous smile—made me want to do crazy things.

He followed me to the other side of the waterfall. He did it much more elegantly, however, managing to swim underneath the power of the water and come back up very close to me. I locked my knees onto his hips, my calves sliding along his outer thighs. It was to keep me from accidentally kicking him as I needed to tread water here, but it was also to keep him at a set distance. Still, he was very, ahem, long, and I felt things brushing against my inner thighs, which could have been seaweed or something floating in the water but I was pretty sure was the creature from his depth.

My eyes traced his body along his perfect pecs attached to monster arms. My soft legs tightened against the meaty muscles of his. A lock of his hair was in his face, getting water into his eye, but he was too distracted by my proximity. I took a hand and quietly moved it across his face and behind his horn. I dared draw my hand along its hard, rough, intriguing surface.

I let my hand slip down his face, following his sharp cheekbone. His giant goofy smile was gone. Instead, he studied me with a clenched jaw. He followed my every move, his rapt attention on me, responding to every blink or cut of my eye.

I was lost in his eyes, and I was about to be lost on his lips. I brought myself closer. When our lips touched, a turbulent rush of spices and adrenaline flooded my system like a waterfall of our own desires finally smashing together, the waters crashing, intertwining, and becoming one surf again. Our bodies aligned, my knees no longer keeping us separate. Instead, my calves twisted and wrapped around his surprisingly thin waist. My legs locked around him as I straddled his thickly ridged abdomen. I knew where that triangle of muscles led. I could feel it against my ass. I was resting on his massive knot of sex.

He now had an arm pulling me close though, the inside of his elbow near my waist, cinching it in, and the bulk of his forearm crossing my back against the opposite shoulder blade, crushing and pressing me hard against his chest. My neck craned to reach his lips.

He was still taking my lead, doing nothing beyond what I had initiated. I knew if I wanted more—and, yes, I absolutely wanted more—that I would have to be the one to press on. I shoved my tongue into his mouth, grazing his teeth. I soon gained entrance; my tongue lost in a space that felt brand new amongst the three twisting tongues.

It was like its own orgy. They caressed my tongue, and then all tumbled into my mouth. It felt uncomfortably full for a moment but undeniably hot. He pulled back slightly, probably to give me room to breathe in the back of my throat. Goodness. He was letting me take the lead, but there was no doubt that he was raring at the bit. Every part of him wanted me. His cocks jumped and leapt against my butt and the small of my back.

I'd never felt so demanded upon. His tongues, thick and passionate, seemed to be trying to swallow my own. He wanted so much of me, and it was so intense, I felt like I was outside of my body as he was trying to come in.

My breasts smashed up against his hard chest, splashing water between us as we made waves. It was only then that I realized I was grinding on him. He had propped up one of his legs so that his members wouldn't be so intense against me. I rode his leg, dragging myself against the thick, defined edges of his thigh. The motion sent my body ablaze. I lost myself in the motion of bucking against him. My mouth let out indecipherable noises when I got the chance to exhale from the intense make-out session.

My hands gripped what they could of his wide shoulders. The water had me slipping, and I was floating in pleasure. My body tightened against his, my core tightening, my mouth pressed deep into his as I moaned in a way that made my body shudder as pleasure rippled from my clit, up the front of my belly, lighting up my chest and clenching my jaw. His teeth lightly clamped on my tongue until all that had tightened gave one last gasp of strength and released.

"Again," I whimpered into his ear, pulling him close with my right leg which was still around his waist.

If he gave his big, goofy smile, I didn't see it as he was so quick to claim my mouth again. He pressed his leg rhythmically slow between my own. I dug my nails into his shoulders, which hardly gave at all, and I got lost in the lapping of his tongues and the lapping of the water one more time.

The buildup was quick this time, and already, my body was ready to reach its peak. I didn't want it to end so quickly, but there wasn't much I could do. I dug into his leg, slick and desperate. My body fell right back into that wave that it had caught a few moments ago, and I rode it, my body stiff and uncontrolled. He let my body take the lead and became my piece of pleasure, getting off as I groaned into his mouth one more time.

I opened my eyes and came to. I had gotten lost in my climax, completely not caring that I had humped his leg into my own oblivion. His face remained hungry on me, curious, mischievous, and proud as he soaked in all that had occurred. I suddenly became a little shy, my desperate need now slaked, leaving me a tangle of post-climax noodles for limbs. I came to the realization of what I'd done.

He didn't tease me at all for getting off on kisses and a well-placed leg. If anything, he seemed pleased. He didn't press back into me, assuming it was his turn to be satisfied. He waited patiently for me, although his hand ran up and down my back in position to easily guide or control my body.

I panted, my face still close to his. "I think I'm ready to go back to your place now."

"Done adventuring?"

I dismounted him and made my way back to the waterfall to slip underneath. "Not by a long shot," I shouted loudly, letting my cheer echo off the walls. The water felt cool on my flushed cheeks as I disappeared underneath the flow.

Chapter Thirty-Three
The Ship

Sara

I put on one of my favorite silky robes, cinched at the waist with nothing underneath. It might have been a cruel trick, but a lot of my body was still screaming to be seen and touched by him. I couldn't help but try to attract him, especially when I walked into the kitchen and saw that he had prepared a small meal and an oversized mug of fah for me.

When I got close to him, I realized he hadn't showered yet. He still had that natural sleepy musk. I had to pull myself away from him, otherwise I'd be against his body, warming it with my own. He seemed to have the same response to me, guarded attraction. Yesterday was amazing.

I sat at the small table that hardly had room for two, crossed my legs, baring a thick thigh, and looked up at him with heavy-lidded eyes. I shrugged and had to pull up the shoulder of the robe so it wouldn't fall completely down and reveal my breast. I took a sip of the fah. It was the perfect temperature.

"Thank you." Yesterday I couldn't be bothered by such a regular need, but I was hungry now. I scarfed down the food.

"May I accompany you to get your things on the ship?" he asked.

I was surprised. I thought he was going to arrange for someone else to go. I was glad he'd changed his mind. Perhaps another olive branch.

"I would like that very much," I said. Then I skipped off to get ready before he could change his mind. Secretly, it made me nervous to return to the ship. I was beginning to connect it with the Orkain.

Vance

Sara was timid and uncertain in the jungle. I'd won. The fears that played in my head now successfully played in hers. Selfish. I should've been able to protect her without crushing her spirit.

She froze when she caught the shine of the drop ship, despite the guard on the ramp giving us the all clear. There was nothing to fear. I signaled for him to give us some privacy, and he disappeared into the jungle.

I took her hand. It was cooler than usual, clammy. She began moving again, and we reached the entrance. "Everything's OK. Why don't you go in and get your things?" I said.

"Alone?" she asked. She didn't seem to think that was a very good idea at all.

"Yell if you need help," I said, keeping it light.

"Sure, of course."

I handed her a bag for her to put her items in before taking guard position.

She was gone for what seemed like an excessively long time. I wasn't entirely sure how much they let the women bring on board. I'd hoped they'd at least been lenient about that part since they intended to leave the women here without setting them up. It felt like she could have packed up half of the contents of the drop ship, but when she returned, she just had the bag I gave her, albeit overstuffed.

"There was still some sunscreen left!" she said, her face greased with some odd-smelling chemical. Her countenance had brightened considerably as well.

"What is that for?" I asked. The smell reminded me of millcress fruit and something acerbic.

"It protects our skin from solar damage. If I stay out in the sun too long, my skin will burn, which also contributes to aging our skin."

"Doesn't your skin age like the rest of you?" I asked.

"Yes, but too much skin damage can show up as wrinkles and spots and makes you look older than you and your skin actually are. I also had some clothes, books, and a deck of cards. I'll teach you Go Fish!"

"I know how to fish," I said.

She waggled her eyebrows. "Not like this…"

I shrugged, happy that she had arrived back in my sight without any harm coming to her. There also weren't any Orkain out here. Usually, they hunted multiple days in a row if not successful, but perhaps they were changing up their routines as well, or perhaps it had been a chance encounter. That would have explained why it hadn't put up a fight at all.

I took the bag from her and slung it over my shoulders. "Anything else you need?"

"No, but I'm not ready to go back home yet either," she said, a glean in her eye suddenly present. Whatever fear she had of the place had dissipated.

"Would you like to see Frustnerdd? It's the town I used to live in before we left for underground."

"Oh yes!" she said. "I'd love to see how you all used to live."

It had been my idea, but hearing her say it like a tourist visiting our tragedy felt a little weird. At least she'd be able to see some of the other people's offerings of textiles and goods, as most of the stores still had products inside of them. We didn't have any sort of looting. We had an excess of goods. Perhaps there were things she'd like to have that would make her feel more at home, or that would make her feel that her room was her own. It wasn't until that moment that I remembered that, while she was coming home with me tonight, that's not where she was intending to stay. That hurt. I hoped she would change her mind.

"I have a second bag if there is something else you need on the ship," I said.

"No, that's good for now. I don't think anyone is going to mess with the leftover stuff, and I'd like the other women to have access to things as well."

She could use the other bag to go shopping in Frustnerdd then.

When we arrived at the edge of Frustnerdd, she exclaimed that she recognized the place. Apparently, her government had showed them photos of the town when they described where they would be staying.

"I hadn't realized it was deserted," she said.

I could see how they could have given her that impression. Even now, nearly a year later, the town was still pristine. The grass hadn't even overgrown around the cobblestone yet. The windows were still streak-free clean.

I considered broaching the topic of re-doing her room, but I didn't want her to think I was pressuring her. Besides, if she was going to stay with me, I still wanted her to be in my room. I was trying to figure out how to make her feel less 'trapped,' as she called it. Perhaps if she had a space that was her own, rather than of someone else's making, she would feel more at home.

Instead, she got really excited over the camping stuff. "We could go camping!"

That sounded like a horrible idea. Sleeping outside during the coolness of the night, or even if with a fire, was probably a dumb thing to do.

"What if we kept to caverns or against warm rock cliffs?" she pleaded.

Her brown eyes looked up hopefully at me, and I had to agree. There was no way I was going to say 'no,' because I had caught what she had said. She had said *we*. Perhaps she did want to stay with me. She seemed to at least be visualizing a future with me. I had hope.

Timidly, I began to pack things up for camping. "I want to sleep where I can see the stars," she said. "Even if that's our backyard."

There it was again. That time it was *our*.

I wasn't a big camper, although I'd gone with friends before. Now I had a lot more survivalist background, for better or for worse. We could make it work. We had fun going through the remnants of town, trying to figure out what each thing was and if we needed it.

"I'd love to sleep near the waterfall," she said.

That did sound nice, however what blurted from my mouth was, "I don't know how to make that safe."

"Of course it's not safe, but we can take precautions. Don't you think that the Orkain will be destroyed…eventually?" She held some sort of multifunctional pot that I couldn't imagine serving any other function *than* as a pot. Perhaps that was my issue, creativity.

I was quiet.

She set down the pot.

"You don't think the Xavians are going to win out?" She had an inflection like it was a question, but I could also tell she was playing with it as a statement, rolling it around in her mind.

Honestly, I guess I hadn't really said it out loud. Maybe I hadn't even thought it. But yeah, I had trouble imagining a world without the Orkain now.

"That's why you want the tunnel system," she said, half a step ahead of me.

Why hadn't I thought that? Why else would you build an entire transportation system underground if you thought the danger above ground was never going to stop being an issue. "They aren't some temporary nuisance. We haven't killed a single one."

"But there does seem to be a limited number of them, right? Once you figure out their weakness, you'll be able to take back your planet."

"There are more than we thought. I don't know if they have any weaknesses."

"That can't be true. And perhaps they don't have the population density to continue on either. Have you seen younger ones?"

"No. We haven't seen any new growth in population, but we don't know their lifespans either.

They travel much faster than us; they're possibly nomadic."

"Well, I believe there will be a breakthrough. I haven't seen a single one of you give up. You arranged for women to come from a galaxy away to keep you all going. I think you can solve your Orkain problem. And until then, we will choose wisely where we camp."

I gave her a grim smile and put the multi-functional pot back on the shelf. We could use a regular pot.

As we left with our camping goods, I ventured the question. "Is this enough?" I asked.

"Is what enough?"

"I want you to know that I never want to trap you. I've been fearful of the Orkain, and so I wanted to hide you away, but I realize now that I can't do that."

"Well, accompanying me to the ship to get my stuff isn't really that grand of a gesture," she said.

I nodded my head sadly.

"But, it's a start," she added.

I took the chance. I put a hand on each side of her and brought her close to me. "I know we just met, and I have a lot to learn, but I want that chance. I want to learn and adventure with *you*."

The breath caught in her throat. I still wasn't sure what she was thinking, but at least she was still here. Still listening.

I continued. "You're the adventure. I'm sorry I don't have a grand gesture for you. Maybe it's not time for that, for us. But we can get to know each other. I don't have much, but what I do have, I'm not going to take from you. If you want freedom, you have it. But I'd love for you to have it with me."

A tear slipped from the corner of her eye and down her perfect cheek.

I searched her face. "Stay with me and we can see how this unfolds. It won't be perfect. I can't even promise to keep you safe from the Orkain flying around. But I can promise to be *with* you. And I think that's what you've been asking of me. Is that right?"

Her chin trembled before she nodded. "I'm never going to be your perfect lover, now at the start or even years from now. But I do like you, and I do want to explore *this*. Is that enough?" it was her turn to ask.

"It's everything," I replied.

I swept her mouth to mine. I held her desperately tight against me. Her soft curves fed my zarata. The connection was undeniable, even if we still had much to explore before, after, below, and around it. I couldn't wait. Sara was my adventure.

She bit my lip, giving me something else to think about. "Do you have a place around here to show me?" she asked.

"What do you mean?" I asked, a little love-drunk from her lips.

"I mean, a place…" she gestured around the jungle with a little wink.

My cocks understood her before I did. They sprung up hard against my pants. Suddenly, I was searching for a place too.

I yanked her off of the trail, leaving behind only the traces of her laughter. I knew exactly the place. It wasn't but a hundred yards. We touched each other over our clothing, reaching for each other every moment we could spare while still navigating the jungle.

At the clearing, we both looked up at the skies and the trees. No Orkain to be found. I picked her up and carried her halfway over the creek, laying her out on a warm, sunny flat rock. And then, I devoured her.

Chapter Thirty-Four
Chilled

Sara

"I don't know why you would want your drink watered down," he shook his head, looking curiously at my drink with ice in it. He returned to cutting vegetables.

"I don't *want* it watered down… I like it cold. Really cold." I sat on the kitchen counter with my iced fyg juice. The drink was nice after our trip back. I was more out of shape than I imagined. And I didn't have a wild imagination.

I had asked Vance to let me take up some freezer space with ice cubes for my drinks, and he had obliged. I was amazed that a place so warm would have tepid drinks. Blech.

He paused to shrug, then continued chopping. I watched in amazement. I didn't have the patience to cut things up so uniformly and neatly. If my vegetables didn't come in some sort of microwavable container, I whacked them a few times with a knife before tossing them into the pan. They cooked unevenly, but whatever. Living and eating with Vance was more like enjoying a fancy restaurant then what I considered 'cooking' in my apartment. More often than not, I drank some wine and ate a bunch of cheese. Sometimes I was fancy and put the cheese on crackers, but I usually saved those carbs for my wine.

Besides, I liked to chew on the ice. I crunched down on one. Vance chuckled.

I was becoming more and more comfortable with him, and he with me. He finished cutting the vegetables, using the flat side of the blade to move the cuttings to one side of the board like a pro. Setting the knife down, he moved the few steps closer to me, parking himself between my legs and leaning in for a kiss.

I smiled mischievously because he was perfectly timed. I put my hands on his shoulders and his hot lips met my cool ones. I pushed the remainder of the ice cube with my tongue against his lips and into his mouth and wrestled his tongues with it. His eyes immediately popped open with the change in sensation. The ice quickly melted with the heat of his excitement.

He pulled from me to curse under his breath before going back in for more. Soon our mouths were one temperature.

"I'm thinking I like that ice," he said, gaining a new appreciation for it.

His hands were clambering over the button on my pants, and soon he was yanking them off of me, my bare ass on the kitchen counter by our vegetables for dinner. I put another ice cube in my mouth and kissed him while his hands squeezed at my hips and the top of my ass.

He stole my glass and drank from it, stealing an ice cube. I thought we were going to kiss again, but he grabbed my legs at the crook of my knees and pulled me to the edge of the counter. He was so quick and rough, it surprised me.

I braced myself with my hands behind me. Vance knelt and breathed cool air between my legs, setting me alight. But before I could arch my head back and imagine what that would be like, he was standing back up, pulling off my shirt, his cold mouth taking in a nipple and sending cold and fiery sparks across my chest. I grabbed at his horns and tried to push him away, but he only groaned and moved to my other breast. The sensations of teeth and ice and hot and cold confused my body, sending zaps of electricity across my skin which burst into gooseflesh.

I flinched as his mouth bit at my sides, his tongues sliding down my belly. He seemed to savor the surprises, my body under his control to do with as he pleased. His fingertips drew swirls on my legs on either side of him as he slowly made his way down, pulling me even closer to the counter's edge until my ass was perched on the corner.

With one long, slow, wide lick, he wet my entrance and my clit, my hands reaching to grab his head and rock him toward me. He had other plans though. He pulled back and opened two of the drawers on either side of us. With fingers locked around my ankles, he put one foot into each drawer like stirrups, opening me up like a book. He flicked the pages with his tongues, and I closed my eyes, throwing my head back and enjoying greedily.

He flicked against my clit until I squirmed with sensitivity, then he pressed a wide portion of his tongue against me so that I could buck with the correct pressure, bringing me to the edge over and over. My hands tangled in his hair until a particular tongue flick knocked me over, my head thudding against the cabinet behind me. I reached up and grabbed the handles of the cupboards while he ate.

If it hadn't been that my hands and feet were tangled in kitchen cabinetry, I would have collapsed and launched off the counter as the combination of heat and ice covered me, sending shocks through my body. I screamed out, confused by the mixture of pleasure and intense cold. They were one and the same. It felt like nibbles on my skin. My legs tried to clench shut, but they were stuck in the drawers. He kept control of my legs as he worked me with the ice cube, the numbness giving way to the lapping of his tongue over my nerves until I was wrenching at the cabinet doors.

I bit my lip as I rode the wave of too much ecstasy, my body screaming to be pleased, to be left alone, to be heard, demanding touch and tongue, each moment quickly passing while feeling like an eternity of need.

His mouth firmly sucking on my clit, his face smashed in between my legs, he positioned my legs over each of his shoulders. With his massive hands on my back, he pressed me even further onto his face. I grabbed handfuls of his hair and let out a squeal as he stood up, raising my feet from the drawers as I sat on his shoulders.

I wrapped my legs around the back of his arms to keep balance as he walked us to the other side of the room, but we nearly toppled as I launched into ecstasy again. He stumbled, but his tongue never lost the place that caused the thrust of my hips. I rewrapped my legs around his strong back, resting calves on muscles, tightening around him until I wasn't sure if he could breathe. He could breathe when he made me cum again.

Vance seemed to need oxygen—something he reminded me of by smashing my back against the wall. The tapestry behind me fell behind the small of my back, trapped.

The shock loosened my legs, and he pulled up to gasp for air. The back of my head hit the wall again as he smashed into me, barely having caught his breath. I used the wall for leverage to push back against him, his tongues reaching into me, curling up against my g-spot. I gasped with pleasure as they pulled out and back in, my channel tightening against them as they splayed and rolled through me.

A tongue pressed against my g-spot as another pressed tight against my clit on the other side, and my body shuddered, starting from the origin to the electrical zips through my limbs and out my fingers, toes, and the top of my head. My juices flowed over his tongue and into his mouth. They coated his beard and dripped down his shirt as he lapped as quickly and as much as he could, my sex exploding, completely unlocked.

Finally, he squeezed my thighs to get me to release his tongue and head so he could get another breath.

My body felt incredibly heavy with the release. I didn't know if I could continue to hold myself up. I leaned against the wall, giving space between my sex, which was on fire, and the enthusiastic tongues of my alien lover. I traced the ridges on his horns, wrapped my fingers around them and stroking them like I wished I was doing with his cocks… Later. I still wasn't finished with him down there.

As my breathing slowed, he gave a few testing flicks of his tongue, relishing in my sensitivity and the reaction he garnered from the smallest movements against me.

In a much shorter time than I would have thought possible, he was lapping at my entrance again, still staying clear of my clit which was swollen with all the sucking. It probably could have used an ice cube at that point, but there was no way I could handle such an extreme right now. I pulled off the wall and leaned forward against him.

He backed up, moving backwards to keep us balanced, all the time licking the edges of my entrance, a wide tongue pressing in and out. He filled me up more and more, deeper, thicker into my channel. It felt full and pleasurable, and I continued to lean into it. He had an ass cheek in each hand, his nails digging in as he pressed me close. He couldn't get enough of me either.

Soon his adjustment for balance had my cheek pressed against the coolness of the opposite wall. My legs were tangled behind his back and knocked against the wall too, but I didn't care. He was thrusting two of his tongues into me as the underneath of another tongue pressed against my clit.

Every thrust of his tongue put more pressure on my g-spot and my clit. My face was smashed against the wall as I laid out on his face, my hips and legs bucking in rhythm with his tongue thrusts, which carried the lifeline and release of my next orgasm. I groaned and panted against the wall, anxiously climbing his face with my pelvis to reach the edge of an orgasm that was growing increasingly farther away. The roll of his tongue against my clit with the pulsing of the tongues in my channel while he fought my thighs for air sent me over.

I slapped the wall and tightened my thighs. His actions grew fiercer, desperate to give me that final smash of ecstasy and anxious for that first gasp of air. My orgasm rolled into a second one before I finally relaxed my thighs. He breathed hot air on my pussy, inhaling the scent of his accomplishments. His face had turned even bluer with the exertion, and he slowly returned to his coloring with each breath. I only caught glances as I continued to use the wall to prop myself up, mostly by my own face. I felt like a wasted noodle atop him.

Vance wriggled me down from his shoulders until my legs were wrapped around his waist and over top of his throbbing cocks. He held me tight. I didn't have to do anything as he carried me to the living room and laid my naked body down on the urish. He then laid beside me, giving me his arm to use as a pillow.

We laid face-to-face with his bulge gently positioned between my legs. I couldn't even keep my eyes open. They were heavy-lidded like I'd been drugged. My whole body was heavy, limp, and yet, I felt like I was floating.

Meanwhile, his fingers moved the damp hair from my face, curling it behind my ear. He kissed the tip of my nose with those lips which had basically destroyed me over and over. He was the perfect mixture of heat, passion, and comfort.

I gave a deep exhale that emptied the breath out of my rib cage and left me feeling even more boneless, my lower body felt numb with pleasure. I fought sleep even as it came like a giant wall. I slammed my fists against it, but in the end, I only remember the soft pecks on my cheeks and nose, his big fingers playing in my hair, and his warm breath on my face as I faded into nothingness and sleep.

Chapter Thirty-Five
Good News

Vance

At the doorstep, I felt a kind of relief from the burn in my chest, replaced with another burn, a desire to see my love. I opened the door to thin, gray smoke emanating from the kitchen.

I rushed inside. The pain that had almost diminished was replaced by a great fear. "Sara? Are you here? Are you OK?" I called.

"Yes, oh my gosh. Of course. I'm all right," she said.

I looked over the scene. There was no fire, just something that appeared to look like black charcoal lumps on a scorched pan. I wasn't sure if Sara was OK though. She was frazzled. The kitchen was a mess. And she looked near tears. She fanned the stove with a towel, which was doing little in a room without ventilation.

I reached over her and turned on the exhaust fan.

"I'm so sorry… I wanted to make you dinner to thank you for everything you've done…" She put her head in her hands and let out a little sob. "Please don't be mad."

"Mad? Why would I be mad?" For a moment, I wondered if there were other meanings to the word. "I'm not mad."

I gingerly put my arms around her, unsure if she wanted comfort in that way. She immediately pressed close to me, burying her face in my chest. Now the pain in my chest was something entirely new as I held her crying figure. I wanted nothing more than to take away all of her pain, to stop her tears. I pulled her away from the stove, picked her up, and carried her to the urish. When I set her down, she did not sit upright but instead cuddled against me, tears still wetting her face and my shirt.

A sniffle escaped, and then a little snort. She giggled at the noise that she had made, and I nuzzled her ear and hair with my nose. I had a feeling that she wasn't crying about the burnt…whatever that was.

"I'm a terrible cook," she wiped her running nose on my shirt, then tried to rub it off with her palm.

I shook my head and took her hand in mine. I kissed the tip of her damp nose. "Yes, you are."

She laughed, then needed to wipe her nose again. This time, she chose her own arm. I rubbed it off with my palm, and she laughed again, sweet melodic notes that warmed the room. I took a thumb and brushed the tears from her cheeks, one by one. Then I gave a tiny kiss where each one had been. Sara pulled close and kissed my lips. Her kisses were chilled, and weak, soft, and gentle.

I circled my arm around her. I loved how it fit along the curve of her hips. I loved the marks on my skin and the echoes on hers.

"Why were you crying? I'm not mad."

"I might have been concerned I was going to burn down your house." She laughed, the relief on her face evident. "I wanted to make you something special. You've been so good to me. I wanted to say thank you, and that I love you."

"I love you too," I said.

"I mean, of course, I do. It's written on my arms, but now I know it too," she explained.

I traced her rotha markings, connecting the dots with the softest of finger touches, sweeping over her skin which erupted in gooseflesh. The electricity felt palpable, ions exchanging between us.

"I have to know," I whispered in her ear. "Will you leave when the Earthlings come back?"

"No, I won't."

"But what about your adventures? Are you sure you're okay here with me?"

"This is the biggest adventure I could take," she confided in me.

"What about me is an adventure?" I asked, unsure.

"Adventure isn't always about brand-new places. It's about exploring further and deeper. It's about taking new paths in your life. Anything I do here with you is an adventure. You're my adventure."

I understood the last part. Sara was my adventure. And her leap encouraged mine. "In Xavia, rotha is generally announced to others with a kumirata, a commitment ceremony."

"That's like the next step?" she asked.

"It's like your marriage ceremony."

"Are you asking me to marry you, Vance?" Sara smiled nervously.

"Marry me, announce kumirata, climb the mountains, be mine," I breathed. Now that I had asked, I was desperate to know her answer.

"Have babies, save the world?"

I heard skepticism, and it stung—Sara wasn't a womb. She wasn't the imported solution to my people's crisis. She was the most fantastic being I'd ever met. And I wanted to be hers as much as she would be mine.

"Sara, all of me is yours. Damn this world and my duties. Rotha is for us to do as we please." Maybe I'd been intent on performing my duties when designing the women's arrival. Life, galaxies, and rotha turned out to be so much more complex. It was changing me. I only wanted her. If there was more, so be it. She was all that mattered.

She smiled at me through shining eyes. "Yes!" She leaped into my arms. "I never expected vacation to end like this, but you're the biggest adventure I could ever have. I want to be a part of your life and your world."

I held her. I couldn't imagine life without her. No matter what life brought us, I knew we could handle it. We were destined to be together. I told her about traditional kumiratas. She told me about weddings. We decided to do something simple. And soon.

"Oh, I can't wait to tell Katy tomorrow!" she said. We were going to her sister's photography showcase. It was the perfect time to share good news.

Sara

To leave now after the chemistry and the excitement and the promise of a lifetime together…would be to run away from the adventure. I knew that now. Anything less than this would be to settle, to leave, to retreat. I was never one to retreat. As soon as Vance had described a kumirata ceremony, I knew that was the next step.

I wanted to share the good news with Xavians and humans alike. Nothing about the American government coming back excited me. I didn't care if I ever saw them again. I no longer trusted them. There was hope and fun for my fellow women to create our own adventures and lives, despite what had happened to us.

And for the Xavians? Our kumirata would mean rotha was not extinct, and any possible offspring would mean a hope for their species to continue in some way. And who knows how that hope would help. How many of them had pretty much given up or decided that this was their lives now? How much difference could be made, if those minds were changed?

#

The next day, I wore a soft blue linen dress with a pearl necklace I had found amongst the jewelry Vance had provided me. I'd been reminded of the pearl necklace Mom had when we were younger, and I was excited to show Katy. We never found Mom's in her belongings. My sister and I hadn't said it out loud, but we were pretty sure she had pawned it as some point when she raising us as a single mother. I hoped it was spent on something important and not for something stupid that kids ask for but don't really need. Our mom had never put a lot of stock or sentiment in possessions, just us.

I had been thinking about Mom a lot lately with this new chapter in my life. Our mom had chosen adventure too when she decided to raise us on her own. She could have dropped us off at our grandparents or some firehouse. She could have gotten pre-occupied by dating, in trying to replace our father, but she didn't do any of those things. And while times were difficult sometimes, what I remember most was how enthusiastic she was to parent us. I never felt like a burden, even though we were easily the best and worst things to happen in her life.

I was beginning to feel that same excitement for my new life with Vance and with whatever little ones we might be blessed with. I wasn't naïve enough to think that my womb was going to save the Xavian race, but I was beginning to feel eager to participate in that part of it. Despite the Orkain, I wanted to have young ones with Vance and to show them this beautiful world. It was more beautiful than Earth, both in scenery and in its people. The government here wouldn't hurt them or deny them based on their inherent qualities. They would be treasured here just as I would treasure them.

But first, I had to break the news to my sister. She had already warned me not to get too close to Vance. I looked down at my arms again. Yep, this was definitely *close*. If there was anything I was guilty of, it was a poor choice in vacation companies. But maybe we could stay and build a life here—both of us. In fact, she'd probably be most improved by remaining on Xavia. On Earth, there was stupid Mike, her ex-fiancé, and a job that she hated. The photography showcase was her attempt at giving this place a chance. I hoped she was giving Drex a chance too.

The differences between Drex's and Vance's homes were stark. Drex seemed to appreciate minimal lines and a modern sleekness—just like Katy. And, Vance, like me, liked the softer things. Another confirmation sign for rotha. It knew to match me with Vance. It knew to match Katy with Drex. I was sure of it.

Katy looked dazzling in a drape dress of jade green, much more elegant than the one I had donned. She also wore a big single pearl on a thin chain of gold. I guessed that either sisters thought alike, or Drex and Vance were comparing notes.

"You look so gorgeous!" I shouted and grabbed her arms, trying not to muss up her dress. I didn't give her the giant bear hug that I wanted.

She was going on about some last photo switch for the end of the show. She was always second-guessing herself. It was my job to tell her to trust her instincts. She showed me both photos, the same subject in both of Bolin mending armor but at a different angle. There really wasn't a difference that I could tell. The others wouldn't be able to tell either, but I let her go on about the pros and cons while I waited for Vance to return so that we could share our news.

Vance and Drex came in with glasses of fage for everyone. They were both good-looking, but I absolutely adored the wider shoulders of Vance. One of my hands received a glass of fage, and the other automatically drifted to Vance's shoulder.

"A toast?" asked Drex, putting his hand on my sister's back.

This seemed like the time. I looked over to Vance. "Should we?!" I asked.

Vance nodded like I taught him, his smile breaking into a grin. "Yes, a toast to rotha," he said.

Drex and Katy didn't respond at first. I took my hand off of Vance's shoulder and flipped over my wrist to reveal my markings. He did the same, parallel to my arm.

Suddenly, Katy was at my side, her drinking abandoned to Drex. "What is that?" she asked. She rubbed my markings like they might rub off.

"You haven't told her?" said Vance. It seemed pretty bold of a question, given that I had gotten them on my body before they had been explained to me.

"Remember how I told you about my parents and how rotha manifested as marks up the arms? This is the start of that. I didn't realize humans could get them," said Drex.

I didn't know Drex well. It was difficult to read him. He didn't seem surprised that we had experienced rotha. Perhaps Vance had already told him? But he did seem distracted by my markings. Perhaps he was wondering if Katy would show markings for him.

"I'm sure your markings will show up soon," I said to Katy.

Katy did indeed look at her arms, but there was nothing there yet. I was certain there would be though. I had seen the way that Drex looked at my sister all the time, even in the few interactions we had had. My sister needed to let go of her past and embrace Drex and this new life. If anyone could be stubborn enough to fight away rotha marks, it would be her. I hoped she wouldn't.

"Congratulations Vance. Congratulations Sara," Drex said, handing Katy back her glass.

"We are going to have the ceremony," added Vance.

I was sure my sister didn't know about that either. "It's sort of like an engagement party."

My sister smiled at me. "I'm happy for you," she said and then gave me a hug, forgetting about not mussing our dresses. "I really am happy for you."

That meant so much to me. While I was glad that I had taken this journey and met Vance and fallen in love, I was also nearly as excited to be sharing the experience with my sister. I would have hated her to be back on Earth, moping around. Here we would be happier. I glanced at my love, Vance. I was sure of it.

Katy took a big gulp of fage, then busied herself with the decision about the seamstress again. Meanwhile, Drex asked Vance and I about the ceremony.

"I want Katy to take photos, of course."

"This will be on the settit though?" asked Drex.

"Yes, we think that's the safest. We don't want to gather outside yet, but I do want you to think about creating an underground gathering hall where we might be able to have more kumiratas... Like your kumirata," Vance nudged.

"We'd like to have it here, actually," I added, realizing that Vance hadn't asked yet.

"We figure it will be good public relations, besides the fact that we want to celebrate with you. Just think, this will be the first announcement that rotha is possible with the human women. It's the first I knew about it, anyway," said Vance.

Drex nodded uneasily. "We still don't know if..."

"I'm not yet," I answered. I wasn't pregnant. "Otherwise, I wouldn't be downing this fage," I laughed.

"What do you mean?" asked Drex and Vance.

"I assume this wouldn't be good for the baby, like alcohol."

"It won't hurt the baby. In fact, it's important for you to feel happy, most especially when pregnant."

"Oh, I like the sound of that," I said. I took another big sip of fage.

"When do you want to do the ceremony" asked Drex.

"As soon as possible. I can't wait to share the good news," said Vance. He wrapped his arm around my hip, and I slid up against him with a sway of my body.

Katy's showcase was wonderful, and I really saw the love that she was already experiencing for the Xavians and their culture. I was proud of her, and I also had my fingers crossed that she would have the same love for a certain person she was sharing a home with. It would be beyond perfect if she would let go of what had happened on Earth and we were able to live our lives together here without regret.

Of course, we were showing our love and gratitude in different ways. That's how we were. Different, but still sisters.

Chapter Thirty-Six
Kumirata

Sara

I prepared for my kumirata in Katy's room. She was discreet, but I could tell that she was still living in this room, not having moved to Drex's room. It felt awkward getting ready for such a wedding-like event, but I didn't blame Katy for that awkwardness. I blamed Mike. He had put this damage and hurt on to this family and for many more events to come. He might not have arrived to the "Death do us part" part, but the ghost of him would be sticking around for a long time to come. Healing came slow. Forgetting might never happen.

Still, Katy was sweet, and whatever she had to wrestle with this morning, I understood but also realized she was keeping under wraps. I didn't want to throw her over the edge. And I didn't want to leave her completely out because of her pain. That's the opposite of what I wanted to do.

She helped me into my dress, which Bolin had secretly been working on using my measurements from the first dress I'd tried on for him. Gulshan had dyed the gown a deep purple using the same method that Sara had photographed for her showcase. Bolin added a bunch of wine-colored beading, which was gorgeous, and in only a week. I was surprised, amazed, and unbelievably grateful. Both of them would be watching on their settits, cheering on me and Vance. Vance wasn't even royalty like Drex, and I was starting to understand how excited and generous the Xavian people were.

It could have easily felt like a lot of pressure, especially at the beginning of such a new relationship, but Vance tried to explain it to me. They all knew it was a new relationship—the spots and kumirata don't mean that the relationship is perfect. It means it's just beginning.

It didn't really have a good equivalent on Earth, except for maybe some sort of arranged marriage. There was an anticipation of the outcome, but it was less wait-and-see and more how-can-we-make-this-work? And as I understood it, the entire community was helpful. I wondered how growing a relationship with such community support would be compared to our relatively behind-closed-doors marriage of the typical American. I couldn't wait to see how we bloomed.

"Isn't Vance wonderful?" I asked Katy, but it was more of a rhetorical question. I knew she didn't know him well, but I wanted her to know that *I* knew him well and would continue to get to know him. That's what this was all about. It was different from a wedding. It seemed in their culture, maybe it was better. It wasn't a destination, or even a milestone. Instead, it was more of a threshold, often the very beginning of a relationship.

Instead of gazing at a ring, I gazed at my own body. The spots on my palms had grown darker, the same shade as on my arms but, contrasting the lighter skin.

"You guys seem really happy," she confessed.

Another thing that wasn't really a destination. Our kumirata wouldn't guarantee happiness. It was a really good chance at happiness, it felt, in this moment though.

I loved the touch of Katy as her fingers ran through and styled my hair. My sister and I had always been close, but now, living away from each other and being more isolated, I noticed and cherished her even more. She braided the hair on the side of my head toward the back, like a tiara, and dotted it with flowers she'd stolen from the decorations that several villagers had arrived with to dress up the living room for the kumirata.

Sara stood back to admire her work. I had been working on my make-up. She gave it and my hair the final touches and then pulled out her camera and photographed me. She bossed me around, making me move from here to there, changing the angles of the window blinds and the artificial light, generally fussing. I wondered if she was this bossy with her clients but figured it was our closeness. I was glad that she brought her camera, and was able to photograph me in this event. I appreciated it even more because I knew how difficult it was for her. This was too much like her moment a few years ago, and it had been stolen from her. I hoped that she would be able to heal and move on. Drex would be so good for that, for her.

She looked at the monitor on her camera then back at me, squinting at my belly. I felt studied and scrutinized, which is not how you want to feel in a ceremonial dress.

Wrinkles between her eyes formed, and she frowned.

"I could be," I said, answering the possible question of a pregnancy. I didn't think I would be showing yet, but maybe I was just bloated. It felt impossible to overeat here. Everything was delicious but very light and healthy. Even the fage had very few calories from what I had gathered. The place was a luxurious getaway, that's for sure.

"One day at a time," I said, brushing it off. It already felt like a lot to think about, and I wanted this day to be about me and Vance. I wanted to celebrate us, before I thought about how quickly our family could be expanding.

Vance

Drex and I were sent into his bedroom to "get ready," but that only entailed looking each other over and admiring what handsome Xavians we were. I wore a burgundy leather vest over my bare chest, with slacks that matched. Drex wore a dark gray outfit that was equally revealing.

"I'm proud of you," Drex admitted as he motioned to return to the living room to coordinate the decoration and broadcast.

"Thanks. You'll get there," I encouraged him. Sara had described him as having the world on his shoulders, and that wasn't far from the truth.

I was standing here on the faith of rotha, so I wasn't worried about Drex. He deserved it as much as I did. Probably more. It made sense that Sara's sister would be my best friend's rotha, and I was going to trust that until I was shown otherwise.

Back in the living room, several Xavians were arranging the lighting and decorations. I know Sara wanted an outdoor ceremony, probably to even be knee-deep in a swimming hole with a waterfall in the background. I swore to give that to her one day. For today, I brought in as much jungle as would fit inside Drex's house. I requested the largest pink and purple gourua flowers off the cliffside—and they did not disappoint. Their sprawling petals, climbing from a pink interior to brilliant purple edges, created a perfect backdrop.

The ceremony began before I felt ready for it. Sara faced me from the other side of the settit, then we walked into the center frame together to signify the joining of our lives. She was gorgeous, and nothing had ever felt so right.

Drex stood behind us and said some words in both English and Xavian. It was in times like this that being important government officials saved us from embarrassing ourselves. We had to be professional. It also gave us an excuse to honestly express ourselves over jokes. Drex didn't disappoint.

"I've known Vance since we were both children. He has always been dutiful in not only serving his people, but in preparing for his rotha. And despite the tragedies that have befallen us, he found his rotha from across an ocean of sky."

I watched my beautiful mate, memorizing the brightness of her countenance and silently promising to always keep her this happy.

"Sara agreed to sleep deeply as she traveled the far reaches of space to find where she might belong. She has found Vance. And they belong together. The fates have called it, and we are here to celebrate that rotha hasn't abandoned us yet. We are here to support this couple as best we can. Please join us," said Drex.

He stepped away, and in the first broadcast interspecies kiss on Xavia, I kissed Sara, my rotha. The background cheering was just that—background, as my lips meshed with hers.

I put my arms around her, and it was many hours into our celebration with Drex and Katy before I thought to let her go. With her on my arm, I was no longer afraid. For the first time in my entire life, I was not afraid of the Orkain flying above my head. They had been the fuel for my nightmares. I had battled them, knew what they were capable of, knew that I wasn't capable of destroying them…yet. However, I also knew no simple Orkain and its talons were going to take my love from me. I knew that I would protect her. There was no doubt about it. I would do everything, be anything, to keep this woman safe. I would protect her. It was part of my being. It was as certain as the zarata and breath inside me. My life and Sara's would always be interconnected, even more than our limbs currently were, even before kumirata. Somehow, now, I was complete.

Chapter Thirty-Seven
Stuck

Vance

Unfortunately, Drex and I quickly found danger outside when we checked. The dark shadow of an Orkain loomed over the field, crisscrossing, seeking where we slept. Even cowering under the trees, I felt exposed. I ground my teeth as we hid.

Underground was the safest. Even if the Orkain were familiar with caves, our tunnels would take away their flight advantage. Hidden, we pretended they didn't exist, if only for an evening. The evening was now over. I couldn't even take my loved one home for our first joining after the kumirata.

"I'm sorry," said Drex gravely, the lightness in his voice gone. The joyous moment had dimmed for him too. In that way I knew he wasn't just apologizing for tonight. He was apologizing for all the nights.

"It's not your fault." None of it was, but I understood. We were the leading faces of the new generation, fresh from presenting a new chapter in our lives…huddled underneath a thicket, fearing for our lives.

I kicked at the thick trunk of the tree, shaking the upper part and its leaves harder than I intended. That guaranteed another several minutes under the tree to make sure that none of the Orkain had caught sight of us and was waiting above. I hated feeling useless. After all the cheering and staring into Sara's face—there was still nothing I could achieve out here.

"You want those tunnels, I know," Drex said. It sounded like he was giving in, or at least providing consolation if he still wasn't going to do it.

I'm not sure which I wanted anymore. Those tunnels sounded like both the safest plan and also like giving up. Our entire civilization would be changed. We'd be an underground people after a while. At the same time, pride wasn't a reason to not adapt. Those who didn't adapt could die off. We were in danger of dying off.

Maybe Drex didn't understand the urgency of it. While Sara and I were probably on a fast-track, Drex and Katy seemed to have gotten hung up somewhere.

"We need more than the tunnels, but that's a start."

"Tunnels are more than a start. They're a huge undertaking. We have to decide if we are going that route first."

Vance understood the sentiment, but they didn't really have any other options. He told him so. "I just don't see where else we can start and really make a difference."

Drex agreed solemnly. He headed back toward the house. There was no reason to still be out and tempting fate.

Sara

I didn't argue when Vance declared he and Drex were going to scout our route home. Given how wonderful the day had been, I didn't want us to run into any trouble—my family had already had enough wedding trauma. I wasn't going to contribute to it by blindly running outside without checking for the flying deathtraps. Besides, it gave me the opportunity to ask my sister about her man.

"How are you two doing?" I asked, stacking my empty plate onto another.

Katy looked down at her empty glass before answering. "I'm definitely enjoying his company," she said.

I knew what she meant by that. "I'm glad you're getting some, sis!"

She laughed awkwardly. She was always a bit shyer about things than I was. "And I'm glad you're happy," she said. She got up from her side of the urish and gave me another hug. "That's why I came here to make sure you'd be okay. I'm not sure if I'm staying when the ship comes back. I might go back home."

"No!" I said, pulling partway out of her hug. What the heck?

"I'm not on Xavia to find love. I'm here to make some money and get out of debt while I make sure you're safe and happy. If they let me go back, I'll probably go back to Earth. Maybe I'll be able to visit."

"But what about Drex?" I knew things weren't going as quickly as things had gone for Vance and I, but I thought things were...going.

"What about him? He is a nice man. One of the sweetest men I've ever known. He cares wonderfully for me and gives me the best orgasms of my life," she said bluntly. "But I can't make life decisions based on being with a man for a few months. I have to make decisions for me, not for *love* or for someone else. We saw how that turned out last time."

"Not all men are like that, Katy. He's not even *human*. He can't be any more different from your ex."

"It's not about being hurt by Mike. It's about not making the same mistake again. I can't throw away my life on Earth because of someone—*anyone*—else. It has to be because of *me*."

"How do you know that jumping into this *isn't* for you? How do you know you're not denying what you want, just for the sake of…what? Practicality?" I retorted.

Her sense of pride had always rubbed me wrong. I still didn't understand why she didn't even ask Mike to help pay for the wedding that he had agreed to and then ruined. She seemed set to suffer in anything that happened to her. I hated that. This felt like more of that.

Before I could voice my concerns, the men returned. Vance immediately closed the distance between us, wrapping me in his arms. I had forgotten the heat of his muscles which melted my own. And those eyes swirled only for me. Katy was being dumb and stubborn. If she felt anything for Drex, she should stay. She deserved this, even more than me.

"We spotted two Orkain out there," said Drex. "We will have to stay the night here."

"We can stay in your old bedroom!" I said to Katy, knowing full well that it wasn't her old bedroom at all. But, for tonight, it would be.

Vance

I carried the remnants of the fage in mostly empty glasses into the bedroom. Staying in Drex's guest room wasn't my first choice, but I was learning to accept that life had a way of subverting my expectations while also giving me more than I could imagine. I mean, I had Sara. I wouldn't dare argue for anything more.

"I had something planned for us," I said as I helped her out of her gown.

"Oh yeah?" Sara said. It wasn't totally unexpected. "You can't do it here?" she asked slyly.

I shook my head. "There were accouterments… I didn't bring them."

She smiled and laughed. She didn't seem too disappointed. Those things would be home when we got back there. Our home. It felt good to say that.

"What are we going to do instead?" she asked. The last word barely escaped her mouth before I approached her aggressively and spun her around and threw her on the bed.

"Oh," she gasped in surprise but didn't yell out. It was good of her. Her sister and the prince of Xavia were across the hallway, and I expected that they weren't going to be partaking in as much ecstasy as I was about to show Sara.

I grabbed handfuls of her meaty thighs and pulled her ass up and toward me. I started low, my nose in her hair, exhaling slowly. I could smell her arousal growing with my face on her ass and on her sex. I brushed my teeth against her ass, grabbing a small mouthful and biting. She hissed quietly.

I stood and positioned her hips against my half-erect cocks. She waggled her ass, snuggling me between her cheeks. I bent down and breathed hard in her ear through the hair that had fallen over most of her face. Then I found her wrists and pulled her hands down between her legs, threading them through. Holding her hands and wrists from the other side, I returned my head to her ass. If I pulled on her hands hard enough, I'd flip her completely over, but for now her face lay against the mattress.

My mouth devoured her. I kissed her cheeks, bit her curves, and breathed on her tight, puckered asshole. With my tongues, I had access to whatever I wanted. It was a veritable feast, and I took my time.

I licked each side of her sex, then squeezed it between split tongues, flicking her hanging clit. Sara shuddered and tried to pull away, but I had a firm grip on her hands and it only forced her face deeper into the bed, smothering her sigh.

I abandoned the sensitive clit for the moment and instead used the bumps on my tongues to tantalize every part except that button of pleasure. I loved playing with her slit, slipping my tongue inside, parallel to her flesh. I could feel her channel above squeezing on nothing, her juices slowly dripping to coat her. The excess fell as drops on my tongue, and I lapped it up like I'd never get enough. I buried my face firmly into her ass, giving my tongues excellent access to that pussy. The farther I pushed, the more I received…more ass, more pussy.

Soon Sara was moaning and struggling to tell me what she wanted. I knew what she needed. I had ignored her clit for too long. It had been sensitive, but now it was longing to be treated with a rough tongue and steady pressure. I pressed a wide tongue on that button of delight. I was rewarded with another squeeze and taste of her nectar, her channel readying itself for me.

I dragged my tongue against her clit and felt her struggle. Her hips began to thrust against me. I had her in such an awkward position, the least I could do was help. I darted my tongue in and out, punching her clit until she was crying out. I struggled to breathe in the thickness of her ass as she bore down on me.

I felt another burst of liquid hit my tongues and drip down the sides as she squirted. I lapped hard as she struggled against me. I still had her hands and she didn't have anywhere to go with my face smashed firmly into her ass. I had almost licked her dry when she transitioned from sensitive to pleasure again. She began working with my tongue, climbing toward *wanting* and then *needing* again. I shoved a tongue in, between her, inside of her.

"Oh Vance," she muttered into the pillow, along with some other choice words or curses that I couldn't quite make out.

She murmured sweetly the entire time as I explored her with my tongue as deeply as I could reach. Her channel pumped hard, forcing me out of her and back into my mouth. Her sweet tang covered my lips. I licked them clean, drawing semicircles around her opening to pump more from her.

Sara whimpered now. Sweat covered her brow, collecting on the bed with face still smashed. She cried out with another orgasm. It took all that was within me to not lick her dry again. But she needed those juices coating her channel if she was going to take me.

When her orgasm passed, it was my chance. I released her hands. I grabbed her by the ankles and calves and slowly pulled her off the bed until she set her hands on the ground, inverted like a plow. I stepped closer to her, and she tightened her calves around my waist as I unzipped and stepped out of my pants.

I had an excellent view of the swollen and pulsing sex where I had had my face moments ago as I licked her off of my lips. I supported a leg on each side of my hips and hiked her up higher so that my cocks were closer against her. Her head was level with the mattress, which I imagined I'd have her slapping against in no time, just like I had with her on top of the bed. I went to drag her out of there to put her in a better position, but she made noises of disagreement. She seemed to want to be cornered and controlled by the furniture.

I placed the head of my thick, bulbous cock against the wet folds of her entrance, pressing slowly forward, millimeter by millimeter, feeling different parts of her give way to make space for me. At the same time, my other dicks were almost impossibly hard. I positioned one, hot and heavy, against her asshole. I wasn't going to enter yet, but I wanted her to feel and understand the force that was behind her, of what *could* happen to her.

"Fuck" she whispered.

I didn't need to be told twice. I took another step until I had filled her to her limits. She groaned, and I felt one of her hands give out for a split second. I didn't think it had to do with her weight. She was strong. She had a weakness for my thick penises inside of her. I felt her ripple tight around me, and it caused me to thrust involuntarily. I wasn't the only one who could perform tricks with the other person's body.

She pushed up into a handstand, threatening my dick with the edges of her thoroughly damp and primed asshole.

With some steady pressure and only a bit of doubt, I popped my cock's head into her asshole. She immediately squeezed around me as she orgasmed from both channels. She dropped to her elbows, changing the angle and the pressure I could exert. I responded by pulling on her legs and driving into her. The pressure came out the other end in cut-off squeals and gasps as I filled her. Not to be forgotten, my smaller front cock lodged her clit against her pelvic bone.

"I need those hip thrusts," she cried out, pleading for the primitive way her humans have sex. Their male humans didn't have penises that could extend and retract within the women's space. Instead, they had to use it as an inanimate spear that they dove in and out with their hips—that thrusting action Sara seemed to really enjoy. I rammed between her thighs, stretching her legs, hips, and her insides. The lengthening and thrusts as I plowed into her was intense and satisfying. I had to pause to keep from going over the edge too soon. She responded by driving her hips into me, wanting more, needing more. *No, my sweet*, I thought. There was no way she was going to cut me off from pleasing her all night. I felt the moment pass before pushing deep into her again.

She tightened around my cocks as I propelled in and out of her until she clamped down and I couldn't move. I know because I tried. She had me in her pussy grip as she came around my throbbing cocks.

I loved making her cum.

I immediately wanted another one. I pulled out and turned her around, her shoulders on the floor. I picked her up and placed her onto my cocks again, holding her as I stood up. My hands supporting her legs, I rolled her sex along my cocks as I bowed my head and bit down on her neck.

She cursed me softly. Her breasts rocked against my pecs as I dropped her down my cocks again, her weight and gravity adding to our pleasure. She was hot and damp and gasping. I couldn't keep my hands off of her. I couldn't keep my face off her neck, breathing in her scent, her hair in my mouth as I grunted with each gyration of my cock, rotating inside my love, stirring her pot until another rush of nectar poured from her and coated us both, dripping down our legs.

She grabbed and held onto my shoulders with clawed hands, clinging on and desperate to pull herself up so she could drop down on my cocks. I pulled her legs to wrap them tightly around me and then plopped down onto the bed so she smashed into me even more. She cried out as her fingers dug into my shoulder blades as my cocks pump into her juicy channel.

"Oh god," she said, her lips curling with an adorable snarl as she received my jets of cum. She lay there heavy, soaking in our quiet joy. We would have so many good nights to enjoy, but I'd always remember this one.

Epilogue

Vance

The evening of Switching Day turned terrifying when Drex called me to tell me Katy had run away from her new host, so I immediately went out looking for her. Switching Day was partially my idea, and it felt like my fault that it was turning out as poorly as it had. I thought the threat of switching hosts would encourage Drex and Katy to commit to each other. Sara had thought so too. We were both surprised when they actually completed the switch. I wanted to scream at them to stand up and say "No, I want to stay with you," but it didn't happen that way. They weren't Sara or me.

News that Drex had actually killed an Orkain was even more shocking. Needing to tend to Katy, he asked Lian and I to deal with the body. I wasn't actually expecting it to be there. Maybe Drex had injured it, but I was sure it would have recovered and left before I arrived. I didn't really think he had taken one down by himself, but when we reached the described clearing, there was indeed a dark lump in the grass. We approached carefully. I knew that it must be gravely injured, if not dead, to still be where it lay.

There was no sign of breath, not even movement of feathers in the light wind. I pulled out my weapon on the approach. Lian was a lot less cautious. His knife stayed on his belt as he marched over to the beast. Before I could stop him, he kicked it hard on the back, between the roots of its two wings. Congealed chunks of blood flew off the body, but that was the only response seen. It was, indeed, dead.

Lian cursed and spit on the creature. He would continue to beat it if I allowed him. The body was much more valuable intact than as an outlet of frustration though. We had never been able to get so close to examine such a beast. It would be of great advantage to us. We needed to get it out of the clearing before its brethren found it.

I grabbed one spiny wing, and Lian grabbed the other. We turned the body over and pulled it onto the heavy tarp I had brought. The Orkain's front was relatively undamaged, armored. His horns and fangs covered the majority of his face, providing protection and a particularly scary visage. His hocked legs were hairy and beast-like. His Xavian chest and arms with massive wings springing from behind were uncanny and disturbing, as nothing else about him was very Xavian or humanoid. It was like a basic torso had sprouted the disgusting appendages of nightmares.

"We're not far from Frustnerdd. Let's put him in one of the stores until tomorrow."

Lian agreed, and we both grunted as we hefted the massive body. Secretly, I was proud. This wouldn't be the last one. We now knew its weakness. Drex had gotten above and killed a prime example of their species. Not a weak or sick one—a hunter. They lived together, and I wondered how organized they were. Would we have to worry about a retaliatory attack? How much trouble would we have to cause to make them flee? I was ready to put up the fight.

Lian complained about the weight, but I did not. I cheerfully dragged the heavy beast along the cumbersome brush, stumbling in the dark. This was a prize of war. I hadn't killed this one, but Drex had. My people had. We had reached a turning point in this war. My head was no longer filled with images of my children wandering in underground caves, but instead, running around free in the jungles of bright-skied Xavia.

I couldn't wait for tomorrow. If I'd had the opportunity, I'd run out now into the darkness with a knife and take on the rest of the Orkain with the treasured knowledge I had now.

We knew how to kill them. We knew where they lived.

My mind buzzed with ideas and possibilities to defeat the Orkain now. There were so many more chances, so many things to try. Everything was looking brighter. Nothing about thinking about Sara and our future children was dim. Nothing with Sara could be dismal or without hope. But now, it glowed with extra triumph. There was a way to that future. I was going to make that future for Sara.

I hadn't been able to see it before her. Now that I had, I was never going to lose sight of it. How could I, waking up to her bright, shining face every morning in my bed?

We secured the dead Orkain body in one of the opened stores and went our separate ways, Lian still complaining. I urged him to get home safely. I couldn't convince him yet what this meant to us. I didn't bother. It wasn't something that I could have been told either. But Sara helped me experience it. The Orkain had brought pain and abyss. I hadn't been able to see light at the end of the dark tunnels that I had wanted to build to surrender, to give up, to hide. Sara showed me that there was no hiding. This was her adventure. This was my adventure. This was our life, and it would only be what we could make of it.

It wasn't time to give up. Now that I had Sara and a way forward, I found the will inside of me. I was going to fight, and I was going to win. The life that I wanted to give Sara and our children, a safe, bright one, full of outdoor adventures and joy…it was all within my grasp. We were going to do it.

From the moment I saw her, I knew I would do everything I could to protect her. I led her to safety, to my home, that very first day. And I did everything I knew to keep her happy and safe. Even if I had to hand dig the tunnels so that she could see her sister whenever she wanted, so she could be with other Xavians without issue, so she could raise our family.

But what I had was not enough. Rotha didn't matter in a world that was crumbling. It was up to me to figure it out, adapt, and find a new way to protect Sara. The ways I had were not going to cut it. She wanted adventure. She deserved adventure. She deserved more than I could provide. She wanted to be places that I couldn't protect her.

I could have given up. I could have sent her home. Or I could stand up.

Given her love, her attentiveness, her strength, and her smarts…she had brought new ideas to me, to our people. She and the other women had injected hope, new ideas, and strength in a world that was dying under the heel of the Orkain. She was brought here under viciously disgusting pretenses, but she'd become nothing less than my savior. In turn, we, together, were going to help the Xavians.

It was awful what the Orkain had done to Xavians, and what the Earth government had done to their women. I didn't comprehend the giant cosmos of it all, but I was thankful for the rotha—that it had brought Sara and I together despite all of this awfulness. Not all life-shattering things had to end badly. Sara had taught me that it was okay to want adventure, to want more out of life. I wasn't going to be left behind. I was going to cling to Sara as hard and as long as I could. She was going places. Now, we were going places. I was so thankful for her bright smile, and the rotha that marked us together.

I didn't know the details of our future, but I did know it was with her. And I was going to spend the rest of my life finding out and coloring in the details with her. She was the love of my life, and she was the hope for me, my people, and this world. Not only was she my world, but she was going to mean the world for so many of our people and our future generations. She was the turning point in my life, and, I knew without a doubt, had helped turned the tide of this war.

And, she would always be mine.

My love.

My rotha.

I would always protect her.

Sara

I woke to the strangest feeling in the world—small flutters of movement inside of me. I wasn't used to it. My newest alien adventure was alive and growing.

We were a bit of an experiment. Our baby would be the first born from human and Xavian DNA. Rotha was a biological connection, an evolutionary advantage for reproduction. It was a good sign for us. And, if the acrobatics in the morning were any indication, our baby would arrive strong and healthy.

I stretched in the rapidly cooling bed. Vance was already up—I wasn't sure if I'd seen him sleep yet. I was a good sleeper. Less so with the little one on the way. We weren't the only ones on the bed. Soft footfalls on the duvet announced a guest.

Moyuki would consider me the guest. I had finally won the big saf over. I had to overlook that she looked like the panther chasing the pet trio in that kids movie, but after that, I grew quite smitten. She was much too large to be on the bed with Vance, and she only joined me in the mornings after I woke, as if she needed my permission before curling into the quickly vanishing curve created by my waist and hip on the bed. I scratched behind her gray ear. She was adapting well to changes, and there were more to come.

The Orkain were a dangerous nuisance. Vance and Drex were planning to drive them off this planet. He told me of their outpost of all young, male Orkain. I worried that Xavians and the humans from our ship might still be alive, kept somewhere in the caves. Drex said they were preferentially taking women. I shuddered at the thought of what they might be doing to them. We had to intervene. Unfortunately, it meant risking the lives of our men—Vance, Drex, Chelk, Lian.

My love arrived, as if planned, with a mug of fah. It hardly steamed over its surface—the perfect temperature. He climbed back in bed with us—all of us. I nestled against him, Moyuki at our feet, our arms and rotha marks tangled together. Our baby growing inside me.

Vance had this reverential view on rotha. He believed it had the strength to build a new community of humans and Xavians. I wasn't sure what I believed. I couldn't deny that my heart and breath were in sync with his. My markings had only gotten more prominent—I loved them. In the course of my life, the universe might have tossed me some unfair things. I didn't feel like I deserved this either. But perhaps better was to come. A world without Orkain?

No matter. I would follow Vance anywhere with anything flying overhead. Because where he was, I was home and on the greatest adventure, all at once. I'd traveled across the galaxy to fall into his arms.

He would protect me in this galaxy and into the next. He was my alien protector. He was my adventure. He was my love.

* * *

Free Bonus Scene

What did Vance have planned for Kumirata night?
And what "accouterments" were needed?

Join Reverie's Revelries and get the spicy bonus
scene, *Kumirata Night,* as a special gift

Reverieharwood.com/newsletter-protector

A Note for You, the Reader

Hi Reader,

Are we really here again? Thank you for reading and investing in the *Rotha Mates of Xavia* series. I'm constantly amazed by the warmth I've received from the romance community.

The first manuscript I ever completed as a young middle-school writer was a romance. I've now returned to the stories that intrigued me, made me cry, and made me hopeful.

I hope *My Alien Protector* has added romance and steaminess…and, a little escape…to your day. Please review on your favorite places to buy books.

Which couple's story do you want to hear next? Send me an email at reverie@reverieharwood.com. If you like booktok or cats, you can follow me on TikTok @reverieharwood. No matter how you reach out, I'd love to hear from you.

Until then, my very best to you,

Reverie Harwood
October 2023